D0000083

Mind Your Manors!

PATRICIA A BREMMER

Mind Your Manors!

by

Patricia A. Bremmer

ISBN 978-0-9745884-7-6

Cover Design by Martin Bremmer

For additional copies contact:

Windcall Publishing/
Windcall Enterprises
75345 RD. 317
Venango, Ne 69168

www.windcallenterprises.com

www.patriciabremmer.com

Acknowledgements

My thanks and acknowledgements to all who helped create "**Mind Your Manors!**".

Martin Bremmer, my husband, who took over my daily tasks so I could steal away to a private place to write.

Jamie Swayzee, for the hours and hours of grueling work on editing.

Detective Glen Karst, who used his expertise in his field to keep my crime scenes believable, while allowing me to abuse his persona in my book.

Jack Sommars, my friend and screenplay writer, for his final editorial review.

Joshua Mackey, from KOGA radio in Ogallala for allowing me to use his name and likeness in the book. What fun!

Eloise Hughes and **Ann Schmitt** models for the front cover. Thanks girls.

Regent Park Nursing Home and staff in Holyoke, Colorado for the tour of their facility and answering my many questions.

Cover Design by **Martin Bremmer.** Martin can take any design from my mind and produce it perfectly on the computer. Thanks Honey!

Chapter 1

"Good morning, Kate," said Melody as she pulled the cords along the window's edge, drawing open the blinds to bring the warm glow of the morning sun into the dimly lit room.

"Kate, dear, it's time to wake up. Breakfast will be ready soon."

Melody Logan, a certified nursing assistant, brought a cheery good morning to each of the residents as she prepared them for a new day. Melody, a sturdy but not quite plump blond in her early thirties, possessed that rare but much desired ability to care deeply about each and every one of her patients.

Continuing with her morning routine, she chose a new set of clothes for Kate, laying them across the back of her chair.

"Katie, come on, let's wake up now."

Many of the residents were given sleeping pills to help them through the night. According to Dr. Raymond

Culbertson, the town doctor, the lack of physical exercise in their lives contributed to the need for less sleep causing restless nights, which then resulted in more naps during the day. The pills helped restore a more normal sleep cycle.

Melody touched Kate's shoulder.

"Kate."

She gently shook her arm.

"Katie."

Kate lay with her back to Melody. Melody touched her hand to Kate's face. She felt cold.

"Oh, no. Not Kate. Not my Katie."

Melody took it hard when death came to take her favorite residents and Kate was definitely one of them.

Katherine Hodges, known by everyone as Kate, came to Wallace Manor six years earlier. She spent her entire life in Wallace, Colorado, a small rural community thirty miles from Denver and only twenty minutes from Greeley. Although Denver continued to grow in all directions, the town of Wallace seemed oblivious to the constant change, remaining untouched over the years. The locals preferred it that way. The self-sufficient town held tightly to the past.

The citizens of Wallace supported their town fully. The strong loyalty allowed the rural businesses to remain while most small towns met with collapse. Even with Denver only thirty minutes away, most chose to stay in

Wallace for all of their daily needs. The beauty and barbershops stayed adequately busy, as did the grocery store and pharmacy. Wallace offered most of what one would want in the city without the traffic and the added bonus of a friendly hello to each customer.

When you took your pet to the vet clinic not only were you greeted by your name, but your pet's name was also remembered. Many small towns lose their medical staff to larger cities, but the attraction to small town living so close to a metropolitan city allowed Wallace to maintain a small group of doctors and dentists who made trips over to Wallace as needed. The one-doctor town had access to several more. The newly constructed assisted living facility connected to Wallace Manor contained nurses and CNAs who were also born and raised in Wallace.

The residents were recognized as parents and grandparents of friends and neighbors in the community.

Melody had fond memories of Kate. Her granddaughter, Abby, and Melody were best friends throughout school. After school and weekends the two girls spent many hours at Kate's home baking cookies and learning to sew and knit. Kate grew one of the largest vegetable gardens in town. Many times she took home the blue ribbon for her produce at the county fair.

She taught the girls the fine details of growing vegetables, but her passion leaned toward her flower gardens. Her flowers consumed more square footage of her yard than her vegetables.

To this day, every time Melody plucks a large ripe tomato from the vine in her own garden, she thanks Kate for the lessons and memories.

She walked to the opposite side of the bed to look at Kate. All the color had drained from the old lady's face. Her snowy white hair remained thick and full while the years sucked the strength from her frail body.

Melody took the brush from her bedside drawer and pulled it ever so gently through Kate's hair, arranging it just the way she liked it. She stroked her cheek as she said her good-byes. She kissed her on the forehead then with a deep breath returned to her job at hand.

Following procedure, Melody checked for vital signs. She went to the nurses' station to make the call.

"Dr. Culbertson's office."

"This is Melody Logan from Wallace Manor. I need to speak with Dr. Culbertson."

"Is this an emergency? He's with a patient."

"Yes, please."

Marlene, Dr. Culbertson's receptionist, tapped on the door of the exam room.

"Yes?" he responded.

"Melody Logan, on line one."

"Excuse me for a moment," he said to his patient.

He went to his office to take the call, preferring to take all calls from the manor in private. In a small town gossip flies quickly and he felt the need to guard family privacy. He wanted the family to hear it from him or the staff, not the gossip line.

"Melody, what can I help you with?"

"Dr., Kate, er... Katherine Hodges passed away during the night. I checked her vitals. There is no palpable pulse, no blood pressure and no respirations."

"I'll be there as soon as I finish with my patient."

Laura Payne, the Director of Nursing at the manor, joined Melody as she returned to Kate's room.

"Would you like me to call the family and the mortuary?" she asked.

"No, I think I can handle it," replied Melody.

"I just thought since you were so close to Kate that maybe you'd like to go home."

"No, that's why I have to stay. I feel like Kate's family."

Laura, a tall, slender, brunette with a keen business sense, handled the nursing staff. She remained firm, but friendly. Most manors have a rapid turnover of employees, but with Laura onboard there were fewer sick calls and no-shows. The staff liked her and didn't want to disappoint her. She made it a point to learn as much about each resident as possible, going on daily rounds just as the aides did.

She also greeted visitors, explaining the changes in their family member who resided within the walls of Wallace Manor. In just one month she will celebrate her twelfth year of employment.

Diane Pratt, a new aide, joined Melody in Kate's room.

"I'm here to help you get Kate ready for her family. I'm not sure what to do," she said with a trembling voice.

"Is Kate your first deceased resident?" asked Melody.

"I'm afraid so."

"We need to clean her up just as if she were still alive. I've got to make a couple of calls then I'll be back to help you."

Diane remained with the body while Melody called Abby.

"Hello."

"Abby, this is Melody."

"Melody, how great to hear from you. What's up?"

Melody paused, before answering.

"It's Grandma, isn't it?"

"Yes," replied Melody, choking back tears.

"Did something happen to her? Is she ill? Did she fall?"

"Kate passed away in her sleep."

Silence told Melody her words hit hard. Then she heard the sobbing.

"I'll call Paul and we'll drive right over."

Next, Melody called Michael from Winegard Mortuary.

Melody joined Diane and they finished preparing Kate's body.

"Her granddaughter, Abby and her brother, Paul will be here soon," explained Melody. "They both live in Denver."

"What happens next?" asked Diane.

"After the family has had their time with her the mortuary will come by and take her body. The rest is up to the family unless Kate has already made the arrangements."

When Abby and Paul arrived, an aide escorted them to Kate's room. Melody stayed with Kate. With the fresh bedding and her body neatly groomed, Kate looked as if she were sleeping.

Abby rushed to Melody in tears.

"Tell me she didn't suffer. I know I should've come to see her more often," she sobbed.

"Abby, she went in her sleep. Yesterday, she enjoyed a trip outside in her wheelchair to look at the flowers. We talked about all the flowers she used to grow."

"Melody, I'm so glad you were here. It's like she always had family around her."

Melody ran her hand down Paul's arm as she stepped out of the room. When their hands met, he squeezed her fingers tightly before releasing them. Abby and Paul said their good-byes then searched for Melody.

"What do we do next?" asked Paul.

"Winegard's will take her to the mortuary. You'll need to visit with them."

Once the brother and sister left, Melody called Winegard's to let them know the family was no longer in the building. She and the other aides walked down the halls closing the doors of any residents who might be able to view the body leaving. Staff members kept the residents who were out of their rooms busy, not allowing them to return until the Suburban carrying the body had driven away. This routine repeated itself often. Wallace Manor and staff experienced the loss of up to ten residents per month.

For some strange reason the population of Wallace rarely changed. For each death there seemed to be a birth. Even though many of the young people moved away after high school never to return, those who did brought with them a spouse. Very often that spouse brought family from a previous marriage or parents who wanted to live nearby. As the families grew the natural balance of Wallace remained.

The same held true for Wallace Manor. When one resident passed on another waited to move in. The aides busied themselves preparing Kate's room for the new arrival. It all seemed so cold and impersonal, yet dying is a natural transition.

Most of the town turned out for Kate's funeral service. Cindy, director of the Wallace Library, stood behind the crowd. Being new to Wallace and with Kate spending the last six years in the manor, the two never met. Many of the other mourners were patrons of the library who Cindy did know. She felt it was a kind gesture to appear at the graveside services of as many citizens as time would allow.

"Where's your boyfriend?" came a voice in Cindy's ear.

The sound of Sheriff Tate's voice made her skin crawl. Having pursued most of the single women in town, he remained perplexed as to why he had not been able to romance Cindy.

"I don't have a boyfriend, thank you."

"Oh, come on now. Don't tell me all that time you spent with Karst he didn't try to put the moves on you."

"Detective Karst and I are just good friends. Not all men are as slimy as you."

Tate's flesh grew red from beneath his collar as it rose to his face. He routinely used women and proclaimed himself as quite the charmer until this ice queen moved into his town.

Cindy saw right through him, having lived in the city most of her life. She quickly learned to spot the snide

Casanova types. She stared straight ahead willing her eyes not to make contact with his. She hoped if she ignored him he would slink away as quietly as he came.

After a few moments, she relaxed the tension in her body until she felt an arm slip around her waist from behind. With one quick movement, she thrust her elbow into his stomach causing him to expel all the air from his lungs with a loud sound. It worked; he removed his arm.

"Well, that's a fine hello," sounded a painful voice.

Cindy, startled, turned face to face with Detective Glen Karst.

"Oh, my God, Glen. I'm so sorry. I thought you were Tate," she tried to explain.

"That's one hell of a thing to say," he whispered. His loud response when Cindy so roughly planted her elbow into his midsection had already disturbed the rows of people in front of them.

"No, no. He was just here asking about you. I called him slimy and he left."

Glen fought to hold back one of his hearty laughs at the thought of Tate trying to pick up Cindy and her response.

"Priceless," he said. "I wish I could've been here."

"What are you doing here?" she asked. "Did you know Kate?"

"No, not really. I do know her granddaughter's husband."

"How do you know him?" she asked, straining forward to catch a glimpse of the man they were discussing.

"They live in Denver and he's an ER doc at one of the hospitals. Unfortunately, we've had to have many discussions about shooting victims and other unsavory deaths. He's a cool guy. I bumped into him last night and he mentioned he'd been in my hometown for a few days and would be back today for his wife's grandmother's funeral. I thought I'd pay my respects."

"How'd you slip away from work?"

"I had an early court case that went much faster than expected. I thought I'd come to the service then run home for lunch before going back to work."

Detective Glen Karst worked for the Denver PD. He and Cindy became friends while investigating a series of deaths in Wallace.

"I haven't seen much of you lately," she said.

"Hell, I've been meeting myself coming and going. Between my open cases, new cases, the dogs and working on the house I barely have time to sleep."

"You do look a little rough around the edges," she said, noticing his two-day old beard.

His hand rubbed the stubble on his face. "I'm thinking about taking on an undercover assignment."

"Isn't that dangerous?"

"No more than anything else. Hell, just driving to work every morning is dangerous. Life's dangerous."

The graveside service ended and the crowd dispersed. Cindy stood with Glen wondering if she should walk away or invite him to join her for lunch. She chose the latter.

"Would you like to go grab a pizza or something?" she asked.

"You know, I'd love to, but I want to check on Mieke."

Glen, every inch a cop, owned two German Shepherds and a Corgi. Mieke, the younger of the two, was retired from the police force after having been shot. Glen adopted her then bred her to a stud dog from the department. In just a few days she'd whelp her first litter.

"Maybe another time then," said Cindy.

"Why don't you follow me home. I've got some meat and Kaiser biscuits. I even think there might be a bag of chips somewhere in the pantry. We can grab a bite while we talk and I can check in on Mieke."

All eyes were upon Cindy and Glen as the townspeople retreated to their cars to drive back to the church for a lunch sponsored by the ladies of the church Kate attended.

"Let's get out of here. I feel a little squirmy planting the seed of gossip," said Cindy.

"I'll meet you at the ranch."

Mind Your Manors!

Glen climbed into his pickup then darted out of town to his slice of heaven in the country. Having grown up in Wallace, when he returned a few months earlier to buy the old Watkins' farm, he felt like he was home again. Now he had a place in the country, fresh air and acres of room for his dogs to run and explore.

Squeals of joy poured from the backyard when the dogs heard his pickup arrive. He thought it best to go inside and change from the suit he wore to court into more casual detective attire before letting his dogs climb all over him. His daily work wear consisted of Wrangler jeans, boots and a blazer.

He would let his girls into the house with him during lunch, knowing they would mind their manners with Cindy if he told them to. They only were allowed to be lap dogs with certain, very understanding, guests. He grabbed some treats and joined them in the backyard for a few moments before Cindy showed up. Somehow he always manages to arrive at his destination much sooner than anyone else, but swears he doesn't speed...much.

The dogs sounded the alarm that a strange car had entered the property. Glen quickly examined Mieke for any signs of distress or labor. She bounced around totally unaware of her delicate condition.

Cindy, feeling very much at home at Glen's house, began setting out food for lunch. He did have a nice selection of deli meats and cheeses. She guessed sandwiches were his mainstay, living alone.

He washed his hands then joined her. He pulled down a bag of salt and vinegar chips from the top shelf of the pantry. Cindy set the table with wine glasses and took a chilled bottle from the refrigerator.

"Help yourself, but I'm on duty today. No wine for me. I'll grab some milk."

He was often chastised by his cohorts for drinking milk with lunch, or any meal, for that matter.

"I'm sorry, I guess I wasn't thinking," she said. "You know, this might very well be the first meal we've shared where you haven't had a beer or glass of bourbon."

"Yeah, well, I didn't say I liked it this way," he said, as he eyed the large bottle of Buffalo Trace bourbon on the counter calling out to him.

"I know you're always accusing me of speeding," he said as he took a huge bite of his sandwich. He swallowed. "But I was concerned when you took a little longer than I expected to get here. I considered calling you to see if you had a flat or something."

"No," she smiled devilishly. "I stopped by the store for this."

She leaned forward to open a bag she set aside on the table. A chocolate pecan cheesecake appeared.

Glen's eyes sparkled as he smiled and said, "Dear lady, you know how to spoil me."

Cindy laughed, "It's no secret in this town that your passion for dessert is cheesecake of any variety. When I went through the checkout Becky was in line behind me. She asked if the cheesecake was for you. I told her we were going to grab a quick sandwich at your place. She said to tell you hi."

"How is Becky?"

"I think she's doing better. She's decided to keep her job at the vet clinic."

"Good, I'm glad to hear it."

Becky and Cindy were unwittingly drawn into a case of Glen's causing Becky extreme confusion and emotional stress. Glen makes it a practice never to draw civilians into a case, but when things happen in small towns, lots of people get involved and many people can be hurt in some way or another.

"You know, I feel bad I haven't been by the hospital to check on Josie but once since she regained consciousness," said Glen.

Josie, Cindy's neighbor, had a bad fall rendering her unconscious, complicated by a broken hip. She was one of the town's people who fell into the hands of the criminal Glen arrested who was responsible for Josie's injuries.

"She understands how busy you are. But she does ask about you often. I think I'll stop in to see her after work. I'll tell her we had lunch. She'll be happy."

Cindy noticed Glen repeatedly checking the time. "Do you have to get going soon?"

"Actually, I do. I need to run out and check on Maggi's dogs then I've really got to head back to Denver."

"Maggi Morgan?"

"Yeah, I had her dogs shipped here from Wisconsin. I'm holding them until she gets back from wherever the hell she is."

Maggi Morgan, a mystery writer and friend of Glen, had her dogs abducted and Glen found them while working a recent case. The dogs had been abandoned at a boarding kennel. He recognized them almost before they recognized him. After the happy reunion he had them sent to him where he's holding them for Maggi.

Cindy, being a library director, has an enormous passion for books and Maggi Morgan is one of her favorite mystery writers. She knew Glen was a friend of hers and they worked together on her books.

"I hate to impose on our friendship, but is there any way I can be here when you reunite her with her dogs? I'd really like to meet her."

"Absolutely. She's locked away writing somewhere. She'll check in with me when she returns. It could be in the middle of the night, ya know. Once I tell her the dogs are here she'll drop everything and drive out."

"That's okay. I don't mind getting a call in the middle of the night if it's to meet Maggi Morgan."

Chapter 2

Bill watched Glen walk to his desk as he slipped on his jacket to go out on a call.

"Where in the hell have you been? Come on, let's go," said Bill.

"Go where?"

"Possible arson in Littleton. Couple of charred bodies."

Glen followed him out the door.

"Why didn't you call me?"

"I did. Why didn't you answer?"

Glen grabbed his cell phone checking the charge.

"Shit. I shut the damn thing off while I was at a funeral service and forgot to turn it back on. I don't think I've ever forgotten before. Wonder why today?"

"Who was the babe?"

"What babe?"

"The babe who made you forget to turn your phone back on."

"Tell me about the arson."

"Tell me about the babe."

"I had lunch with a friend of mine at my place when I went home to change and check Mieke."

"Okay, if you don't want me to know."

"Look, it was Cindy, the library director. You met her. We were at the same funeral. She asked if I had time for a pizza. I wanted to check Mieke and change so I told her to follow me home and grab a sandwich. End of story. Now can we get back to work?"

"Okay, okay, you don't have to be so damn touchy about your private life."

"Yeah, well, around you the word private doesn't exist."

Bill and Glen worked several cases together. Their personalities clashed frequently, but Glen trusted Bill's instincts and abilities as a cop. He trusted him with his life.

Bill's untidy, overweight and balding appearance contrasted Glen's neat, muscular body.

Glen wore his sandy brown hair cropped close. Bill, in an attempt to cover his balding head, allowed the left side to grow longer to comb over the bare skin. This effect made him look worse, especially on windy days. Glen ripped him frequently about the comb-over, calling Bill "the flag" while it flapped in the wind. His favorite vice, jelly donuts, managed to appear on most of his neckties and sometimes down the front of his shirt fitting tightly over his bulging belly.

Glen worked out daily with Russian Kettlebells and running with his dogs. They resembled the pair from the old television show the Odd Couple. But when the two cops worked a case, rarely did the bad guys slip away.

When they arrived in the quiet Littleton neighborhood the streets were abuzz with spectators. After the fireman extinguished the flames they entered the remains of the house. Two bodies were discovered in what appeared to have been the living room. The police on the scene treated it as a possible homicide. Now the two detectives had the gruesome task of trying to find evidence while the CSI crew and fire investigators sifted through the wet ashes.

The condition of the bodies created confusion as to the gender. By the size of the larger corpse, it was safe to assume a male. The smaller one could have either been a female, a young male or a male with a slight frame.

"What've we got here?" asked Glen.

A young fire investigator responded, "We're pretty sure it's arson."

"What makes you so certain?"

"The fire seemed to have been set in multiple spots throughout the house for maximum burn. Based on the smell and apparent burn patterns, an accelerant was likely used. Tests will confirm that."

"How many individual spots?"

"Well, the best we can give you now is the bed in the master bedroom, the basement entertainment area and the living room where the bodies are located. There was also evidence of some trailing of thc accelerant throughout the house. Our guess is it started in the bedroom moved down to the basement and finished with the living room."

"Our vics must've been dead before the fire started," said Glen.

"Unless they were passed out from drugs or alcohol," added Bill.

"Yeah, but the middle of the day in a neighborhood like this...I think we can rule that out for now."

"Who called it in?" asked Glen.

The first officer on the scene responded, "The guy who lives next door to the north." He checked his notebook, "Tim Mertz."

"Where's Mr. Mertz now?"

"He's in his house with a victim advocate. He wasn't feeling well. He's an old guy."

Glen left Bill at the scene while he strolled next door to have a chat with Mr. Mertz.

Glen rapped on the door.

"Come in," called the feeble voice.

The advocate, Helen, returned to the room carrying a hot cup of tea for the witness.

She acknowledged Glen's presence as the detective on the case. She placed the cup of tea on the table nearest the old man's chair.

"Be careful, it's hot," she warned then stepped back to allow Glen the privacy to do his work.

"Mr. Mertz, the first officer on the scene told us that you called in the fire."

"Yes, sir."

"How did it catch your attention?"

"Well, I was letting Sparky out to go to the bathroom. Sparky, Sparky. Where's Sparky?" he asked with panic in his voice.

"He seemed frightened by all of the commotion and ran under your bed. I closed the bedroom door so he wouldn't slip out with people coming in and out to speak to you," said Helen.

"Okay. Thank you. I hope he's all right. Do you have a dog?"

"Actually, I have three. Two German Shepherds...."

"Yes, of course," he interrupted. "You're a police officer, you're supposed to have German Shepherds."

"I also have a little Welsh Corgi that I rescued," answered Glen.

"You're a nice man, rescuing that little dog."

"Thanks, now you were letting Sparky out to go to the bathroom. Then what happened?"

"Sparky, Sparky, here boy. Where's Sparky?"

Glen glanced over at Helen who shrugged her shoulders. She understood the position Glen was in at this point when his only witness showed signs of dementia. He also realized that post-traumatic stress could cause similar reaction—if Mr. Mertz was indeed overwhelmed by the incident.

"Would you go see if you can coax Sparky out from under the bed and bring him here, please."

Soon Helen returned with the small mixed breed dog. Sparky had wiry hair and brown spots on his white body, most likely some Jack Russell Terrier hidden somewhere in his pedigree. She handed Sparky to Mr. Mertz. His face showed an immediate calm, relaxing the tension.

"Now, were you letting Sparky in or out?"

"In."

"Does Sparky run loose or do you keep him on a chain?" asked Glen having noticed the chain strung across the porch.

"Always on a chain. Believe it or not I can't keep up with the little guy like I used to. I'm not sure if I could catch him if he started to run off."

"Mr. Mertz..."

"Call me Tim."

"Tim, did you notice anyone next door when you let Sparky outside?"

"You mean the house that burned?"

"Yes sir, do you know who lives there?"

"I like to keep to myself. I'm not one of those nosey neighbors."

Just then Bill walked in to see how the interview was progressing.

"Hello, young fella, are you here to ask me questions, too? I was telling this nice man. What's your name?"

"Glen."

"I was telling...er...this nice young man that I'm not one of those nosey neighbors. I like to stick to myself."

"Did the next door neighbor have a dog?" asked Glen.

"No sir. I don't trust anyone without a dog. She didn't have any kids either. But that's good. I don't like the noise when kids live next door. The last family that lived there had three kids and they were always on my front lawn. They broke my favorite rose bush, they did."

He started to stand.

"Let me show you my roses."

"Bill here's, allergic to roses. Maybe we should talk more about your neighbors," said Glen.

"Which neighbors do you want to talk about? I like to mind my own business you know."

"Excuse me a minute," said Glen.

He took Bill aside.

"I'm getting nowhere here. This is gonna take some time. Have you found anyone else, a little more with it, who we can question?"

"Officers already went door to door and no one's home. There aren't many homes on the block. Yeah, if everyone went to work this guy might be all we have."

"I assume we're widening our search."

"I already have the uniforms doing just that," answered Bill.

Bill spent the next few minutes sharing the information from the scene with Glen.

Helen had gone into the kitchen to fix Mr. Mertz a sandwich. When Glen returned to him he was munching away as if he hadn't eaten yet that day.

He sat on an ottoman so he could make direct eye contact with Mr. Mertz.

"Glen, that's your name. Right?"

"Yes, Mr. ... er...Tim, that's right."

"You want to know about the fire, don't you?"

Glen was amazed at the change a little food could make.

"What can you tell me about the fire?"

"I was letting Sparky here in and I saw the smoke. Black smoke just pouring out of every window. Then I saw her car in the driveway and worried she might still be inside. I knew I couldn't do anything to help her so I called 911."

"That's good, Tim. You did the right thing."

"Can you tell me who lives with the woman next door?"

"She lives alone. Well, at least she's not married, but she has men there all hours of the day and night. I'm not nosey mind you, but I do notice things. From that window right there I can see most everything that goes on in that house. She never closes her shades. A real nice looker, if you get my drift," he winked at Glen.

"How old would you say she is?"

"Oh, about thirty. Nice looker. She likes to sun bathe in the summer out back. Girls these days sure don't wear much clothes. Let me tell you, one time she was out there stark naked laying in the sun. I couldn't believe my eyes. I kept an eye on her though. I didn't want some thug coming in and bothering her."

Glen struggled to hold back a smile. The old gent still had an eye for the ladies.

"Does she have a name?"

"Of course she does. Her name is Carol. She's a nurse or a doctor because she wears those hospital clothes."

"You mean scrubs?"

"I don't know what you call them, but that's what she wears."

"Did she have a man with her today?"

"Yes, sir. Two of them. One inside and the other pounding on the door. Mad he was. Do you think he's the one who set the fire?"

"He could be. Can you describe him?"

"Tall, big guy with blond hair, kinda tough looking."

"Do you have any idea what kind of a car he drove?"

"Didn't drive a car, had a motorcycle. A Harley. I know because I used to work on them when I was younger."

"Do you know Carol's schedule?"

"She works all night. Comes in about eight in the morning. Sometimes alone and sometimes with a man."

"Is it usually the same man?"

"The blond used to meet her here a lot, then not so often. She's been bringing a lot of strange men home. All of them have different cars."

"Do you know which hospital she works at?"

"Nope."

"Do you know her last name?"

"Smith, but I'm not sure if that's her real name."

Glen shot a look at Bill. "I'm on it."

He started a phone search for a Carol Smith at the local hospitals. He hit it on his second call.

"Can you give me a description of Carol?" asked Glen.

"Pretty girl, blond hair and the biggest blue eyes."

"So you've visited with her.

"Oh yes, she's come over to use my phone a time or two when her cell phone wasn't working."

"Thank you, Tim, you've been a big help. I may be stopping by to visit with you again. Here's my card. Call me anytime if you think of anything else, no matter how small, okay?"

"Yes, sir. Any time. I sure hope Carol's gonna be okay."

Glen didn't have the heart to tell him Carol's condition. Since the charred house standing next door was uninhabitable, Mertz would have no way of knowing Carol hadn't simply moved away.

"Well, let's head next door and see what the nozzle monkeys have come up with," griped Bill.

He had no use for firefighters. After a thorough job extinguishing the smoldering spots, they also totally demolished the crime scene, making the detectives' jobs nearly impossible.

The fire consumed all trace evidence except for possibly the nature of the accelerant. Now they could only hope the post-mortems could give them something to go on. The two detectives will work closely with the fire investigators for the insurance companies, who stop at nothing to avoid paying insurance claims, hoping desperately to find and charge someone with arson if there is the slightest inkling it could go in that direction.

Glen and Bill drove back to their department. The fire had also devoured the day. Exhausted, without much to go on, thc two parted ways in the parking lot.

Hide and watch, Glen thought, as he knew the phone calls from neighbors, friends and relatives would start pouring in and at least part of the puzzle would come together.

As Glen drove through downtown Wallace he couldn't help but notice the increase in traffic. Off in the distance he heard the sound of the high school band performing for the Friday night game.

It had been years since he attended a high school football game. He thought about how quickly the summer had passed by and now classes had begun. When he was a boy school started in September, the day after Labor Day. Now, classes begin in many schools across the nation in mid-August.

He slowed his pickup then pulled into the high school parking lot. He rolled down his windows to listen to the sound of the band. The roar of the crowd and the cool evening air took him back to his youth.

He decided to stay and watch the game for a short while. He paid for a ticket then stood next to the bleachers scanning the crowd for a familiar face.

He found Dr. Janet and Dr. Phil, two vets from the clinic he takes his dogs to. He had become good friends with them over the years. It had been weeks now since he spoke with them after he uncovered the town's serial killer. He was certain many people were angry with him and in denial that he could possibly accuse one of their own of committing murders, including an attempt on Glen's own life. After all, Sheriff Tate disliked Glen and had maliciously passed around his own set of rumors accusing Glen of being involved.

He climbed the stairs of the bleachers until he reached the row where his two vets sat cheering on the town team.

"Glen, come join us," Janet waved.

He excused himself as he passed seated spectators while he moved sideways down the row to the spot next to Janet. She scooted closer to Phil, making room.

"What've you been up to?" she asked. "Haven't seen you since, well, you know." She looked around to see who might have their eyes upon them.

"I'd just as soon not mention it any more," said Glen.

"Gotcha," said Janet. "I feel the same way. How's Mieke? Should be any time now if I remember correctly.

"Glad you brought her up. Am I supposed to count from the first day of her standing heat or the last?"

"Most generally the first, but it would not be impossible for it to be the last day. A lot could depend upon how many pups she's carrying. Since we did a surgical insemination I'd say go with that date."

"I could bc wrong, but I think she'll have a small litter. She's not terribly big," said Glen.

"Don't let size fool you. This is her first litter and she's more fit than the average dog. Those muscles have a way of holding things in pretty tightly sometimes. How's her appetite?"

"She's been eating a lot less this week. This morning she didn't eat at all. I stopped home to check on her at lunch time and she was out bouncing around, playing with the other two."

"Don't be surprised if you find yourself up all night delivering puppies since she skipped her breakfast. Have you been taking her temp?"

"Nah, I thought I'd start tomorrow."

"Famous last words," laughed Janet.

Glen had trouble focusing on the game. Janet caused him concern about Mieke.

"I think I'll go home and check on her. Now you have me worried."

"Call if you need anything. We've both got our cells with us," said Janet.

Glen smiled and waved at a few of his neighbors as he found his way through the crowd to the parking lot. He hesitated and looked back at the game in session in time to watch the home team score a touchdown. For a moment, he thought about returning to the game then he remembered his psychic friend, Jennifer Parker.

"Follow your instincts. Listen to that small voice inside telling you what to do. It's never wrong."

She repeated those words often to him during times of doubt.

He turned on the lights in the kitchen then opened the back door to let the dogs in. Cheyenne and Taffy came bounding inside, excited to see him, but no Mieke.

He grabbed a flashlight to search the backyard. She did not respond to his calls. He stopped, closed his eyes and let his conscious thought drift away. As he stood in the silent blackness of the evening he heard panting at the far end of the yard. He walked in the direction of the sound and it grew louder.

Mieke had carved out a perfect hole large enough for her and the litter of puppies she was about to give birth to. Glen gently rolled her back to search for hidden puppies beneath her. He examined the ground around her. The dry soil told him birth had not yet begun.

He scooped her up in his arms and carried her into the large bathroom where he had prepared an area for her and the pups. The other dogs wanted to join them, but he insisted they remain at the door. Cheyenne obeyed while Taffy marched straight up to Mieke to sniff her curiously.

Always prepared, Glen had anticipated the need for the other dogs to feel a part of the process. He had cut a piece of woven wire fencing and made a half door for the bathroom. He had leaned it against the wall until needed. He scooted Taffy out then hung the new door on the pins he attached to the doorframe.

He examined Mieke closely, no sign of a pup coming just yet.

"You stay put. I'll be right back."

He darted off to his room to slip into old jeans and a t-shirt. He grabbed his cell phone, a glass of bourbon and returned to her side. Towels, blankets, suction bulb, scissors, iodine and dental floss filled the delivery kit on the bathroom counter. He looked at his watch and waited. Two hours of hard labor and panting without a puppy means a trip to the vet clinic for a c-section.

He sipped his bourbon and she lay her head on his leg.

"So, what shall we drink to?" he asked.

Her tail thumped on the floor.

"Okay, here's to a happy, healthy litter."

His phone rang.

"Glen, what's the damn emergency? You sounded anxious."

"Maggi, where the hell have you been?"

"Writing."

"I know, but where?"

"My little secret, remember?"

"Why didn't you answer your cell phone?"

"I didn't take it with me. I wanted no distractions. So what's the big emergency?"

"No emergency. I have a couple of friends staying with me who want to see you."

"Oh, Glen, you know how I feel about meeting people and signing autographs. Now I'm glad you couldn't reach me."

"They're still here. They said they're not leaving until you come by."

"You poor dear. Are you stuck with these two, really?"

"Yep."

"Can it wait a few days for me to unwind?"

"Sure, if that's what you want."

"Who are they? Are they friends of yours?"

"Yeah. The guy's name is Bailey."

"And the woman?" Maggi's heart began to race.

"Oh, her? He calls her Bridgette."

"Oh, my God! Glen, I love you! You found my dogs! I can't believe it!" she screamed into the phone.

After a moment of silence Glen heard Maggi crying.

"Are you okay, kiddo? They're fine. They'd just like to see you, but if you still want to wait a few days, I don't think they'll mind."

"Wait? You son of a bitch. I'll be right over."

"Whoa, girl. I've moved since you disappeared and vowed never to speak to me again because I didn't rush home to find your dogs."

"Moved? Where?"

"Wallace."

"Where in the hell is Wallace?"

"Get a pen and paper and I'll give you directions."

"Can't you just bring them to me? I've been driving all day."

"No, I'm about to deliver a baby. Now take these directions down quick and get off the phone."

"Baby? What's going on?"

Without answering her question he blurted out the directions and told her to call back if she got lost then hung up the phone to catch the first puppy. He cleared the sac away from its face then held the pup in front of Mieke for her to clean. Soon the wet squirming puppy cried out, causing the two onlookers from the other side of the wire door to take notice.

Glen placed the puppy against Mieke to find a nipple and take in his first meal. He patted her head then slipped back to the kitchen for a refill of his bourbon.

"One down and I wonder how many more to go? Could be a long night," he muttered.

Then he remembered his promise to call Cindy when Maggi arrived to pick up her dogs. He almost didn't call, but he had warned her it could be the middle of the night and she said she didn't care.

"Hello," said Cindy.

"Were you sleeping?" asked Glen.

"Glen, hi. Yes, I had just dozed off. What time is it?"

"Around ten. Maggi's on her way over."

"I'll be right there, bye."

Glen met Cindy at the door.

"Come with me," he said.

He walked her to the bathroom. She peeked in wondering what was going on then he heard her say, "Oh, how cute. How many?"

"She's just starting."

Cindy poured a glass of wine and joined him on the floor of the bathroom. They talked about dogs from their childhood years. A knock at the door interrupted their conversation. At the same time, the second puppy was about to make its way into the world.

"Can you let Maggi in?"

"Why don't you do it? Then you can properly introduce us," said Cindy, a little nervous.

"Okay, if you want to stay here and deliver this pup."

Cindy looked down to see the amniotic sac bulging as the contractions pushed the puppy out.

"I'll answer the door," she said.

"Come in, Maggi," said Cindy.

"Are you the one having the baby?" asked Maggi.

When she took a moment to look at Cindy, she realized she wasn't pregnant and if she had just given birth moments ago, she looked too good.

Cindy chuckled, "I'm Cindy, and it's Mieke that's having a baby. Well, actually two."

"No shit, Glen's delivering twins? Why not get the poor woman to the hospital? You do have a hospital in this town, don't you?"

"Maybe you should come with me."

"Hell no. I came for my dogs and I'm outta here. He's not gonna rope me into helping with some screaming woman pushing two kids out."

Cindy enjoyed Maggi's strong personality.

"Maggi," Glen called from the bathroom. "Get your ass in here. Now!"

Obediently, Maggi followed Cindy to the bathroom where she dropped to her knees in awe of the new puppies. Suddenly, she felt a pang of stress in her gut.

"Are these the two named Bailey and Bridgette that wanted to see me?"

"No, Maggi. I truly do have your dogs. Give me a minute to get this second pup settled then we'll go get them."

She followed Glen to the barn where he kept the two Bernese Mountain Dogs. They were beside themselves barking and whining when they recognized Maggi.

Glen opened the gate and they burst forth knocking her to the ground, rolling her in the dust of the barn floor.

"Is she okay?" asked Cindy.

"She's fine."

Maggi's tears mixed with the powdery dirt causing mud to run down her face. Glen helped her to her feet and the three humans and two dogs returned to the house.

Cindy poured a glass of wine for Maggi while she washed her face. The three of them stayed up the remainder of the night watching and helping Mieke give birth to eight puppies.

Chapter 3

The two ladies helped Glen clean the bathroom floor after the birthing. He had to coax Mieke to go outdoors with the other dogs. She had no intention of leaving her puppies. He was relieved she whelped on a Friday night so he could spend his next three days at home with her. By then he felt he could transition her and the pups to the back porch, where he had installed a doggie door opening out into a pen in the backyard.

Until this time, he kept the gate open allowing all three dogs access to the back porch and the entire yard. With Maggi's dogs leaving, he could open the barn door part way to give Taffy and Cheyenne shelter when he was at work. These arrangements would have been impossible at his home in Denver. Living in the country with numerous outbuildings had wonderful advantages.

The aroma of brewing coffee met Glen at the door on his way back into the house. As he stepped into the kitchen he found Cindy busily preparing breakfast.

"What's going on?" he asked.

"It's been a long night. I'm sure we're all ready for breakfast," she replied.

"Darlin', you got that right. Where's Maggi?"

"She said she needed a shower to help wake herself up. She's using the one in your bathroom. She didn't want to disturb the pups in the main bathroom."

"Man, a shower sure sounds good. Do I have time before breakfast?"

"Go ahead, I have everything under control," said Cindy.

Glen glanced at the table already set with dishes and glasses of juice. Bread stood at attention in the toaster slots waiting to be lowered. Cindy had bacon frying in one pan while scrambled eggs were firming in another.

"That was rude of me. Do you want me to help before I shower?"

"Nope. I told you I have everything under control. Just don't be long. I don't like to serve cold food."

Glen pulled out a chair and sat down to remove his boots. He tugged his shirt from the waistband of his jeans as he headed off to the bathroom. Mieke had gone ahead of him and was busily nursing her pups when he walked in.

Glen adjusted the shower temperature to hot and stepped in.

"What the hell?" yelled Maggi from the master bathroom.

With his head under the stream of hot water Glen didn't hear her.

"Who's messing with my hot water?" she yelled again.

Still no response. She rinsed her soapy hair under cold water and hurried from the shower. She wrapped herself in an oversized terry towel. Shivering from the sudden cold water she joined Cindy in the kitchen.

"Did you turn on the dishwasher or something?" she asked.

"No," said Cindy, surprised by the wet shivering Maggi dripping on the kitchen floor.

"Damn old farmhouse. I ran out of hot water right in the middle of my shower."

Cindy poured a hot cup of coffee for Maggi while she towel dried her long black hair. She held the hot cup tightly to warm her hands as she sipped it slowly.

"Hope I didn't take too long," said Glen as he joined them.

Maggi turned to complain to him about his lack of hot water. He wore his blue jeans, no shirt and a towel wrapped around his neck.

"You jerk," said Maggi, as she threw the towel from her hair at him.

"What'd I do?"

"You took all the hot water."

"What do ya mean?"

"I was in the shower rinsing my hair and the water turned icy cold. Just look at me, I'm turning blue."

She jumped up to show him how cold she was when the towel covering her body fell open. She caught the towel before it fell off in front of him.

Glen released one of his hearty laughs.

"I guess if you want to show me your blue body, I'm game."

"Arrgg," said Maggi as she stormed off to get dressed.

"Is she always like that?" asked Cindy.

"Nah, she's really pretty nice, but she does have a quick temper and mornings are not her favorite time of the day."

Cindy filled the plates while Glen set them on the table.

"I can't believe you went through all of this trouble. I plan to make it up to you."

"Yeah sure, that's what men always say."

"I'm not like most men. When I say I'm gonna do something, I do it."

"The hell you do," said Maggi as she re-entered the room. "I can't count the number of times you cancelled dinner plans at the last minute with Debbie and me."

"That was because of work."

"It's always because of work. You need a new excuse."

Cindy sat down to watch the two of them squabble. She could hardly believe she was having breakfast across the table from her favorite mystery writer. The event proved to be quite entertaining. She had new insight into the personality of Maggi Morgan.

"If you don't want a spanking you'd better back down. Now eat."

Maggi's mood improved with a little food in her stomach.

"What are we doing today?" asked Maggi. "We should go out and celebrate the return of my dogs."

During the night, while they delivered the puppies, Glen told Maggi the story of how he came to find her dogs in Wisconsin. Cindy helped fill her in on the deaths in Wallace and how Glen single-handedly solved the crimes. Glen disagreed and quickly pointed out he couldn't have accomplished it without Cindy, Becky and Josie.

"Maggi, I'm planning to stay home to tend to Mieke and the pups. I'm not going anywhere."

"What about work?"

"I have three days off."

"What, no cases in dire need of your attention?"

"Yes, but Bill can handle some of the investigation."

Cindy began to clear the table, still amazed at the way they talked to each other. One might have thought they were once married.

"Bill. How is good old Bill?" asked Maggi.

"I take it you don't like Bill?" asked Cindy.

"Let's just say Bill likes me a little too much. He makes my skin crawl."

"All men make your skin crawl," teased Glen.

"That's not true."

"When's the last time you were on a date?"

"I don't have time to date. I'm too busy writing."

Glen winked at Cindy. He knew how to get under Maggi's skin by pushing all the right buttons. He made a game of it. Her reactions, at times, could be quite entertaining. He had the utmost respect for her as a mystery writer who could spin remarkable tales of suspense.

Maggi caught the wink. She looked first from Glen then to Cindy, who now turned her back to them, as she headed to the sink with the dishes.

"Spill it you two. Are you an item and I missed something?" asked Maggi.

"I think the one thing we all have in common is the lack of desire for a relationship at the moment," said Glen. "Cindy is one amazing woman and definitely too good for someone like me. We're becoming great friends."

"How'd you two meet?" asked Maggi.

"I'm the library director for Wallace. Glen told me he needed to do research for a book he was working on and I offered to help him."

"Glen, writing a book? No way. That would take time away from his job. Nothing nor no one comes between this guy and his work."

"You're so right. He was working on a case when he told me he was researching material for his book. I guess you could say he used me," she said, smiling.

"That's more like it. It's not that he can't write. You should see some of the stuff he gives me for my crime scenes. Someday, if he ever decides to retire or if he gets shot one more time, he may sit down and actually write a book. Then he'll make me work to stay ahead of his fame."

"So you really think he can write?"

"Honey, he's a very talented writer."

"Not to change the subject but would you ever consider giving a book talk at our library?" asked Cindy.

"Here? In Wallace? I didn't think anyone here would read..."

"Maggi, watch yourself," Glen interrupted.

"I was going to say read my mysteries. What did you think I meant?"

"On the contrary, many of the patrons of our library are huge fans of yours."

"Sure, in that case, I'd love to. Just give me a few weeks to get my life back to normal. I need to spend some time with my dogs and decompress from my writing."

Their conversation was interrupted when Glen's cell phone rang.

"What's up?"

"Are you coming in today?" asked Bill.

"Today's my day off, so don't count on me. How's the investigation going?"

"Since when does your day off stop you?"

"Since Mieke had her pups."

"Glen, we've got another homicide on our hands."

"I'm not listening. Find someone else."

"Come on, I need you."

"Ain't happenin'. I asked, how's the investigation going?"

"We talked to everyone who knew this Carol Smith from the hospital. Seems she got very friendly with lots of the male patients. She was always bragging about how, after they were released, she'd go out with them. She targeted the ones with money, married or not."

"Any idea who the boyfriend was who got toasted with her?" asked Glen.

"Not yet, we're working on it. When old man Mertz told us she had a cell phone we tracked down her provider and we've now got a list of her calls in and out to her cell.

I don't know how she had time for work with all the calls day and night."

"Anything I can do from here?"

"I thought you didn't want to work?"

"I said I wasn't coming in. That doesn't mean I can't work from here."

"Lot of good you can do from there. Hell, you don't even have a computer. There's probably not a computer anywhere in your podunk town."

Maggi looked at Cindy.

"See what I mean," she whispered. "He can't stay away."

Both women listened to Glen's side of the conversation trying to determine what type of case he might be involved with. Cindy, because of curiosity about Glen's work, and Maggi, looking for ideas for a plot.

"There's a computer at the library I can use. I can check in on Mieke and work from there," said Glen.

"Okay, I'll email the list of people who made cell phone calls to Smith. Narrow it down to the men and..."

"Who the hell do you think you're talking to, some rookie? I know how to handle an investigation. I'll get back to you with my findings. Go ahead and send the email. I'll be at the library in a couple of hours."

Glen set down his phone and noticed the smug smile on Maggi's face.

"Don't say anything," he warned.

The women laughed.

"Look Glen, if you want me to stay here today and take care of your dogs, it's the least I can do to repay you for bringing my babies back home to me," offered Maggi.

"That goes for me, too," Cindy added. "I don't know much about dogs, but I'm sure if you left me with instructions I could carry them out."

"Tell you what, Maggi, if you could stick around until say, noon, I'll be back by then." He turned to Cindy. "I'll keep your offer on hold in case something develops with this investigation."

Maggi took her dishes to the sink.

"Addicted, that's what he is. He's an adrenaline junky and catching the bad guys gives him a high," said Maggi.

Glen rose from the table to dress for work. As he passed Maggi, he slipped the towel from around his neck and snapped her on the backside with it as he hurried out of the room.

Cindy was surprised to see the less serious side of Detective Karst. She finished clearing the table and Maggi helped her with the dishes. She smiled as she thought about her next writer's group meeting where she would announce she washed dishes with the famous mystery writer Maggi Morgan.

At the library, Glen searched the list of cell phone owners for men's names. There were very few women so he had his work cut out for him. His first plan of action was to call each and every one of them to determine who might be missing. His list totaled thirty-two different men. Bill was right; this woman was busy. He wondered then if she prostituted herself or if she dated these men for free meals and gifts.

One by one, he placed calls to the names. He explained he was following through on a missing persons investigation. He wanted to confirm their names and addresses. His search narrowed down to ten men who didn't answer their phones. He knew his next step would be to visit those men. Saturday might find more of them at home rather than at work.

He promised to relieve Maggi at noon when the library closed. Possibly, he could take Cindy up on her offer to dog sit until he could return later in the day. He'd make it up to her with a nice dinner.

At the front desk he learned Cindy had already left the building. As a matter of fact, she left over an hour ago. One of the librarians told him she had gone to Denver to visit Josie at the hospital.

If he could reach her by cell phone, and if she was finished with her visit, maybe he could still ask her to watch the dogs. It was worth a try.

Josie sat propped up in bed munching away on the caramel corn Cindy brought to her. The elderly woman, with the spunk of a wildcat, seemed more like a kitten, with the color washed from her face and her body immobilized.

"Thanks for bringing the caramel corn. They won't give me the food I ask for here," complained the eighty-year-old woman. "They treat me like I'm some old lady. If they bring me oatmeal or milktoast one more time for breakfast, I'm gonna throw it at them. Why do they bother to give you a menu choice if they won't bring me what I want?"

The nurse who stepped into the room heard her comments. She reassured Cindy, "It's not that we don't want to give her what she wants, it's just that after being unconscious for so long and having broken her hip, the doctor wants to make sure everything is functioning properly before he allows her to eat foods that may be too greasy or cause digestive problems."

"I hope I didn't do something wrong by bringing her a treat then," said Cindy.

"No, I think they're about to lift her dietary restrictions."

"How much longer will she be in here?" asked Cindy.

The nurse looked at her chart. "I believe the doctor plans to release her from here in the next few days if she continues to improve the way she has so far. She's one tough cookie."

"There's nothing wrong with my hearing. Don't talk about me like I'm not here," barked Josie.

Cindy turned the conversation back to Josie.

"If they're going to release you in a few days, where will you go? Surely you can't go home. You can't walk, can you?"

"Not with this new hip. I'm wheelchair bound. I reckon I can manage."

The nurse interrupted, "She'll be going to a nursing home. Probably in the town where she's from."

"I don't need no damn nursing home. That's for old people. I just broke my hip. If I were younger and broke my hip I wouldn't be going to a nursing home."

"No matter what age you were, if you broke your hip and had no one at home to care for you, you'd be going to some type of full care facility."

"I wish I could help you out, Josie, but I can't take time off of work," said Cindy.

"I'm afraid you'd have to take a lot of time off of work," said the nurse. "She's going to need care for two, maybe three months."

"You might as well shoot me now cause I ain't gonna be worth anything to anybody after three months in a nursing home. If the food doesn't kill me, I'll go insane."

When Cindy's cell phone rang she was relieved to take a break and step out into the hall.

"Cindy, Glen. I'd like to take you up on your offer to help out with the dogs today if your schedule will allow. I've got to go into Denver to visit with some people about my case."

"Sure, Glen. I'm about finished here anyway. I'll go straight to your house from here."

"Great. Hey, how's Josie?"

"You know what? I think it would cheer her up to talk to you. Do you mind?"

"Hell no, I don't mind. Let me talk to the old broad."

When Cindy handed the phone to Josie she had a surprised look on her face.

"Someone would like to speak to you," she said.

"Hello?"

"Hey, kiddo, how's my favorite female detective?"

"Damn it, Glen, why haven't you been in to see me?"

"I've been chasing bad guys. It's a lot harder when you're not around to help me. When are you getting out?"

"Never! They're gonna put me away in an old folks home."

"What do ya mean? Why?"

"Cause they say I can't take care of myself. That's why. They're planning to kill me. I hope you're gonna be around to put them all away after I'm dead and buried."

"Nobody's gonna kill you, Josie."

"The hell they're not. Wouldn't it kill you to be locked up with a bunch of screamin' dying old people?"

"That's what bourbon's for. Ya drink enough of that and you won't care where you are."

"I ain't never had a drink in my life," she stated proudly.

"Well, maybe it's time you start. I'll bring ya a bottle."

She laughed.

"You might be right. At least I'll be in Wallace so you can stop by more often to visit me."

"Darlin', I promise to do just that and I keep my promises. See ya soon."

The smile beaming on Josie's face after having talked to Glen told Cindy she made the right choice having him speak with her. He had a way of making Josie feel special. She so admired his work as a detective, having read every crime book and magazine she could get her hands on. She loved meeting a real live detective. Having helped him with a case, even if it meant she ended up in the hospital, was well worth it.

Glen relieved Maggi when he returned home with a pizza. After lunch she helped him move Mieke and the puppies to the back porch, making it easier for Cindy to dog sit. He was unsure if Mieke would go outside for her. Maggi, having had dogs for so many years, was a pro at handling them. Cindy seemed a little nervous around the large German Shepherds.

With Maggi's dogs loaded in her car, Glen gave her a hug and kissed her on the cheek. Cindy pulled up just in time to witness the embrace. She wondered if they were a little more involved than they let on to her. Maggi waved good-bye to Cindy as she drove away.

"There's some left over pizza in the kitchen if you're hungry," said Glen.

"Thanks, actually I am. I didn't stop to eat on the way over. I was hoping to see you for any last minute instructions before you left."

"Maggi and I moved mother and pups to the back porch. All you have to do is listen for any signs of distress and keep an eye on Mieke to make sure she's acting okay. I'm sure everything will be fine. Actually, I could probably leave them alone and she'd be okay, but I don't want to worry about her while I'm gone. I really do appreciate your help. I plan to make it up to you in a big way."

"That's two."

"What's two?"

"You owe me for breakfast this morning and now this. That makes two."

"You got it," smiled Glen.

He walked her into the house. Glen put on his concealed holster clipped to his belt, hung his badge around his neck and put on his jacket to cover his gun.

"Just call if you need anything. Since you stayed up all night, feel free to take a nap. You can sleep in my bed if you want."

"Why, Detective Karst," she teased.

Glen blushed. "The bed in my guest room is piled with boxes I was sorting through."

"I'll be fine. Do you want me to fix supper for you? What time will you be back?"

"Don't bother. I can't give you a time. I'll be home as soon as possible."

Glen drove to the first house on his list. He parked outside. Calling the man's cell phone one last time, he finally received an answer.

"Mr. Brady?"

"Yes."

"Mr. Brian Brady?"

"Yes. Who is this?"

"My name is Detective Glen Karst. I was wondering if you'd mind stepping outside for a minute. I'm parked across the street. I'd like to ask you a few questions."

When Glen saw he was a small man with dark hair he knew that, not only was he not the victim, but he also did not fit the description of the suspect.

"What's this all about?" asked Brady.

"Do you know a Carol Smith?"

Brady looked back to the house. "Why?"

"She was found dead and your phone number was on her cell phone."

"I don't know anything about her death. I only saw her a couple of times. If my wife finds out, you'll be looking at another dead body."

"I may want to talk to you downtown in a few days."

"Sure. Great. Yeah, anything. Can I go now?"

"Yeah, go on back inside."

Glen had an uncanny ability to read people. He had interrogated enough criminals to understand the body language of a guilty man. He felt this man was only guilty of cheating on his wife with a hot little blond number. He was able to scratch him off of his victim list.

As Glen turned the corner to approach the second house on his list he saw flashing lights. The yellow tape sectioning off the yard told him something was up with this man.

He parked his pickup out of the way and walked up to the first cop he saw, with his credentials in view around his neck.

"What's going on?"

"Dead female inside."

Chapter 4

After double-checking the address of the house against his list, Glen knew he was on to something. He stopped at the officer posted at the door who logged Glen's name and time of arrival. Moments after he appeared on the scene, Bill walked in.

"Glen, what the hell are you doing here? How'd you find out about this so fast?"

"I accidentally stumbled on to it while working my list of names. Is this the other homicide you started to tell me about?"

"No, there's a new one on your desk waiting for your attention. I just got the call for this one. What do ya have so far?"

"Not much, I just got here myself. A white female in the kitchen, someone slashed her throat," said Glen. "Who got the warrant?"

"Corporal Dix," replied Bill. "Forty-five minutes start to finish. Not bad."

Mind Your Manors!

Out of habit, Bill checked the lock and the doorframe for signs of forced entry. The CSI crew busied themselves in the kitchen taking pictures and dusting everything imaginable for prints. On the floor next to the body lay the murder instrument, or so it would appear. The perp used a knife from the rack on the counter top.

Bill bagged the weapon, to later be dried and then boxed with "bio hazard" written all over it. He took great care to disturb none of the blood on the knife.

"You know, you'd think as often as these big knives are used in the movies to kill people, women would learn to hide them rather than leave them out in plain sight," he said.

"Jennifer says its bad feng shui to have knives exposed in the room," said Glen casually, while his eyes scanned for details of the murder.

"Don't go bringing your psychic friend in on this investigation, we don't need to know about her feng shit," snarled Bill.

"I said feng shui not feng shit," corrected Glen in an annoyed tone.

Jennifer Parker, a psychic who helped Glen on several cases, proved to be invaluable as a resource when all other avenues failed. He grew to admire and respect her talents. She instilled in him the ability to go within himself to learn more about a crime to aid in solving it. He wished the department would put her on the payroll.

Not only did most of the other detectives not believe in her work and refuse to spend time communicating with her, but she also had no desire to devote her life full time to solving crime. The pain and the anguish she experienced while working a scene was not something she wished to live through on a daily basis.

If a case touched Glen in an emotional sort of way, or if they were up against a clueless crime with nowhere else to turn, he might seek out her advice and guidance. He tried not to abuse her assistance. Over the past few years they became very close friends. If he wasn't so wrapped up in work, she is the type of woman he might like to get to know a little better. Not many women can remain as mysterious as Jennifer Parker.

In the beginning, his sergeant forced him to work with her at the request of the parents of a missing girl. When Glen realized she was not a fraud, he feared she could read his every thought. Since then he learned that ability escaped her.

He wondered what she might feel or see if she were here today. He has never brought her into a case where a body still remained at the crime scene. Having both the body and the weapon, she might make short order of the entire situation.

On several occasions she worked with him to improve his psychic abilities. She told him everyone is born with the gift, some more than others, but those who wish to develop it can learn to.

Glen looked around the room as the crew worked feverishly gathering evidence. Bill had stepped out of the room to talk to the first officer on the scene.

Standing over the body, Glen reached for the bagged knife on the portable table set up in a "clean" area for evidence. The "clean" area is a place that is likely unimportant to the crime at hand and is duly processed anyway, at the beginning of the search. He checked one more time to be sure no one was paying attention to him then closed his eyes. His pulse quickened, he found himself short of breath; he sensed fear. He could smell it like a dog can smell fear on a frightened human.

He relaxed and allowed himself to drift into the feeling. He had the sensation he was out of breath from running. He felt someone grab him around the throat. He dropped the knife as he spun around to his attacker, prepared for combat as he opened his eyes.

The sound of the knife hitting the floor caused the other officers to look toward the sound. Glen stepped back away from the body. A little shaken by what had just happened, he realized no one had grabbed him, but he felt what the woman lying on the floor must have felt moments before her death. He needed a glass of bourbon.

"Are you okay, Glen?" asked one of the members of the CSI crew.

"Yeah. Sorry guys. I guess the bag slipped out of my clumsy hands."

Bill walked back into the room.

"What the hell happened to you?" he asked.

"Nothing. Why?" responded Glen.

"You're white as a ghost and look at you, you're sweating. Are you having a damn heart attack or something?"

"No, really, I'm fine. Must've been something I ate. I'm gonna check out the backyard."

Glen stepped outside for a breath of fresh air to calm his nerves, even then cognizant of where he stepped and his surroundings.

Many times he witnessed Jennifer lose the color in her face and appear distressed and frightened at a crime scene. He had no trouble imagining what Bill must have seen on his face.

He tried to shake off the feeling and return to his work. As he walked toward the middle of the yard he turned to the house, feeling with all the instinct within him that the killer had stood in this very spot. Now he had to decide if the missing husband or stranger killed the woman and why.

Bushes overgrown against the house would give cover to an intruder. He ran his hand over the tops of the bushes. As the leaves parted his eyes focused on a bit of white, but only for a split second then the parted leaves closed to conceal it. He brushed back the bushes more carefully to expose the white paper of a cigarette butt, gently releasing the bushes he stepped several paces away. He photographed the bushes and house for reference, and then moved in for closer shots until he had the butt perched gingerly on the branch.

Reaching into his pocket for an evidence envelope he then, using his pen, gently coaxed the butt into the envelope. He could tell upon closer examination it had not been out in the weather.

Feeling more confident the intruder entered from the back of the house, Glen continued to search for more evidence to confirm his theory. The door handle and jambs had already been dusted for latent fingerprints. A privacy fence separated the yards adjoining the homes. He walked to the edge of the yard; as he looked toward the street he noticed the fence did not include a gate. The driveway stretched from the street to the side of the house. The garage doors did not open to the front of the house but to the side. Where the driveway ended and the yard began, the homeowners had tilled the soil in preparation for a flowerbed or to plant additional grass or sod.

He squatted down for a better look at the freshly tilled soil. He found two tire tracks. It took him only a moment to recognize a motorcycle made them. The impressions were obviously too deep and wide for a bicycle and with only two tracks, not four, it obviously was no car.

He called for Bill on his radio.

Along with Bill, a tall thin officer walked up to Glen.

"What's up?" asked Bill.

"Check out the tracks. What do you think made them?"

As Bill squatted down to examine them, the other officer said, "Looks like the tracks my bike makes."

"So, it appears someone with a bike lives here. What's your point?" asked Bill.

"Think about it. Carol's neighbor said a blond burly guy on a bike was beating on her door that day just before the fire. The guy who lives here had his number on Carol's cell phone. I couldn't reach him by phone today, that's why I drove over here," said Glen.

"So you think this guy might be our big burly blond?" asked Bill.

"Could be. Any idea where the man of the house is today? Has no one been able to reach him to tell him about his wife?" asked Glen.

"Don't jump to conclusions, old man. We still don't know if the woman on the floor lived here and if our missing guy is her husband."

"Can't be all that difficult to find out. Did you look for pictures of the family?"

"Yes, and there are none setting out," said the officer, still listening to their analysis of the crime.

"How about the bedroom? What'd you find in the there?" asked Glen as he walked past them to the house.

He ran upstairs to search for the master bedroom. Locating it he walked to the closet, inside were clothes for both a man and a woman. He checked the sizes for the woman. They were most likely the victim's. When he checked the size of the man's clothes, he believed they belonged to a larger than average man. But then his only witness to size was an elderly man suffering from dementia.

Glen questioned the head of the crime scene crew.

"What can you give me?" he asked.

"We found photos of the woman confirming this is her home. No signs of forced entry. You've already seen the probable murder weapon."

"What about the man who lives here? What can you tell me about him?"

"Lots of suits tells me he's a business man. By the looks of the electronic equipment and furniture in this house, I'd say they're doing pretty well."

"Any photos of him?"

"We found photos of her with several men. Could be brothers and a father, could be her husband is one of them or he could be the one taking the photos. We did find lots of nice camera equipment."

Bill joined Glen.

"This was no robbery," said Glen. "There's no sign of forced entry, no theft of the electronic or camera equipment."

He opened the top drawer of the bureau, finding her jewelry box. He opened the lid with his pen.

"No sign of missing jewelry. Every piece is laid to rest in such a way that it would've been impossible to rifle through it without disturbing it," said Glen. "It appears the only crime committed here was murder or rape and murder. My guess is, when the M.E. gets finished with the vic, we're gonna find out there's been no rape. The only plan was to kill her."

"We've gotta find this husband," said Bill. "I'm looking at him as our prime suspect."

"I'd have to agree," said Glen. "Let me know what you find out. I've got to get home."

"Hell, Glen, you can't just walk away like this."

"Watch me. It's my day off and I'm gonna try to salvage what I can. You've got plenty of help for the grunt work; I'll see you on Tuesday morning. By then we should have more to go on. Let me know what you find out from the neighbors and the family when you make those calls."

Bill watched Glen as he drove away. He wondered what happened to his work-around-the-clock partner. His concern for Glen's health surfaced. He would make it a point to speak to him about it on Tuesday. Maybe a few days off would do him good.

Glen's stress level zoomed upward at the crime scene. He felt the need to relax and give his experience some thought. He picked up his cell phone to call Jennifer. He wanted to explain to her what happened and hoped she could shed some light on it. As he was about to press the speed dial number for her, he stopped.

A fearless competent officer of the law described Glen. Somehow calling Jennifer made him feel he might be showing a sign of weakness. He'll tell her about it sometime when their paths cross by chance. The last thing he wanted, at this point in his life, was to be dependent upon a woman. After all, he'd been a cop, a good cop, for several years before he had even heard of Jennifer Parker.

He envisioned Jennifer the day she stood in his house looking out the window. At that moment, he thought of her as a woman for the first time, as he studied her slender silhouette against the light shining through. He remembered her long flowing hair, her slight waist. A loud horn blast in heavy traffic jarred him back.

His thoughts turned to Cindy who so graciously offered to take care of his dogs. He contemplated ways to repay her. As he drove past Winegard's Florist, flowers seemed appropriate. Circling the block, he parked in front of the store.

Inside he met Vanessa for the first time. Vanessa Winegard, a well-dressed woman in her late forties, greeted him with a smile.

"May I help you?" she asked.

"Yes, I'd like to buy flowers for a friend."

Glen's badge still hung from the cord around his neck. When he finishes for the day he generally removes it and slips it into his pocket before going out in public. Today, his mind preoccupied with thoughts of Jennifer and his experience at the crime scene caused a lapse of awareness.

Vanessa asked, "Are you here on a case?"

"Excuse me?"

"Your badge. I wondered if you were working on a case here in Wallace."

"No," said Glen as he took off his badge and slipped it into his pocket. "I live here, just forgot to go back anonymity."

"I'm not sure we've met," she said.

"I'm Glen Karst. I bought the old Watkins farm."

"We may not have met, but I've sure heard about you. Sheriff Tate's not...shall we say...overly fond of the way you cracked down on the deaths around here by stopping..."

"Yeah, I reckon we'll let that rest," Glen interrupted.

"I'm sorry. My name is Vanessa. Vanessa Winegard. My husband and I own this shop. Actually, my husband also owns the mortuary."

"That's why the name sounds familiar," commented Glen.

"You said you'd like to buy flowers for a friend. Is she a special friend?"

"You mean a romantic friend?" asked Glen. "No, she's been helping me out a lot lately and I just wanted to show my appreciation with some flowers," as he perused the selection of roses.

"Would you like a bouquet or an arrangement?"

"What do you suggest?"

"You could go either way. An arrangement is hands-off, but a bouquet seems a little more personal."

"Let's go with a bouquet," said Glen.

"What type of flowers would you like?"

"It definitely has to be roses. You see, I have a theory on women and roses. There's only one flower that you give to a woman and that is a rose, period. The color and number denote the occasion such as red and white are strictly for the lover, though red can cross over to Mom on the most special occasion. All other colors are for everyone else. Always a dozen at the minimum, unless you're making a special point to a lover, then two dozen offset in a simple arrangement is wonderful."

"I agree," she went in back to look in the cooler. Glen followed.

"What are those?" he asked as he pointed to a small lavender-colored rose.

"Very good choice. Those are lavender roses, very, very fragrant and very pretty," she said.

"Those are nice."

"Are you wanting to take these with you now or do you want them delivered?"

Glen thought about it for moment then realized if he had roses delivered to Cindy's house the entire town would immediately find out, especially if she wasn't home and they were delivered to the library or a neighbor's home.

"I'll wait and take them with me. Take your time. I'm in no rush."

Glen strolled around inside the small floral shop admiring Vanessa's handiwork.

"How long have you had this shop?" he asked.

"Almost twenty years."

"Have you always lived in Wallace?"

"No, my husband's from here. We met in college and moved back when his father wanted to retire from the mortuary."

"I take it that was his course of study."

"Actually, not. Chemistry was his major. He wanted to work in the agricultural field on pesticides and fertilizers. You know, that kind of thing. Then his dad convinced him to take over the family business that his grandfather had started. At first, Michael fought the idea, but soon realized he could make more money in the family business, giving him more freedom than working for someone else in a lab somewhere. So here we are."

"I suppose he grew up with it so handling dead bodies probably didn't seem that unusual to him," said Glen.

"That's true. It was much harder on me. I tried to help him in the beginning, but being around sad people bothered me. I'm a pretty happy person. Flowers make people happy so it seemed like a good move for me when the floral shop went up for sale. Actually, the two businesses sort of compliment each other anyway."

"Indeed they do," agreed Glen.

As he looked out the window onto main street, he saw Sheriff Tate drive past.

"You say ol' Tate is still pissed off at me?" asked Glen.

"Oh yeah, he really doesn't like you. I think you hit him where it hurts and that's right smack dab in his ego."

Glen laughed, "Little man, big ego, doesn't make for a good combination."

"Here ya go. What do you think?"

"Great job. What do I owe you?"

"Is fifty-seven dollars fair?"

"Absolutely."

Cindy heard Glen walk in. The dogs had run anxiously to the door at the sound of Glen's truck a mile away. She sat up in bed to look at the clock, shocked to see it was nearly five o'clock. She had checked Mieke a few times then quickly fell back to sleep.

Glen tapped on his bedroom door.

"I'm awake, come in," said Cindy as she smoothed the blankets on his bed.

"I'm sorry, did I wake you?"

"No, well, yes. But that's okay, it's time to get up or I won't sleep at all tonight. You must be exhausted, you've been up the entire day."

"I'll sleep when I die," he said.

She followed him to the kitchen where he poured a tall glass of bourbon. He went to the living room to the chair where he set her roses.

"Here, lovely lady, these are for you. Thanks again for helping out."

Cindy smiled, "Why, Detective Karst, they're lovely."

"What's with the Detective Karst shit, you usually call me Glen?"

"I know, but the flowers took me off guard and I wanted my thank you to be proper or something. I'm still sleepy; just ignore me. How was your day? Did you find out what you needed to?"

Glen took a large swallow of his drink.

"I'll tell you about it over dinner. How's everything with the puppies?"

"Fine, she's a good mom. She barely leaves them."

"I'll feed them, then why don't you let me buy you dinner in town tonight," he said.

"Sure, that sounds good. Can we stop by my house first so I can freshen up?"

"Not a problem. A shower sounds good to me, too. Something about dead bodies makes one want to feel clean, got to wash off the day."

"You found a dead body today?"

"Yeah, a woman had her throat slit. I'll tell you about it at supper."

"You know what, Glen. I think I'll head home now. Why don't you shower and meet me at my house."

"Good idea, I forgot about your car. I'll see you in less than an hour."

Glen rang Cindy's doorbell. As he stood on her step waiting for her to answer, he felt sad looking at Josie's empty house next door. It must really be tough to be old and all alone. He promised himself to make it a point to visit her often until she could return to her normal lifestyle. Many residents move into a manor with a medical problem, but not many leave alive.

"Where are you taking me?" asked Cindy.

"Do you have a craving?"

"Nope."

"Then let's go to Fouraker's Steak House. A nice big steak sounds good to me," he said.

"Oh no," said Cindy as she glanced up from their table.

They had just been seated when Sheriff Tate walked in with a promiscuous bleached blond on his arm. He strutted across the restaurant to his table bobbing like a peacock during a mating ritual.

"Are you okay? Do you want to leave?" asked Glen.

"No, but he's gonna make a big deal out of this, you know."

"Let him."

Cindy knew Glen had a stressful day, no sleep and was now on his third glass of bourbon. She wondered if he had the ability to control himself in the event Tate made one of his crude remarks.

"Glen what're you doing here?"

A hand touched Glen's left shoulder. He turned, half expecting to see Tate standing over him.

"Darrell, what the hell brings you to my town?"

"Who says you own the town?" he teased.

Glen rose to shake hands with Darrell and his wife.

"Cindy, this is Dr. Darrell Hooper. We see far too much of each other in the ER in Denver when we're investigating cases. And this must be your wife?"

"This is Abby." Cindy shook hands with both of them.

"We're just getting started, would you like to join us?"

Glen shot a glance at Cindy for approval.

Cindy, anxious to make new friends who were not from Wallace, had already begun to make room at the table for them.

"What brings you to Wallace?" asked Glen.

Abby responded, "When Grandmother died Darrell spent a few days here with me. We stayed on the farm in her house and he fell in love with it. He talked me into coming back here to live."

"No shit! Hey, that's good news. What about your job in Denver?"

"I quit."

"What's your plan? Are you going to work here or have you made so damn much money you can afford to retire?"

"Grandmother left my brother and me a tidy little nest egg. Enough for us to live on while we decide what we want to do. She kept Grandpa's farmland so we're gonna continue to lease it out."

"That's what I do with my land," said Glen. "I like it that way."

Cindy asked, "Who was your grandmother? You look familiar to me."

"Kate Hodges."

"That's where I know you from. I went to her funeral."

"Did you know my grandmother?"

"No, but I feel I should get to know everyone here. I do try to attend most funerals when my schedule allows. I'm the director of the library."

"I absolutely love to read, so I'll be spending lots of time there," said Abby.

The four of them chatted until they closed the restaurant. Abby and Cindy became fast friends. Cindy hoped they would spend more time together. Glen and Darrell enjoyed conversation that didn't involve discussing the point of entry or type of weapon used to create the damage.

As they walked to their cars, a voice came from behind Darrell.

"Aren't you the new Doc in town?" asked Tate.

Darrell turned to him, "Yes, I'm a doctor, but I'm not practicing yet."

"A word of warning. If you want to make it in this town, you might want to choose your company a little better. This guy's one dangerous son of a bitch. You have to watch out for someone who turns on his friends."

Darrell looked at Glen in surprise.

Tate turned to Cindy, "I knew you were lying to me when you said you weren't putting out for this sorry excuse for a cop."

Glen grabbed him by the throat, knocking him against the brick wall.

"Glen, stop it!" yelled Cindy. "He's just taunting you."

The veins in Glen's neck stood out as he released his grip on Tate's throat. The smell of alcohol on Tate's breath and his slurred speech told Glen he probably wouldn't remember what happened by morning. The temptation to work him over was strong, but Glen forced himself to walk away.

"Another time," he vowed.

Forgiveness was easy for Glen because he knew people. Forgetting was not.

Chapter 5

The following Tuesday Josie moved into a room at Wallace Manor. Melody helped her to settle in.

"It says on your chart your name is Josie. Is that short for Josephine?"

"Land sakes, girl, don't you dare start calling me Josephine. You tell those others out there the same thing. I want to be called Josie. Not that I'll be here long."

"I'm expecting to have the pleasure of your company for the next couple of months while your hip heals," responded Melody in a caring voice.

"Don't you know these places kill people?"

"Now, Josie, we have lots of patients here after a surgery, some much younger than you and even some older, who go back to their homes."

"Do they pay you to say that?"

Melody knew Josie would be a challenge to win over, but she was up to the task. She busied herself in Josie's room unpacking her clothes and hanging them in the closet. She felt Josie's eyes on her, watching every move, sizing her up.

"Would you like a snack or a book or magazine?"

"You have books here?"

"Yes, ma'am, we have our own little library. If you can't find it here, we can call over to the big library and have them bring over whatever it is you'd like to read."

"What kind of snacks do you have?"

"I can bring you some fruit or candy. How about a nice piece of chocolate?"

"What I'd really like is a cup of tea and a couple of cookies. I don't eat chocolate candy. Never had a yearning for it. Mother used to make fudge and she said I was the only child within a hundred miles who refused her fudge."

"Do you have any family nearby?"

"No, it's just me. I don't even have a cat."

"You're from Wallace, aren't you?"

"Born and raised. I have that nice little brick home on Mulberry. You know the one. All the roses out front. I sure miss my roses."

Josie had a far away look in her eyes.

Her words saddened Melody, recalling memories of Kate and her bountiful flower gardens.

"We have flowers out back. Maybe when you feel up to it I can take you out there in a wheelchair. We can sit and enjoy them together."

"You seem too young to appreciate flowers. Kids your age are too busy to enjoy the small things in life, like the smell of a sweet rose or the taste of fresh vegetables right from the plant. Wal-Mart's your answer for everything."

"Not me. I have a huge vegetable garden and lots of flowers. When I was in school my friend's grandmother taught us all about gardens. I could live in mine, but unfortunately I have to work."

"Who was your friend's grandmother? Maybe I know her."

"Katherine Hodges."

"You know Katie? We went to school together. She used to beat me out every year at the county fair with the stuff from her gardens. I'll swear, you know Katie. How's she doing?"

Melody brushed a tear from her eye. "Kate died not long ago."

"Did she live here?"

"Yes, for six years."

"And it killed her didn't it? I told you."

"I'll go get your tea."

***

Back in Denver, Bill joined Glen at his desk. He set his coffee down. Glen eyed it, worried that Bill would knock it over. Almost as soon as he had the thought, Bill sat on the edge of the desk and his gun brushed against the flimsy Styrofoam cup, spilling the contents across Glen's desk. He jumped back before it dripped onto his lap.

"Damn it, Bill. Do you always have to bring food to my desk?"

"You have more room on yours than I do."

Glen glanced across the room to Bill's desk buried in files, loose papers and old food containers.

"Maybe if you weren't such a slob you could eat at your own desk."

"Yeah, but I'm a loveable slob. You couldn't get along without me."

Glen handed him a napkin to wipe the white powder and jelly from his mouth. As long as Bill remained superior to some of the other detectives, Glen chose to overlook his gross appearance and eating habits.

"What'd you find out while I was gone?"

"On which case?"

"Let's start with Carol," said Glen.

"Definite on the arson, definite on her ID, we're still trying to ID the guy."

"I don't suppose there was anything left on his fingers for a good print?" asked Glen.

"Nope, the guy was a big chunk of charcoal. We're hoping to find some match on dental records."

"Where are you starting?"

"I guess with the names on her cell phone. Thank God she left that in her car."

Glen opened his notebook and tore off a sheet, handing it to Bill.

Bill licked his fingers then took it from Glen.

"What's this?"

"A list of the guys who didn't answer their phones. No sense in wasting time on the men I've already confirmed living."

"Good point, thanks. I'll get someone on this right away," said Bill.

"What's next?"

"The vic who was stabbed. Her name is Monica Steele, husband, Gerald Steele. Her family said they weren't getting along. Her co-workers confirmed it. They've been married eight years, no kids, no dog. She told her friends and family she wanted to file for divorce."

"Sounds like our guy has motive," said Glen.

"Yep. Her sister told me that she found out he was having an affair," said Bill.

"Probably with Carol. Why else would he have been on her cell phone?" said Glen.

"There's more," said Bill. "He had an accident with his motorcycle and spent a few days in the hospital with a minor head injury."

"Did you find out if he's a big blond guy?" asked Glen.

"Yes, on both counts," said Bill.

"Did Carol's family give you any information on Gerald's family?'

"Only that he has none. He grew up in the system. He bounced from foster home to foster home. Seems he had a temper and couldn't control it."

"That's a new one," said Glen sarcastically. His heart went out to kids, especially kids with a tough start. If he wasn't a cop he'd be working to fight the system and improve it. Instead, he arrests what the system creates.

"So, we can confirm Monica's marriage to Gerald. He finds a babe on the side, his wife finds out and wants a divorce. Gerald has a temper; he loses it and kills his wife. The scene didn't look fresh when I was there. Do we have a time of death?"

"It can only be narrowed down to the same day as the fire."

"Son of a bitch. The bastard kills his wife then finds his girlfriend with another man. He loses his temper again and sets the two of them on fire. This guy's mine," said Glen. "If that's what happened. Still a lot of ifs to prove."

"We're on this together. I can't let you have all the fun."

"Have you run a check on his accounts?" asked Glen.

"Yeah, he's hiding out somewhere. No activity yet."

"He probably had some bucks stashed somewhere in that big house," said Glen. "Let's go catch us a bad guy."

Glen got up to leave.

"Wait, don't you want to hear about the other case?"

"Tell me in the car. Let's go."

***

"Knock, knock," said Cindy as she entered Josie's room. "Are you up for a little company?"

"Yes, I am. You can't believe how boring it is in here."

"How long have you been here?"

"What time is it?"

"Almost noon."

"Then I've been here two hours. Noon, huh? Where's my lunch. They probably forgot about me."

"I'm sure they'll bring it along soon. Look, I brought you some roses. Glen bought them for me last Friday. They smell so nice. I chose some of the best ones to share with you. I thought they would mean a little more to you coming from Glen, knowing he picked them out."

"Why's he giving you flowers? I'm the one who's locked up in here?"

"Oh, Josie. Give him a chance. He's been working on a tough case. He'll be in to see you. He promised."

The idea of Glen working on a new case perked her up. "What's going on? What kind of crime? Is it in Wallace again?"

"No, this one's in Denver. A woman was found dead in her home. It was all over the papers."

"Was she married?"

"Yes."

"Then the husband did it."

"What makes you say that?"

"Glen's not the only one with gut instincts, you know. Tell him to come in here so we can discuss it. Two heads are better than one. I'll need to know more about the crime scene."

"I'm not sure how much he can share with you. It's still an open investigation," said Cindy.

"That's okay. He knows he can trust me."

Just then the aide, Diane, walked in carrying a tray.

"Lunch time," she said as she brushed the bangs of long blond hair from her eyes. "How's a little meatloaf and potatoes and gravy sound today?"

"Like real food," Josie said. "Will I get fed like this every day or is this just a first day treat?"

"I think you might like the food here. The cook is very good. We have lots of family members come by to eat with the residents because it's all so tasty. Maybe your family will be stopping in to have meals with you occasionally."

"That's not going to happen," said Josie.

"Why not? I'm sure once they taste the food they'll make a real habit out of it."

Josie positioned herself closer to the tray as she picked up her fork to taste the potatoes.

"It's not happening because they're dead," she said nonchalantly.

"Oh," said Diane, taken off guard. New to nursing homes, she was still unaccustomed to many of the comments from the residents and the brutal honesty in which they delivered them.

Cindy winked at her.

"Josie has no family, she's outlived them all."

"That's right. I've been too busy to die. Up until now I've avoided the grim reaper. But this place is probably his second home. I 'spect I'll be seeing lots of him 'round here. But I ain't goin' without a fight. You tell him that when you see him."

Diane left Cindy and Josie to continue her rounds.

"Is she gone?" asked Josie.

"Yes," replied Cindy.

"No. Is she really gone? Look out in the hall to be sure she's not listening in on police business. You know that no one in this town can keep a secret."

Cindy smiled at Josie and checked the hall.

"She's really gone."

"Good, now tell me more about Glen's case."

"I don't know any more."

"Are you withholding facts from me?"

"No, Josie. I wouldn't do that. I really don't know any more about the case. You should know Glen well enough to know he doesn't discuss his work."

"Yeah, I guess you're right. He probably doesn't want you to know. We'll just have to keep it our secret. I wonder when he'll be in to discuss it with me?"

Cindy rolled her eyes and thought, what a pistol.

"I've got to get back to the library. You take care of yourself. I'll be back to see you. Everything's fine at your house. I've been watering your houseplants and looking after your lawn. So don't worry about a thing."

As Cindy strolled back through the manor she stopped to watch the residents. At one table in the dining room she saw a group of chatty gray-haired women all talking at the same time while they ate. A few men seated at other tables comparatively were much quieter than the ladies.

Looking around the dining room, she realized the women outnumbered the men three to one. It must be true that women live longer than men, she thought.

The residents varied from those as capable as herself, only needing assistance after a surgical procedure, to those who were fragile and physically disabled, to those who appeared to have retreated within themselves in an almost vegetative state. In a manor this size, the residents were mixed more often than not. No special wings or different dining areas; they all shared the common rooms and the lobby.

Cindy knew Josie would never be happy until she returned to her home.

Back at the library, Cindy gave Glen a call.

"Cindy, what's up?"

"Hi, Glen. I just came from the nursing home. Josie's there."

"How's she doing?"

"She's not a happy camper. Your phone call the other day cheered her up so much. I was wondering if you could stop by there on your way home tonight just to say hi."

"I'd be happy to. Thanks for the heads up. I gotta go, I'm in the middle of something."

Bill and Glen were at the bank where Gerald worked. They learned he was the branch president by the plaque on the door to his office. Glen approached a teller.

"I need to speak to your president, please."

She appeared nervous, then responded, "I'm sorry, he's not in. Would you like to speak to Mr. Sloan, our branch vice-president?"

"Sure, that would be fine," said Glen.

She escorted the detectives to Mr. Sloan's office.

"These two gentlemen would like to have a word with you."

He stood to shake their hands.

Glen closed the door.

"What can I do for you, gentlemen?" he asked.

"Can you tell us where we might find Gerald Steele?" Bill asked.

"Do you have business with Mr. Steele? Maybe I can assist you."

He kept his responses businesslike and proper.

"We really need to speak directly to Mr. Steele," said Glen.

"I'm sorry, he's not in."

"When do you expect him back?" asked Bill.

"I'm not exactly sure."

"Is he ill?" asked Glen.

"Look, if there's some banking matter that I can help you with, I'd be more than happy..."

Bill showed him his badge.

"Now, can you tell us when the last time was you saw Mr. Steele?" asked Bill.

Mr. Sloan had a look of relief on his face not having to continue with the charade.

"He was here last week. Then he just didn't show up for work yesterday. We haven't been able to reach him by phone. I assumed, since his wife died, he was too busy with funeral arrangements and I'm sure he's under a great deal of stress."

"What do you know about his wife's death?" asked Bill.

"Only what I've read in the paper. Of course, there's been talk in the office when we didn't hear from him. We were wondering if he was all right or if something happened to him as well. Can you shed some light on this for us?"

"Actually, that's what we want from you," said Glen. "Can you check his accounts to see if he's had any activity since last week?"

"I'm afraid in order to give you any information regarding his account I need his permission, or a search warrant."

"No need to be specific. He's missing and we wondered if he'd used his account. Oh, and by Colorado law you cannot be held civilly or criminally liable for providing account information that is material in a police investigation. Here's a copy of the statute. "

Mr. Sloan hesitated as he studied the faces of both men. He turned the computer monitor preventing them from seeing the screen as he checked Gerald's account.

"No activity."

"Do you have a photo of him?" asked Glen.

"On the wall in the hall. All of our employees are pictured there."

"Was he planning a vacation or trip?" quizzed Bill.

"No, he took some of his vacation time shortly after he was released from the hospital."

"Do you know where he went?" Glen asked.

"No, could've just stayed home to recuperate longer. I'm not sure. Is he really missing?"

"It appears that way," said Glen.

Once out on the sidewalk, Glen said, "Hell, that didn't get us anywhere."

"Well, at least we know he didn't show up at work either and he's still not spending money. We also know he went on a vacation. Do you think he took his wife or his girlfriend?"

"We know that he took time off," said Glen. "Let's check with Monica's family."

Bill called Monica's mother. She assured them that Monica had not gone on any vacation with him. She was unaware that Gerald even went on a vacation.

That tidbit of information told the men Gerald probably took time off work to play house by day with Carol then went home to his wife at night. All the while, the wife assuming he'd been working all day.

It was time to call it quits. Glen parted ways with Bill in the parking lot. They would resume the investigation the next morning.

As Glen drove through Wallace he remembered his promise to stop by to see Josie. He parked his pickup and sat there looking toward the door. He pressed his head back against the seat and closed his eyes. He searched for the burst of energy he needed to lift Josie's spirit. He wished he had a glass of bourbon.

He slid out of the pickup and walked down the street to a bar. Inside he recognized no one. He sat on a stool and ordered a double bourbon. He sipped his drink while he thought about Josie. How he hated to see her in a place like that. He had flashbacks to his childhood when his great grandmother lived in that very same facility. The smells and the sounds frightened him. Nearly ten years old he thought he could handle it. Several of the residents perked up when they saw a child. They reached out for him, eager to touch him and talk to him. He froze in his tracks. His father tried to coax him to talk to the people, but he remained too afraid.

That was the one and only time he visited his great grandmother before her death shortly after that day. Now, as an adult, he had to face the ghosts of his past.

He sees death almost every day in his line of work, but death among the elderly seems so sad. He wondered how many deaths those walls had actually witnessed.

His thoughts turned to Jennifer. What happens when she enters a nursing home or a hospital? Do the dead come forth in droves to speak with her? He decided to ask her the next time they talked.

He tipped his empty glass, not realizing he had finished it off while deep in thought.

Not wanting to stall any longer, he walked back down the street. Inside, he was surprised to see the light cheery atmosphere that had replaced the dark gloomy rooms he remembered. As he walked through the lobby, he saw residents playing cards and watching television. He paused to study the numerous birds fluttering around the aviary. Further down the hall, he noticed aquariums containing colorful backgrounds and fish quickly darting in and out of the rock formations.

Life...he witnessed signs of life everywhere. Not the morbid place of death he expected to walk into. No longer did he notice the smell of the elderly and dying. It reminded him of a hospital, clean and sanitary. It comforted him to see the changes time can bring. He felt better about Josie's temporary housing.

At the nurses' station, he asked directions to Josie's room.

"Hi, I'm Laura Payne, I'm the director of nursing. Josie's only been here part of the day and you're her second visitor. She's one popular lady. Follow me. I'll take you to her room."

Glen appreciated the professional demeanor of the attractive tall brunette. He wondered if she was married. He noticed the absence of a wedding ring.

Before Glen could step back away from the counter, he felt someone tugging on his jacket. He turned to find a woman in a wheelchair who had silently rolled up to him.

"Do you know when Rita will get here?" she asked.

"I'm sorry. I don't know Rita," he responded in a gentle voice.

"You must know Rita. She said she was going to get a ride with you. Where is she? I've been waiting."

Laura intervened.

"Sally, Rita's not here yet. Maybe she'll come a little later. Mr...," she turned to Glen.

"Karst, Glen Karst."

"Mr. Karst didn't bring her today."

"Oh, then where is she?"

"I'm not sure, but we'll keep an eye out for her," said Laura in a comforting tone.

They walked to the end of the hall to Josie's room.

"Josie, you have a visitor," said Laura.

"Detective Karst," said Josie. "I knew you'd be coming soon. Now let's get down to business. Tell me about your case."

Laura was taken back by Josie's comments.

"Are you really a detective?" she asked, concerned that yet another disgruntled resident or resident's family member may have turned them into the state, causing a detective to investigate charges against the facility. It had only been a year since the Bangert Company took over Wallace Manor. A decision made by the town council in an attempt to improve the situation and maintain a tighter budget.

Glen smiled. "Yes, I am. Josie and I are old friends. I won't keep her long. I'm sure supper will be coming soon."

Laura sighed with relief. "Yes, it is. Supper should be in about fifteen minutes. You're welcome to stay and eat."

"Maybe some other time. I have animals to care for at home."

Glen walked over and gave Josie a kiss on her cheek.

"Lookin' good, Missy, lookin' good."

"Now I feel good, getting a kiss from a looker like you."

Glen blushed.

"Let's get to work," she said. "Fill me in."

"Now, Josie, you know I can't do that. You're on leave. You're not assigned to this case."

He hoped his choice of words would appease her, at least for the time being.

They chatted briefly about her surgery and her trip over to Wallace Manor. Their visit was cut short by the arrival of an aide to wheel her to the dining room for her first meal with the other residents.

Glen stood to assist when his phone rang.

"Glen, have I got..." said Bill.

"Can you hold a minute?" Glen interrupted. He stopped the wheelchair and squatted down to Josie's level.

"I've gotta go, dear. I'll be back as soon as I can." He kissed her on top of her snowy white hair.

She squeezed his hand, dropping it as she left the room.

"Okay," he said to Bill.

"You're not gonna believe this."

"What?"

"We got an ID on the male vic with Carol from his dental records."

"Who is he? Was he on the list?"

"Yes, sir. None other than Gerald Steele himself."

Chapter 6

Parked in front of his house, Glen remained in his pickup replaying the last bit of evidence reported by Bill. He rubbed his burning eyes then punched both fists simultaneously on the steering wheel.

"Just figures, damn it, nothing's ever easy," he said.

Then he thought, just because he's dead doesn't rule him out as the perp in his wife's homicide. But then who did him in? This new piece to the puzzle put them back to square one.

He slipped out of his pickup and walked to the house feeling as though he'd been sucker-punched. Where were his instincts when he needed them?

Inside, he changed then fed the dogs. Mieke and her pups were doing fine. She did a great job caring for them. At this point they were hands off. She nursed, bathed and cleaned up after them. The heat lamp he hung over the bed allowed the pups to move in and out of the warmth as they felt the need.

As he picked up each puppy, an even number of males and females, he noticed a few spots of blood on the carpet. He assumed it came from Meike until he noticed the wrist area on one puppy had what looked like a tiny wound. Upon closer examination so did the other leg. He checked each puppy and found the same tender tissue.

"What the hell?" he said.

Then he realized the dewclaws were missing.

"Too bad you can't talk," he said to Mieke. "You could explain this to me. I know you didn't remove them."

Knowing someone had been to the house and performed the minor surgery on the pups told Glen one of the vets must have paid him a visit. He returned to the house in search of a note.

He found a small piece of hot pink notepad paper fastened to the refrigerator by a magnet advertising the local grocery. He pulled it down to read:

Glen, I'm sure it slipped your mind to bring the pups in for dewclaw removal when they were three days old. I had a farm call near here so I thought I'd stop in and handle it for you. I hope you don't mind.

Take care,

Janet

Glen checked the date on the calendar hanging on the kitchen wall. The pups were three days old. Having been so involved with his case, it totally slipped his mind. He saw the note he had written on the calendar to remind him to take the pups in today.

"I'll be damned. Gotta love livin' in the country," he said.

He poured a glass of bourbon then sat down to call Janet.

"Good evening, sweet lady," he said.

"Glen, I was wondering when you'd be home. I didn't want to call and bother you at work. I really hope you don't mind that I removed the dewclaws. I got to thinking about it afterwards and didn't know, if for some reason the pups were to be police dogs, if they needed to keep them. I know there are certain breeds, like racing greyhounds, where they leave them on. I didn't check Mieke to see if she still had hers."

"Damn it, Janet you just rendered those pups worthless for police work."

Janet remained silent.

Glen laughed. "Hell, I'm just foolin' around with you. I want to thank you for handling it. I don't know where my head was. Can't believe I didn't get it taken care of myself."

"You son of a bitch, don't freak me out like that!"

Glen's laughter grew louder, "Come on that was funny."

"You are gonna send me a bill for your services, aren't you?" he insisted.

"Yeah, and it'll be double because of your smart-ass attitude. How are the pups doing? Everyone stop bleeding okay?"

"Yeah, they seem fine."

"Good. Gotta go, I'm on call and there's a horse down with colic."

Another good deed for the day from yet one more resident of Wallace. How could anyone from the city understand the kind of life one lives in a small town? Of course, there is the annoying fact that everyone knows everyone else's business, but when someone needs something there are a dozen neighbors willing to help. That fact remained unchanged since his boyhood days.

He remembered when a farmer had an accident or became ill at harvest time, the neighbors showed up early in the morning with combines, trucks and grain carts to take over the harvest before attending to their own. With a large crew of neighbors they could quickly knock off multiple fields in just one day, donating their time and fuel.

After breakfast the next morning, Melody kept her promise to Josie. She wheeled her out into the garden to enjoy the huge display of chrysanthemums. The fiery colors of autumn were approaching when the flowers burst forth in bloom. The lavenders and yellows were offset by rusts, dark purples and burgundies.

"Oh my, look how beautiful they are," said Josie, admiring the way the colors lined the walkway.

"I think mums are some of my favorite flowers," said Melody. She reached down and plucked a large yellow blossom to hand to Josie. The contrast between the two women, young and old, frail and plump, one in the prime of life while the other nearing the end, disappeared as they shared their love of the garden.

"I have other residents to check in on. Would you like to sit here a while longer or do you want me to wheel you back inside?"

Not yet sure of her surroundings and fearful of being forgotten, Josie suggested she go back inside.

"Would you like to take a nap before the show starts?" asked Melody.

"What show?"

"Oh, I'm sorry. I forgot this is your first full day with us. Several of the residents like to gather in the commons area to listen to the radio at ten."

"I can listen to the radio any time. Take me to that library of yours."

She pushed Josie toward the religious section of the small library.

"I ain't no Bible thumper. I might believe, but I sure don't need to keep reading about it. I want a good murder. Where's your true crime section?"

"I'm afraid we don't generally have much call for true crime. How about mystery?"

"That'll work."

Melody left Josie to thumb through the collection on the shelf. She'd stop back in a few minutes to see if she needed anything.

***

"When do you want to take a look at this?" asked Bill, as he tossed a folder onto Glen's desk.

"What is it?"

"It's that other homicide I was telling you about."

"Who's on it?"

"We are, if you want it. I've started the investigation," said Bill. "I've got some guys checking stuff out for us."

"Don't you think two open cases are enough for us to handle right now?" complained Glen, still upset about Gerald's death.

"Yep, but everyone else is just as busy. Sarge thought we could handle it."

Glen flipped open the file. Inside he saw the photo of a mutilated body of a man. He read on to discover the victim was a minister or preacher of some sort.

"What the hell happened?" he asked.

"We've got his wife in custody."

"Do we have a confession?"

"Not yet. That's why Sarge wanted you to handle it. He has some asinine idea that you'd be better interrogating the woman than I would. Something about how the ladies like you. Hell, police work is police work. I've gotten my fair share of confessions from women."

Glen studied Bill's crumpled appearance and said, "Yeah, I'm not sure why he said that."

"What?" whined Bill. "I didn't have time to iron my shirt this morning. Besides, I wear my jacket when I'm not at my desk."

Glen took the file then headed to one of the jail's interrogation rooms. He sat down at the table to read before one of the guards brought in the wife.

Glen knew she had been picked up a few days after Earl's death. She was missing from the scene. The parishioners went to check on him when he didn't show up for the Sunday morning church service. They discovered his car missing and the door locked. Two men knocked, but no one answered. About to leave, one of them noticed blood on the doorframe.

They walked around the house looking in the windows. The drapes were drawn throughout. When they peered in the bedroom window, the split in the drapes allowed them to see the foot of a person lying on the bed. They rapped on the window. No movement.

The house belonged to the church; extra keys were in the office next door. One of them jogged back to the church to retrieve the key. Cautiously, they let themselves in, not wanting to touch anything in case they were entering a crime scene.

Everything in the house appeared neat and tidy—until they stepped into the bedroom. There on the bed, they discovered the body of their pastor, Earl Coughlin. On the floor, next to the bed, lay a claw hammer covered with blood and scalp hair.

There was no sign of Norma anywhere in the house. They were positive someone had broken in, killed him and kidnapped Norma. They notified the police. An autopsy revealed large amounts of whiskey in his system along with multiple doses of sleeping pills. A condom wrapper was found on the night table near the whiskey bottle. They obviously engaged in sex before the intruder broke in. Or worse, maybe Norma had been raped.

She was declared missing. A quick check of her credit cards disclosed activity in Fort Collins. The local police were contacted and given a description of her car from the information the parishioners had given the Denver police.

A car was dispatched to her motel. An officer knocked on the door. No answer. Having gotten a keycard from the front desk, one officer used it to open the door while his partner stood ready with his gun drawn.

"Mrs. Coughlin," he called out, as he pushed the door open.

No response. They feared the worst. When they stepped inside they found her sitting on the edge of the bed in a bloodstained dress weaving a tissue between her fingers. She was non-responsive. They requested an ambulance.

"How the hell could she check in to the motel and no one thought to report the fact that her clothes were covered in blood?" asked one of the officers.

"No one wants to get involved, I guess," said the other.

Norma was taken to the hospital for medical clearance and SANE exam, wherein specially trained doctors and nurses examine victims of sexual assault and collect evidence, as well. Her examination showed no signs of violent rape. Other than her mental state, she appeared to be in good physical condition. Because of her mental state, the officers kept her at the hospital on a seventy-two hour emergency mental health evaluation, with a cop on scene around the clock. By the time she was to be released, the lab had the results of the blood on her clothes and hands. It was definitely Earl's blood. She was arrested and taken to jail after the psychiatrist said she was not an immediate risk to herself.

Glen stepped outside the room while the guard seated her. He preferred to make an appearance after he observed the demeanor of the suspect through the two-way. He wanted to be sure they didn't shift into acting mode when he entered.

So far, all he noticed was that she stared straight ahead at the wall not moving, other than weaving the tissue in her hand over and under her index fingers.

"Good morning, Norma. I'm Detective Karst. I'm here to talk with you about the last few days."

She looked at him without saying a word.

"Is that okay?" he asked.

She nodded.

Immediately, Glen noticed her eyes, dull and lifeless, almost as if she were on drugs. He quickly checked to see if a drug screen had been performed. It had and she was clean.

"Norma, do you know why you're here?"

She shook her head.

"Before we get started can I get you something? A cup of coffee, a Coke...?

"Tea," she whispered barely moving her mouth.

"You'd like a cup of hot tea?"

She nodded.

Glen went to the door and requested a cup of hot tea.

"Before we talk, I have to advise you of your rights, okay?"

Once she convinced him she understood her rights and agreed to waive them to speak with him about the case, he proceeded. He began his line of questioning with topics unrelated to the case. He asked her about her birthday, family members, schools and her current occupation. He continued along those lines of questioning to determine her lucidity before he moved on to the questions more pertinent to the case.

"Norma, can you tell me who Earl is?"

She nodded.

"Who is he?" he decided to ask her a question she was unable to answer without speaking.

"My husband."

"Good. And where is Earl now?"

"Sleeping."

The body had been found in bed.

"Is Earl at home in your bedroom sleeping?"

She nodded.

"Norma, why were you in the motel in Fort Collins?"

She shrugged her shoulders.

"Did you drive yourself there?"

She nodded.

"Norma, you know Earl's really not sleeping, don't you?"

A tear rolled down her cheek as she nodded.

"Tell me what happened, I know there are reasons for everything."

She did not respond. She stared straight ahead fumbling with the tissue between her fingers. He continued after having made the effort to give her the chance to tell the story on her own.

"Norma, did you hurt Earl?"

She nodded.

"Norma, I need you to speak to me."

"Yes," she whispered.

"Why did you hurt Earl?"

She shrugged her shoulders.

"Words, Norma, I need to hear your words."

"I didn't want him to hurt me anymore."

"Tell me more," coaxed Glen.

For the next two tear-filled hours she told an all too familiar tale of emotional and physical abuse.

Glen confirmed what he suspected the moment he looked into her eyes. She was a battered woman. That unmistakable look he saw so many nights when neighbors would call in an incident of domestic violence. He'd look into the eyes of the abused women refusing to press charges against their abusers. What kind of animal would do that to a woman? He found no justification for it and loathed the cowards who did it.

He thought back to a time before he was an officer of the law, quite a big younger and a lot cockier. He walked past a window of an apartment where he heard screams. He looked in and witnessed a man beating a woman. He raised a ball bat to hit her when Glen burst in through the closed door, shattering the wood trim. He yelled for her to leave while he lost his temper on the drunken husband. He stopped short of beating him with the very bat he planned to use on his wife. The following week, when he visited his friend at that same apartment complex, he watched the same woman come out of the door and leave in a car with the man who had beaten her.

He understood what Norma had probably experienced at the hands of her husband. Several more hours of investigation and interviews provided evidence of the history of abuse that Earl had viciously carried out against Norma. Glen was actually proud of her for finally ending it and told her so, weaving in the "you didn't have to kill him" speech. Glen's report of the evidence and surrounding circumstances indicated clearly that Norma acted in self-defense and then suffered post-traumatic stress disorder. He sent her back to her cell and reported to his sergeant. The District Attorney's office found nothing to charge her with. He signed off on the case.

***

Diane found Josie in the library so intently focused on a book she didn't hear anyone approach.

As Diane gently touched her shoulder Josie jumped with a start.

"Girl, don't do that to an old lady like me. Can't tell how much longer the ol' heart can take a jolt like that."

"I'm sorry, Josie. I thought you might like to join the others, the show's about to start."

"Okay, let's see what all the commotion's about. I never listen to the radio at home. All those damned commercials. I like my record player. No commercials there."

"Opal, this is Josie," said Diane as she parked Josie next to her.

"Nice to meet you," said Opal. "You're new here, aren't you?"

Josie, surprised to find another resident who appeared to be mentally with it, responded, "I got here yesterday. What's the big deal about the radio show?"

"Why, it's the Josh Mackey Show. Don't tell me you live in Wallace and don't know who Josh Mackey is."

"I'm afraid I don't. I never listen to the radio. It's either my books or my record player when I'm not out tending my garden or doing other chores."

Opal looked over the top of her glasses at Josie seated in the wheelchair.

"Hip surgery," explained Josie. "What are you in for?"

"My family thinks I need someone to look after me. I forget things."

"That's no excuse, we all forget things. What else is wrong with you?"

"Nothing, the doc says I'm as strong as a horse."

"Good morning, Wallace," said the voice of Josh Mackey over the radio.

Josh, a young man in his late twenties, moved to Wallace from Denver. His love of entertainment landed him a job on the local radio station. The female residents of the town revered his celebrity status. With a kind heart he brings a smile to everyone who listens to his show. His commentaries on the talk shows stir up controversy in the small town. He likes to liven things up a bit, keeping it interesting.

One day, while visiting the nursing home to meet some of the residents, he discovered they rarely listen to the radio. They had the same feeling Josie had. The modern music and the many commercial breaks turned them off. He planned to do something about it.

Now, from ten to eleven every morning, he airs a broadcast designed for the seniors in the area. He plays music from the thirties, forties and fifties. He welcomes the listeners to call in requests and to send him stories of their youth growing up in Wallace, which he then reads through, picking the best to read on the air.

During the broadcast he also wishes a happy birthday or anniversary to the senior citizens. His show has increased the listener base and brought a ray of sunshine into the lives of the lonely.

As he played music from the Big Band era, Josie closed her eyes to remember her life as a young girl. Song after song touched her. She laughed at the stories of stealing melons and turning over outhouses.

When the show ended at eleven she was disappointed.

"Well, what'd you think?" asked Opal.

"It was wonderful, absolutely wonderful. What a special young man he is."

"Wait until you meet him," said Opal.

"What do you mean?"

"He comes by every Wednesday afternoon. He brings treats and sets up his equipment and plays the old radio story shows. You know, like the Shadow and the Lone Ranger."

"He doesn't."

"Yes, he does. You'll just love him."

Josie and Opal sat and talked until suppertime. The next morning they shared breakfast together. During the meal, Opal introduced her to a number of the other residents who, like Opal and Josie, still had their wits about them.

Later in the afternoon the group invited Josie to join them in a game of cards. They played rummy until the aides made them stop. They needed to eat and get ready for bed.

When Josie was tucked into bed she hoped the night would pass quickly so she could visit with her new friends. Before she met Detective Karst and worked on his case with him, she didn't have much company. Older people are quickly forgotten when they fail to keep up the pace with the rest of the community.

The next morning Darcy stopped in to check on Josie.

"Who are you?" she asked.

"Hello, Josie. My name is Darcy," said the redheaded mother of three young boys, a single mom in desperate need of work to support her children after her husband skipped out on them. She took the job at Wallace Manor, but didn't really like it.

"Land sakes, how many of you are there?"

"How many what?"

"How many different nurses?"

"Actually, I'm not a nurse. I'm just an aide, but there are about thirty of us."

"Let's get going, we're burning daylight," said Josie, anxious to visit with her new friend.

She looked down the hall to see what was keeping Opal. Her breakfast remained untouched in front of her while she waited.

"Josie dear, you should eat something," said Diane.

"I'm waiting for Opal," said Josie.

Diane stood next to Josie for a moment. She adjusted her scrub top and straightened her long blond hair. She wasn't quite sure what to say.

"Opal's not coming to breakfast. Why don't you eat and then I'll take you out into the garden."

Cindy stopped by to see Josie.

She found her sitting at the table chatting with the ladies she had played cards with. When Josie looked up and saw her, she waved.

"Can you take me out of here?"

"No, I'm sorry you have to stay until you're better."

"Not out of the manor, out of the dining room. I want to talk to Opal."

"Who's Opal?"

"She's a lovely lady. We had the best time yesterday. She didn't come to breakfast. I want to be sure she's feeling okay. She's in room one thirty-seven."

Cindy wheeled Josie to the door of one thirty-seven. The bed was empty, not even a sheet covering it. Cindy knew immediately what had happened.

"Where is she? I'm sure she said room one thirty-seven," said Josie.

Laura came by to introduce herself to Cindy.

"Hello, I'm Laura Payne, the director of nursing. May I help you with something?"

Cindy noticed the dark eyes and slender body, every hair in place and her meticulous makeup. She seemed so out of place working here. It would have been more believable if she had told Cindy she was a model.

"Hi, nice to meet you. I'm, Cindy the library director. Josie was looking for her friend, Opal."

"May I speak to you a moment?" asked Laura.

The two stepped away from Josie.

"Opal passed away in her sleep last night."

"I was afraid of that," said Cindy. "What should I tell Josie?"

"The truth, but please take her to room to tell her, if you don't mind."

Cindy pushed Josie slowly down the hall to her room.

"Did you find out what happened to Opal? What room did she move to? We had plans for today."

"Josie, Opal died last night."

"That's impossible. She was as healthy as a horse. Her doctor told her so. She just forgot things. There was nothing wrong with her. She was murdered."

"Josie, I'm sure no one killed your friend. It was just her time."

"You're wrong. She was murdered; I can feel it. Murdered!"

Chapter 7

Darrell and Abby were having morning coffee while they sat on the porch of her grandmother Kate's farmhouse.

"I can understand what Glen sees in living out here," said Darrell.

Abby never dreamed she'd return. She had her fill of small town life while growing up. An athletic girl, she played volleyball and girls' basketball. When not playing ball, she joined the other cheerleaders performing for crowds at the boys' games. She competed in mock trial, the debate team and remained an active member in 4-H. Her grandmother would have been disappointed had she not entered projects in the county fair. Abby knew Kate hoped she would one day take her place as the blue ribbon winner for produce.

Abby couldn't wait to leave. She thought the city had much more to offer; besides, she could never see herself married to one of the local boys. She went off to college to become a registered nurse, where she met

Darrell during his internship. The two hit it off immediately. As soon as Darrell advanced beyond his intern status they were married. He insisted she stop working at the hospital to stay home and start their family. Over the past few years, nothing seemed to work as Abby failed repeatedly to conceive.

Darrell hoped the slower paced country life and returning to her roots might help Abby relax and if she were meant to conceive she would. All the tests and procedures they'd endured to determine the cause of her infertility showed no answers. They agreed to let time and Mother Nature take over.

"We really need to get a subscription to the Denver Post," said Darrell. "There's just not much here."

He turned page after page of the Wallace Journal. Sports took up the majority of the paper, a small amount of local news and local events—nothing about the world outside of the rural town. He was surprised to find the page on births, deaths and hospital notices.

"I didn't know they devoted so much space to who's in the hospital and when they were dismissed. Look at the size of the announcements for births and deaths. Can you imagine if they tried this in the Denver area?" he chuckled.

"Maybe you're about to find out small town living is not for you," said Abby, wondering if he was fascinated or just mocking the community.

"No, don't take me wrong. I think it's quaint. I like it. It's nice to know the big news is…" he looked for a name, "Rachel Wilson was released from the hospital on Wednesday, instead of writing about all the crime that happened during the night."

Abby leaned into his shoulder while he continued to read. She sipped her coffee and watched a pair of squirrels playing on the front lawn beneath the large oak tree that stood for many years. She remembered when her grandfather hung a tire swing from its strong branches and would push her and her brother, Paul, for what seemed like hours. She had a new appreciation for her past, seeing it through the eyes of an adult.

"For such a small community there's sure a lot deaths in the paper," said Darrell.

"What do you mean?" she asked.

"Look, there were four elderly people who died."

"That's for the whole week," she said as she looked over his shoulder. "You're used to the Denver paper that lists deaths for each day."

"I suppose you're right."

"Did we ever get the autopsy reports back from Grandmother?" asked Abby.

"I think they're on the table. I didn't open yesterday's mail. I was too busy scraping dead mice off the floor in the laundry room," he said.

"One little mouse," she said. "He probably died five years ago. Big deal, you sissy."

He pulled her over his shoulder onto his lap where he kissed her gently. His kisses grew more passionate as he began to unbutton her blouse.

"What do you say we work on that family plan?" he suggested.

"Why Doctor, what are you suggesting?" she teased.

He carried her into the house, not making it past the sofa in the living room where he made love to her.

While Abby showered after the romance, Darrell sat at the dining room table going through the mail. He opened the autopsy report. Everything seemed to be in order but the large amount of hypnotics in her system confused him.

Abby stepped into the room while drying her hair. Walking up behind him, she slipped her arms around his neck and kissed him on top of his head then placed her chin on his head to read the report he had opened.

He asked, "Did Kate have a sleep disorder?"

"No, not to my knowledge. Why?"

"I'm confused about the fact that the tox screen on the autopsy report showed drugs in her system."

"I suppose I can check in with Melody. She'd probably know. How about bacon and eggs for breakfast?"

"Sounds good. Can we have pancakes with that?" he asked.

"Boy, the way you eat no one would ever guess you were a doctor," she teased.

After breakfast Darrell asked if they could stop by the nursing home to talk to Melody. As a doctor, he couldn't understand the need for sleeping pills for residents of the manor. He wondered if Kate had other medical conditions that could be genetic. A full medical history could only help to keep his wife healthy and possibly find some strange overlooked link to her inability to conceive. He worried about her health knowing both of her parents died young from cancer, leaving her to live with her grandmother.

The first thing Darrell noticed about Wallace Manor was the décor. It looked more like a hospital than the nursing homes in Denver where he did a rotation as an intern. He theorized, since it was the only nursing facility in town, the need to glamorize it to compete for clients didn't exist.

They strolled through the lobby hoping to catch a glimpse of Melody assisting a resident. Darrell noticed a small cluster of women walking the halls at a rapid pace for exercise. He wondered why, if they were in such good physical health, they were residents.

Cold stares followed their movement to the nurses' station. No one manned the desk. They waited. Finally, an aide stopped. It was Darcy.

"Can I help you?" she asked.

She smelled of cigarettes. She must've just stepped inside from a smoking break in the garden. She lacked the same cheerful attitude that Melody poured forth. Obviously, this was just a job for her.

"Is Melody working today?" asked Abby.

"Yeah, she's here somewhere. I'm sure she's busy. Did you want me to find her?"

"If it wouldn't be too much trouble," said Abby, feeling like they were intruding.

"I guess I can page her. I hate using the intercom system, but if you want me to, I will."

Darrell stepped forward.

"Yes, please do," he said in a firm tone.

He disliked lazy employees, especially those dealing with sick or elderly patients. He preferred they work at a job not requiring them to come in contact with another human being in need.

When his hospital refused to let employees smoke on the company grounds, even the parking lot, he praised the decision. If hospitals are all about health care why don't the employees care about their own health? Abby gave him grief on more than one occasion about his prejudice toward smokers.

She felt he needed to ease up and enjoy life more. His professionalism made him too stiff and structured. His response was always the same, "Wouldn't you prefer a doctor who was stiff, educated and professional as opposed to a laid back, casual doctor who might make an error in diagnosis?"

She had to agree.

"Melody, please come to the nurses' station. Melody, please come to the nurses' station," announced Darcy. "She should be right here."

Darcy disappeared down a long hall and into a resident's room.

She was right. Melody popped out of a room down that same hall and made her way to where they were standing.

Surprised to see Abby, she hugged her and said, "Hi, what are you doing here?"

"Darrell had a question about Grandmother. Do you have a minute?"

"Sure, but not very long. It's a busy day and we're a little short-handed."

"Can you tell me how Kate's health was at the end?"

"Well, not much change over the last six months or so. She was coherent and alert. Her emotional health was good, considering she had trouble with her mobility. I actually thought she could go on that way for a few more years. But you never know. Some days they just decide to give up and the next thing you know they're gone."

"Did she have any pain or difficulty sleeping?" asked Darrell.

"Oh, she had a little arthritis but that's not uncommon at her age considering how hard she worked her entire life. Sleep problems...no. Why?"

"Her tox report came back showing she had sleeping pills in her system. Can you explain that?"

"Sure. Dr. Culbertson prescribed them."

"Why? If she had no sleep disorder?" asked Darrell.

"Standard procedure."

"What do you mean standard procedure? Since when is it standard procedure to pass out sleeping pills to the elderly?"

Melody felt uncomfortable discussing Kate's condition any further.

"Maybe you should speak to Laura. She could give you more answers. I just follow orders. I'll take you to her office."

They followed her down the hall to Laura's office. She popped her head in to tell her she had visitors. Laura, on the phone, raised one finger in the air to signify she'd be with them soon.

"I heard rumors that you might be moving back. Is there any truth to that?" asked Melody.

"Actually, we've already made the move. We put our house in Denver on the market, put our furniture in storage and moved in at the farm. When we get more settled we'll invite you over for dinner."

"Are you planning to resurrect the garden?"

"Absolutely. What about you? Do you remember everything Grandmother taught us?"

"She'd never let me forget. I saw her five days a week here. I still can't believe she's gone."

Laura stepped out into the hall.

"Can I help you?"

"Laura, this is Abby Hooper. She's Kate Hodge's granddaughter and this is her husband, Darrell."

"Come in and sit down, please," said the ever-gracious Laura.

Abby noticed Darrell couldn't resist admiring the beauty Laura possessed. He almost forgot what he wanted to speak to her about.

Abby broke the silence, "Kate's autopsy showed sleeping pills were in her system. My husband was wondering why?"

He regained his composure.

"Yes, why would Dr. Culbertson prescribe sleeping pills to the elderly?"

"Occasionally, we have a patient with intense pain and the pills help them get through the night, especially after having undergone a surgical procedure."

"What about Kate? I'm not aware of any surgical procedure, sleep disorder or emotional need for a sedative to help her sleep."

Laura eyed Darrell cautiously. His choice of words set off alarms.

"Are you a doctor?"

"Yes, as a matter of fact, I am."

"Why is it exactly that you ordered an autopsy on Kate? Did you suspect something other than old age?"

"Isn't it customary to perform autopsies on the deceased residents?" he asked.

"No, it's not. Most families understand once they come here due to the ailments of old age, they seldom leave. Some families find relief that their suffering on earth has come to an end. It varies among families of different religious beliefs, but, all in all, autopsies are rare occurrences here."

"Is it a common occurrence then to administer sleeping pills?"

"Dr. Culbertson has a theory that disturbed sleep patterns add to the confusion and disorientation of their days. He feels that allowing the residents to have an entire night of restful sleep puts them on a better schedule to cope with daily activities. We have no one falling asleep during mealtime or sleeping the day away only to remain awake all night and possibly disturb the other residents. It's been working out well."

"So, he routinely gives them to every resident, every night?"

"Yes."

"I can't believe it," he said angrily. "Are the families aware of what he's doing?"

"I'm not sure, probably not. By bedtime we usually don't have any family members visiting," she said.

She feared Dr. Hooper had the potential to disrupt the operation of the nursing home.

"How often does Dr. Culbertson examine the residents?"

"Excuse me?" she asked

"How often does he make rounds?"

"Here?"

"Yes, here?"

"About once a month."

"That's it? He's giving drugs to people that he only sees once a month?" The anger mounted in his voice.

"If we have a resident exhibiting any signs of illness or discomfort we take them over to the clinic to see him."

"When was the last time he examined Kate?"

Abby watched as both Laura and Darrell tried to remain professional but their tones expressed anger. She now feared Kate might not have been receiving adequate care. Already feeling guilty about not visiting more often, she now added to that guilt wondering if she should have found a place for her in Denver where she could have watched her more closely.

Laura checked Kate's records.

"You have to understand, Kate was in excellent health," she tried to explain.

"So good that she died?"

"No, what I'm trying to say is, she had no reason for the past year or so to be taken to the clinic. She complained a little about her arthritis and being too frail to walk around and take care of her own meals."

"She hadn't been examined by the doctor for over a year?"

Laura said nothing.

"Come on," he said to Abby. "It's time to pay the doctor a little visit."

He stormed out with Abby at his heels.

***

"Good job on the confession," said Bill. "That was record time. How'd you get the dame to admit to killing her husband so fast?"

"The son of a bitch abused her. Didn't you see her? Didn't you look into her eyes?" said Glen, still annoyed.

He never understood how some veteran cops are oblivious to such obvious signals. He is never wrong about people, ever, and often assumes that other cops are the same. Most are, some are not.

"No, I have to admit, I just read through the paperwork. I never actually met her. So you think he got what he deserved, huh?"

"No, he deserved worse. He deserved to be locked up where he could be abused and raped by other inmates. Then he deserved to die."

"Yeah, I had a feeling when I saw you this morning that something was eating at you. I know how you overreact to women being abused."

"Kiss my ass! There is no *over* in a situation like this. If all men felt the way I do about women and the need to care for them and protect them when necessary, there would be no assholes on the streets who beat, rape and kill them."

Glen stomped off to get a cup of coffee and calm down.

When he returned he had his temper under control.

"Anything new on the arson case or the slasher?" asked Glen.

"You still think the two cases are connected, don't you?"

" Of course, don't you?"

"I'm beginning to agree with you," Bill said. "As a matter of fact, I got a call this morning from Monica's sister. She said she wanted to talk to us. She should be here any time now."

"What's up with that? She didn't give you any reason?"

"Nope."

Glen scoured the report from the insurance investigators, the crime scene crew and the notes he and Bill had made. He hoped something would jump out at him, something he missed that could connect the dots between the slashing and the arson—something more than circumstantial evidence.

He recounted the facts. Carol Smith and a male friend, boyfriend or lover, Gerald Steele, were both found dead, bodies charred beyond recognition in the living room of her home. The only eyewitness to the possible suspect was an elderly neighbor suffering from possible Alzheimer's or another form of dementia.

Witness, Tim Mertz, described a large blond male with a Harley Davidson motorcycle pounding violently on the door prior to the fire.

Glen still believed Steele killed his wife during a possible argument when she announced she was filing for divorce after learning of his affair with Carol Smith. But he knew that wasn't the only possibility...prove what isn't, Glen, prove what isn't, he reminded himself.

What more could her sister bring into the investigation to help them solve the mystery?

He was about to discover the answer.

"She's here," said Bill. "She's at the front desk."

"Are they sending her back here?" asked Glen.

"No, I told them to escort her to the soft interview room. I thought she'd be more comfortable speaking to us in private."

"Then let's go. I don't want her feeling uneasy sitting there alone," said Glen.

He slipped his jacket on and Bill did the same. The two men walked in to find Monica Steele's older sister.

"Good afternoon, I'm Glen Karst and this is Bill Thompson."

She stood and extended her hand.

"Before we begin, can we get you anything? A cup of coffee? Tea?" asked Glen.

"Water would be fine."

Glen requested a bottle of water.

Bill opened his notebook.

"You're Kimberly. Right?"

"Yes, sir. You're the officer that came to my house to ask me questions."

"That's right. Good memory. Some people say we all look alike," he tried to ease her tension.

She looked first at Bill then at Glen. "No, I don't think so."

Glen chuckled, "Dear Lord, I hope I don't look like him."

She smiled. Glen watched the tension leave her face. An officer came into the room with her bottle of water.

She opened it and took a sip.

"What do you have for us?" asked Glen.

"I'm not sure if you can use it," she said. "But we were clearing Gerald's clothes out of the closet to give them to charity. I was emptying his pockets out onto the bed before putting them in a box. I found this note in one of his coat pockets."

She handed it to Glen.

Bill leaned over to read along.

Glen smoothed the crumpled paper.

I know who you are and where you live. You'd better stay away from Carol or you're going to have to answer to me. If you don't want any harm to come to you or your pretty little wife, back off Jack. You're only getting one warning and this is it.

Chapter 8

Chatter grew louder among the women gathering in the commons area of the Wallace Manor. At any moment Josh Mackey would make his entrance. One never knew what to expect. Over the past months Josh might arrive dressed in his normal work attire of jeans, a t-shirt, and tennis shoes or he may don one of his many costumes he collects.

Today Josh appeared wearing a tuxedo. He spent much of his time in thrift stores in Denver attempting to find something to bring a smile to the ladies at the manor. The men looked on, waiting for the show, not sharing the giddiness of the women.

He distributed the treat of the week, sugar free candy; the orange slices so many of the residents grew up with. He walked from table to table, wheelchair to wheelchair, shaking hands with the men and kissing the ladies on their cheeks. He wasn't sure who gained more from his visits, he or the residents.

Josie, admiring his good looks and charm, planned to enjoy the weekly visits. He brought balloons or flowers to the residents who celebrated birthdays during the week. He led the other residents in song to acknowledge the special date. He didn't press them for their ages, but some were more than anxious to announce they'd made it one more year.

The hour, as always, flew by too quickly and it was time for Josh to return to work. Applause followed by thank-yous rang throughout the room as he threw kisses and bid them farewell.

The residents were then prepared for the dinner hour followed by the evening rituals at bedtime.

Josie, although anxious to return to her home, felt the stay here could be very tolerable. She could play cards and chat with the other residents. Having been the town historian, she had much to share and learn. She enjoyed being wheeled to the garden on sunny days to read and she agreed the food was exceptionally good for a nursing home.

As the days passed, she met many family members of the residents who joined them for lunch. She knew most of their relatives, if not from the manor, then from the years she lived in Wallace. How she loved to share stories about her youth to those who would listen.

***

Abby sighed with relief when she and Darrell marched into Dr. Culbertson's office earlier in the week to discover he had taken a few days off and would return on Wednesday afternoon. It gave Darrell the opportunity to calm his anger and plan his words carefully.

A few days later, as they waited in the lobby for a chance to visit with the doctor, Darrell couldn't help but notice how difficult it was for him not to offer his assistance to the patients who were ill. After years of working in ER, he never realized how much he might enjoy the slower pace of treating patients, other than those suffering the pain and anguish imposed upon them from car accidents or violent crimes.

Finally, they were called into an exam room.

Dr. Culbertson entered. His smile caused his small eyes to disappear into his chubby well-scrubbed cheeks. His balding head and round midsection gave him the appearance of a smiling Buddha. He extended his hand to first Abby, and then Darrell. "I'm Dr. Culbertson, how may I help you? My nurse said you have some questions for me concerning Kate Hodges?"

"Yes, she was my grandmother," started Abby.

"Kate was a lovely woman and a joy to take care of," he responded.

"Just how much care did you actually give to Kate?" asked Darrell.

"I beg your pardon?" Dr. Culbertson said with a questioning tone. "Is there a problem?

"You tell me. Why did she need sleeping pills?" asked Darrell.

"Oh, that's standard procedure," said Dr. Culbertson. "They're administered to all of the residents at the manor to assist them with a good night's sleep."

Darrell bristled at his condescending tone.

"Prescribing sleeping pills or any other type of sleep aide is not standard procedure for the elderly," insisted Darrell.

Dr. Culbertson winked at Abby.

"Seems your husband has been surfing the Internet. Sometimes, it's best to leave medicine to the professionals and avoid self-diagnosis from unreliable sources online."

His words infuriated Darrell. Abby feared he'd lose his composure at any moment.

"I *am* a member of the medical field, Dr.. I'm an M.D., same as you and I don't need to surf the Internet to discover you're making a lethal error in judgment," said Darrell.

"I beg your pardon. I've been caring for patients like Kate for the past thirty years. Don't you question my judgment, young man. I don't care if you're a doctor or not. I know how to look after the health of my friends and neighbors in the community. Now, I'm sorry Kate died, but it was nothing more than her time to go. Her death had nothing at all to do with prescribing sleep aides. I suggest you return to..." he paused to search his memory for Darrell's mention of where he'd come from.

"I'm one of your neighbors, but I sure as hell am not one of your friends. And you can be damn sure you will never ever, touch me or my family for any medical reason."

Abby remembered going to Dr. Culbertson when she was a child. She liked the sweet jolly man and never gave his medical abilities any thought. Her mind flashed back to local gossip about a couple of malpractice claims, but her grandmother brushed them off to greed and misunderstanding.

"I believe your actions should be brought up to the State Medical Board," said Darrell.

"Now, wait a minute. Let's not fly off the handle. Maybe we can talk this over. It is possible you younger doctors may have differing opinions and I'm sure I could learn from your more recent educational experiences," responded Dr. Culbertson. "Besides, I'm planning to retire very soon."

"How soon?" asked Darrell.

"As a matter of fact, I've recently begun interviewing for a successor," he lied.

"How soon?" asked Darrell again.

"As soon as I hire a replacement. It's not easy finding a doctor willing to relocate here in Wallace. We have several visiting doctors, but the good citizens of this town need someone around for emergencies."

"I guess I'm your man then," blurted Darrell.

Abby's mouth fell open. He had not once discussed staying permanently or becoming the town doctor.

"Darrell, do you know what you're saying?" asked Abby.

"Tell you what, Darrell," said Dr. Culbertson. "Why don't you stop by my office in the morning and bring your resume and we'll talk on a more civil level. I'm sure we can reach an arrangement we can both be happy with. Say, ten?"

"I'll be there."

Darrell guided Abby out of the office to their car.

"What in the hell was that all about?" she asked before getting into the car.

"Just get in. I don't want to talk about it here. People are watching," he said.

He drove down the street to Pizza Hut. This time of the day the restaurant was nearly empty.

"You order," he said. "I'll be right back."

He stepped into the bathroom to wash his face and calm himself. He gazed into the mirror, realizing he still carried the look of anger on his face. He leaned back against the wall taking deep breaths. What had he just done? Was he up to following through with his offer to take over Culbertson's practice? Could he really live and work in such a rural area? How could he let his temper take over the way it had?

When he felt his pulse return to normal and the tension leave his face he returned to the table to join his wife.

"I'm sorry," he said as he kissed the top of her head. "I'm not sure what got into me back there."

"Are you planning to apologize?" she asked.

"Yes, but I know I'm right and I know he shouldn't be seeing patients any more. He's not competent. For God's sake, Abby, he's nearly seventy years old. How many lives could be in danger if his memory lapsed? Did you notice his hands trembling?"

"My whole body was trembling when you lost it in there. Did you ever think maybe you caused it?" she pointed out.

"How would you feel about me practicing here? I won't if you don't want me to."

"I don't know. I've noticed you're getting a bit edgy being home all the time. Sitting on the porch swing or fixing screens and shingles doesn't seem to suit you. How can you go from the hectic pace of the ER to the sedentary life on the farm?" she asked.

"You're right. I need a happy medium and I think this might be it. I'd be willing to give it a try if you are," he pleaded.

"Okay, I'll agree. But what makes you think he'll even suggest you as his replacement after the way you behaved today?"

"He'll hire me. I'm sure of it."

***

The investigation into the death of Monica and the arson at the home of Carol Smith kept Glen and Bill busy. One by one, they checked out the names on her cell phone. Nearly all of the men had alibis and were surprisingly very cooperative.

When they left the home of the final man on the list, Bill said, "Man, I wish all of our interviews were so easy. No slime bags here."

"It helps that they're all married and will do anything to make sure their wives don't find out," Glen pointed out.

"I suppose you could say we've got'em by their balls," laughed Bill.

"That was the last one, I think it's time we come up with a new list of suspects," said Glen. "Let's go by the hospital and see who might have been friends with Carol. Maybe if we're lucky she bragged to the wrong person about her escapades."

Inside the hospital they were directed to a lounge area where they could interview the nurses on duty who might have information about Carol's busy lifestyle.

Each nurse they spoke to had nothing to add. Either they were not close to Carol or, if they were, Carol never revealed to them the names of the men she had relationships with outside of the hospital. The mysterious blond man apparently only existed in the mind of Tim Mertz.

Glen stopped by the coffee machine hoping a little caffeine would enhance his thought process. He watched the busy staff hustling up and down the long halls. Patients, doctors, nurses and orderlies kept the halls in constant motion.

Then it occurred to him.

"What?" asked Bill.

"What do you mean?" asked Glen.

"I know that look. You've got an idea. Spill it," said Bill.

"Who says our big guy has to be a patient? All of the men we spoke to gave us a brief account of their hospital stays. Maybe Carol was also seeing someone at work."

"Don't you think one of the nurses might have said something to us about that?" Bill pointed out.

"Not if she had to keep it a secret. Not if he was married. Or how about a married doctor?" said Glen

"That's a good theory," said Bill. "I'm sure some hotshot, high paid doctor wouldn't want it to get back to his wife. Might hurt his reputation."

"Or his wallet," said Glen. "Come on."

Glen crumpled his paper cup and tossed it into the trash.

"Where are we going?" asked Bill.

"To canvas the parking lot."

"What are we looking for?"

"I'll know it when I find it," said Glen.

Bill hated Glen's evasiveness, but had learned to keep his mouth shut and follow his lead. Glen was rarely wrong.

Glen walked slowly through the parking lot.

"It would help if you told me what we're looking for," complained Bill.

As they patrolled the staff parking area, there, glistening in the sun, stood a Harley Davidson filling the parking slot assigned to Dr. Gruber.

Glen stopped.

"Hell, any one of these docs can own a bike," said Bill.

"I know, but my gut tells me this one might belong to a large blond guy with a temper," said Glen.

The two detectives went back inside to inquire about Dr. Gruber at the main information desk.

Dr. Gruber did not answer his page. Finally, a nurse responded.

"Dr. Gruber took the remainder of the day off. He said he was feeling ill."

They rushed outdoors just in time to watch a large man wearing a helmet speed out of the parking lot.

***

The next morning at exactly ten o'clock, Darrell walked into the clinic to visit with Dr. Culbertson. The lobby was empty. He went to the desk.

"If you're here to see Dr. Culbertson, he's not taking patients today," said the nurse.

"Is he in?" asked Darrell.

"Yes, but he asked not to be disturbed. He'll be in meetings all morning."

"Would you tell him Dr. Darrell Hooper is here to see him."

She disappeared down the hall turning into an adjacent hall.

Knocking on Dr. Culbertson's door, she announced, "A Dr. Hooper to see you."

"Send him back," he said.

The nurse returned to Dr. Hooper then escorted him to Dr. Culbertson's office.

Both men stood, not saying a word until the nurse exited the room. Dr. Culbertson closed the door.

"How can we work through this?" he asked. "At my age, I don't have the energy nor the desire to fight a malpractice suit, even if I don't believe I'm in error."

"I can understand that. A man of your stature within the community would probably much rather go down without a blemish on his record."

"Precisely."

"Might I suggest you retire immediately and turn your practice over to me?"

"It's not that easy. Don't you want your accountant to look over the books?"

"Money's not the issue here."

"Wouldn't it look better if we worked together for awhile until you became familiar with my practice?"

"Not necessary."

"What will I say to everyone?"

"Look, that's not my problem. We can do this nice or we can do it dirty. How do you want to play it?"

Dr. Culbertson stared out of his office window. For many years he had the opportunity to play God in his small community. He brought babies into the world and then treated their grandparents on the way out. The citizens knew they could count on him. He went to church with these people; he sat with them at ball games. How could he just walk away? He knew he didn't stand a chance with the medical board. In the past there were mistakes he'd made along the way, but everyone still trusted him. He reassured them in his confident manner that he did all he could. The lack of autopsies allowed him to hide any and all of his medical errors.

With his reputation at stake and a clean reputation in a small town is of utmost importance, he turned to Dr. Hooper.

"You've got me over the proverbial barrel here. I'll do it your way."

"Fine," said Darrell, proud of his conquest over Dr. Culbertson.

"Close the clinic for the remainder of the week. Tell your staff I'll be working with them from this day forward. Make an announcement in your local paper. It'll be our little secret."

Working as an ER doctor in a large Denver hospital, Darrell found the job rewarding. He held the lives of his patients in his hands daily. He knew his talents and abilities surpassed doctors like Culbertson, but his choice left him bitter regarding the lack of recognition. Then he arrived in this town to find the incompetent doctor, by his standards, being treated like royalty. He craved a taste of the glory. He wanted the praise that accompanies a job well done. He needed to experience it.

He knew he would be providing better medical care to the community. No one would lose. Dr. Culbertson reigned supreme for many years; the time had arrived for him to step down. Allowing him to maintain his reputation and pride made Darrell feel his decision was more than fair.

"Shall we begin," he said to Dr. Culbertson.

Reluctantly, the older doctor nodded his head. He took a deep breath, ran his fingers across his balding head and straightened his shoulders as they walked out of his office.

"Betty, I'd like to introduce you to your new boss, Dr. Darrell Hooper."

Betty, surprised, said, "What are you talking about? You're not leaving are you?"

"I've been thinking about retiring for some time now. Dr. Hooper is willing to take over the practice so I'm ready to step down."

"When?"

"Effective today," he said. "Maybe it's not too late to get in a game of golf this afternoon."

Betty shook hands with Darrell, "Dr. Hooper, welcome to our town."

"Thank you, I think I'm going to like it here," he smiled charmingly.

She blushed, wondering how nice it would be to look at this handsome doctor every morning when she came to work.

"Now if you'll excuse me, I think I'll start to pack my office," said Dr. Culbertson.

"No rush on that. Take your time," smiled Darrell, wanting to begin his practice on a favored note.

"Betty, please show Dr. Hooper around for me, would you, dear?"

Too interested in spending time with the new young doctor she completely missed the sadness in the voice of her former employer.

Happily she escorted him through the clinic, introducing him to everyone. Next, she took him across the street to the hospital.

She beamed with pride as she explained to the staff the surprising change of medical care in the area. Not only was she spending time with the new doctor, but also had insider information about the switch.

From the hospital they went to Wallace Manor. Betty walked Dr. Hooper to Laura's door.

"I'm sure you want to meet the Director of Nursing. She's really nice and so pretty," she said.

Betty tapped on the door.

"Come in," Laura said.

"Laura, I'd like you to meet Dr. Hooper. He'll be taking over Dr. Culbertson's practice."

Laura glanced up from her desk, unable to disguise the look of shock on her face.

"I know how you feel," said Betty, "It came as a big surprise to me, too. Can't believe Dr. Culbertson kept it a secret this long. Who would've guessed he was ready to retire?"

"Dr. Hooper, so we meet again," said Laura.

"You two already know each other?" asked Betty.

"Yes, we've met. His wife's grandmother was Kate Hodges."

"No kidding?" Betty turned to face him. "You're Abby's husband?"

"Guilty," he said, not taking his eyes off of Laura.

He studied her nearly black eyes and perfect complexion. Something about her captivated him. In all the years he'd worked at the hospital no pretty nurse or female doctor stirred up this kind of emotion in him. Not that he would ever consider cheating on his wife, he loved Abby, but this woman intrigued him.

"I'll show Dr. Hooper around from here. Thank you for bringing him by," said Laura.

Betty, disappointed to end the tour, said, "That's good, I have work to do at the clinic."

She hoped to impress Darrell with her efficiency.

"I'm not sure how much of our facility you've already seen or what you would like me to show you," said Laura.

"Let's start with the residents," he said. "I want to meet every one of them."

He stepped back from the doorway to allow her to lead the way.

As she walked she felt his eyes upon her. She stopped and waited for him to catch up to her. Her comfort level increased while he walked beside her.

One by one, she introduced him to the staff and the residents. He made predetermined guesses as to the employees who would be caring workers and who would be more like the one he met earlier, Darcy.

Along one hall they met Vanessa delivering flowers to one of the residents.

Laura stopped her.

"Vanessa, I'd like you to meet Dr. Hooper. He's replacing Dr. Culbertson."

"What?" she said, shocked by the news.

Laura gave her a second to regain her composure.

"Dr. Hooper, this is Vanessa Winegard. She owns the floral shop and her husband, Michael, owns the mortuary."

He extended his arm to shake hands.

"I guess we'll be seeing a lot of each other," she said.

"Why, are you ill?" he questioned.

"No, but when a patient of yours dies I expect our paths will cross."

"Let's see if we can keep that head count down, shall we?" he responded.

That stiff professional side his wife warned him about did not fit the casual atmosphere of the town.

Vanessa and Laura both sensed he would be a difficult person to work with. Laura knew she'd be expected to stay on top of everything. Not that she hasn't been doing a wonderful job for the past eight years, but she wondered if her best would be good enough for the new doctor.

Chapter 9

Glen awoke to the sound of Taffy scratching at the edge of the bed. He rolled over to check the time. Panic filled his body as he leaped to his feet, realizing he'd overslept. His internal alarm system rarely let him down. Today was no exception as he slowly gained his composure and became aware that it was Friday, his day off.

With his hands raised high over his head, he went into a full-length stretch.

"Hell, I must not have moved a muscle all night," he moaned.

He refused to accept the possibility his body might be fighting back from all the abuse he'd given it over the years. Late hours, no sleep, lots of bourbon and red meat topped off with hundreds of slices of cheesecake would undoubtedly take a toll on anyone.

He let the dogs out and checked on the puppies that were growing quickly. Their eyes and ears were opening. Mieke made his work at this stage in their development nearly hands off.

When he opened the refrigerator he noticed a tall pitcher of extra strength iced coffee, his own concoction made by grinding French roast coffee coarsely then adding it to a coffee press. Next, he adds hot tap water and honey leaving it set in the press eight to twelve hours with the plunger up. Finally, he extracts the cold brewed mixture from the coffee press pouring it into a glass carafe to be stored in the refrigerator until he's ready to drink it. He took a big swallow. As it hit his empty stomach it sent a chill throughout his body.

He dressed for a morning bike ride. He used to run but switched to the bike when his knees began to complain about the impact. Today he opted to leave the dogs at home. As Mieke's pups were getting older, she no longer had the same desire to stay cuddled next to them every hour of the day. She whined when the other dogs went with Glen to ride. He thought his decision to ride alone would ease her anxiety.

The crisp fall air made him feel alive as he pedaled along the country road. The birds busily flew from tree to tree alerting each other of his presence. A quarter of a mile up ahead, he spotted a group of deer meandering across the road, preparing to settle in after their morning of grazing.

He glanced over his shoulder as he heard the rumble of a vehicle coming up behind him. A hill blocked it from his vision, but the sound told him it was approaching quickly. Realizing the driver might not be prepared to meet a bicyclist in the road, he moved closer to the ditch that skirted the edge of the road.

The car sped past him then the driver slammed on his brakes and threw it into reverse, spraying Glen with gravel.

"Out looking for dead bodies in the bushes?" asked Sheriff Tate.

"Somebody has to," said Glen sarcastically.

"I've got my eye on you, big shot. Cop or no cop, one false move from you and you'll find your ass in my jail."

"You're not man enough to take me in and your jail's not strong enough to hold me."

Tate seethed.

Glen knew how to taunt the incompetent local sheriff who had an eye for the ladies when it should have been on crime. For years he let criminal acts go undetected while bragging that his county had a low crime rate. Once Glen moved into the community he exposed Tate for who he was. The locals were not quite sure where to devote their loyalty.

Tate, at a loss for words, stomped on the gas pedal, once again sending out another spray of gravel.

Glen expected as much and had already turned his back to Tate's car before the stinging tiny pebbles ricocheted from his body. He envisioned snapping Tate in two and feeding him to his dogs. Then he dropped the fantasy to continue his ride. The many years of working homicide allowed him to get into the minds of the murderers and to do it best, he had to learn to think like one. This was one of those incidents when he could rationalize how the mind of a killer really works.

After his ride he stepped into the shower to scrub away the stress of his encounter with Tate. Through the sound of the water spraying and the lathering of his head with shampoo, his keen ear caught the sound of his cell phone on the kitchen counter.

"Damn," he said. "Whoever it is will just have to wait."

He sped up his shower then, wrapped in a towel, went to pick up his phone, checking it for a voice mail.

Jennifer Parker had called. He quickly returned her call before he even listened to her message.

"Jcnnifcr, Glen."

"Good morning, Detective Karst. I thought I'd call and see how your new babies were doing. I wondered if they were up for visitors."

"Absolutely. I'd love to show them off. Today happens to be my day off."

"I know, that's why I called."

"How'd you...never mind? Why do I keep asking?" he laughed.

Glen still remained amazed at Jennifer's psychic abilities. He would never feel comfortable wondering what she really knew about him that she just wasn't telling. She has told him many times she cannot read his mind, but somehow he doesn't totally believe her.

There have been too many times when they spoke on the phone and she knew his mood or some event that had happened to him or was about to. The problem with her psychic visions is they don't always come with a calendar. She can have a vision and not be certain if it has already happened or if it will occur in the future.

On several occasions when they've worked together he's been tempted to ask her questions about his future. He knew it would be futile. Ethically she could not divulge much to change the course he set for himself and his life.

She waited until he'd share something personal with her about an event that happened in his life and she'd respond, "I know."

"So, are you coming over to see the babies or not?" he teased.

"I would like that, provided I won't be interrupting your day."

"Jennifer, you know better than that! No way could you interrupt my life and, if you did, it would be a welcome interruption. What time can I expect you?"

"Would an hour from now work?"

"Sure, tell ya what. I'll take you to lunch in Wallace and show you the big town. Do you eat pizza?"

"I have, on occasion, eaten a slice or two. I might prefer a salad if that's alright with you."

"Yep, they've got a great salad bar."

"Wonderful. I'll arrive in an hour prepared for the grand tour and I'd be happy to dine with you for lunch."

"Okay then, it's a date."

He hung up the phone. A date, he thought. I wonder what it would be like to date her. She's pretty easy on the eyes and has a great figure, but how do you date a psychic? His mind wandered to birthdays and Christmas. No way could he surprise her with a gift. Just holding an object belonging to a missing person conjures up all sorts of visions of where they are and what might have happened to them. A gift package would probably be way too easy.

Feeding the dogs and doing his other morning chores caused him to drop his thoughts of Jennifer. He finished getting dressed and straightening up his already meticulous house.

The doorbell rang.

When Glen went to let Jennifer in, to his surprise, he found Maggi and her two dogs at the door.

"What the hell brings you out here so early in the morning?" he asked.

Maggi tossed back her shoulder length black hair and shoved past him. The two Bernese Mountain dogs followed her, wagging their tails in excitement to see Glen.

"I came to see my babies. How're they doing?" she asked as she headed off to the bathroom. "Where are they?"

"I have them on the mud porch out back."

"Mud porch? I hope you're taking good care of them. I worry, you know. You're gone all day at work. What if something happens?"

"Maggi, nothing's gonna happen. You worry too much."

"Me? What about you? You're always on my case about being careful. Hell, Glen sometimes you can be damned annoying about it."

"And with good cause, wouldn't you say?"

"I'm fine, I really am. One little episode that put me in the hospital and you go off the deep end."

"That little episode nearly cost you your life if I remember right."

Before their argument could continue the doorbell rang again.

"I see you have company," said Jennifer. "Should I come back?"

"No. I don't have company, just Maggi."

"I heard that," she said, joining them with a puppy in her hands.

"Jennifer," said Maggi. "What a surprise. Glen didn't tell me you were coming over."

"How could I? You wouldn't quit bitching long enough."

Maggi curled up her lip, shooting an angry glance at him.

"And this must be one of Mieke's offspring," said Jennifer, taking the small puppy from Maggi.

"I see she hasn't lost any of her psychic powers," said Maggi.

Glen glared at her.

"You look different," said Maggi. "What's different about you?"

She walked in a circle around Jennifer scanning her entire body.

"Your hair. You have long hair. How did you grow your hair out so fast since the last time I saw you?"

Jennifer smiled at Glen.

"What?" said Maggi. "What am I missing?"

"Jennifer wears a wig in public to maintain the integrity of her job," said Glen. "I've convinced her to leave it at home during her off hours."

"Turn around, let me see," said Maggi. "Why in the hell would you cover up that gorgeous hair? I love the auburn color and the length, oh my God, it's so long. And, wait a minute. I don't think I've ever seen you in blue jeans either."

"I believe it is a more appropriate attire for the farm. The time you spent with me in Omaha and at my home recuperating I felt uncomfortable letting my hair down, so to speak."

"Are you here to help Glen with a case or …are you two…?"

"Maggi, chill," said Glen, annoyed with her insinuations.

"I came by to see the puppies," said Jennifer.

"Speaking of dogs," said Maggi. "Did Glen tell you I have mine back?"

"Yes, he shared that with me. I'm so happy for you. I knew how desperately you missed them."

"I do have one question for you," said Maggi.

Glen knew that tone and once again shot Maggi that "watch what you say" look.

"Why can you help Glen find all those dead bodies and sometimes live ones, but you couldn't help me find my dogs?"

"I'm sorry, but I can't always pick and choose what I see. From what I learned from Glen, your dogs were in no harm. So often I pick up on frightened energy from a crime scene or a person being held captive. Your dogs were not putting out that form of energy."

"So you only pick up on negative stuff?"

"Not always. It's really difficult to explain."

"If I picked up a deck of cards and chose one, could you tell me which one it was?"

"Sometimes."

"Can you pick lottery numbers?"

"I don't know, I've never tried."

"Why the hell not?"

"I don't need the money. My life is full the way it is. There is so much more to life than material possessions."

"How do you live?" asked Maggi.

"What do you mean?"

"Money. How do you make your money? Does Glen's department pay you?"

"No, that's strictly volunteer work. I sell my books and I collect payment for my services when I give talks at seminars. Of course, I have a large insurance settlement from the death of my husband."

"What? You were married?"

Glen stepped in, "Yes, Maggi. Jennifer was married. Why not? And why the third degree? Back off."

"Fascinating. I find it all so fascinating. I might choose to add her or someone like her to one of my mystery novels. Now, back to this lottery thing. Today's Friday. There's a drawing for the Powerball tomorrow night. What will the numbers be?"

"I'm afraid I don't feel comfortable choosing the winning numbers using my gifts."

"Okay, what about if you agree to not keep the money. I'll go buy the ticket and give it to Glen to hold. Then, if you win, we'll split it and each give it to the charities of our choice."

"Maggi, give it a rest," barked Glen.

"No. If I'm supposed to believe this stuff, I want proof. I'll give my share to a dog rescue shelter. Where will you give yours?" asked Maggi.

"I'm not sure. I've not given it any thought. I would not like to make a practice out of such a thing. Gambling is not what being psychic is all about. I suppose I would donate it to the psychic school in London that I attended."

"Maggi," Glen warned.

"Glen, chill. I'm not going to drop it. All she has to do is shoot six numbers at me and I'll let her be."

Jennifer noticed Glen's discomfort, as he wanted to protect her.

"Okay," said Jennifer. "What must I do?"

"Pick five white ball numbers between one and fifty-five for the drawing tomorrow night, September fifth."

"That's all. You just want five numbers?"

"Yes."

Jennifer handed the puppy to Glen then walked to the window to stare out, blocking her focus from her surroundings.

"One-four-seven-fourteen-eighteen," she said.

"Great, now choose a red number from one to forty-two," instructed Maggi.

Jennifer turned to her, "Twenty-three."

Maggi jotted down the numbers.

"Are you about done now?" asked Glen.

Jennifer was a welcomed guest in his home and he didn't appreciate Maggi imposing on her.

"Yep, I got what I wanted. I'll pick up a ticket when I get back to Denver."

"Glen and I will be dining in Wallace for lunch, would you like to join us?" asked Jennifer.

"Maggi's dogs are in the backyard. I don't think it's a good idea for her to leave them in her car while we eat. It's going to be pretty warm in another hour or so," said Glen, hoping Maggi would pick up on the hint.

"Sounds like fun. I'll just leave the dogs here and come back for them after lunch."

Maggi behaved herself for the remainder of the visit. She and Jennifer played with the puppies while Glen called Bill to check on the status of their cases. It might be his day off, but his mind never rests.

"Are you girls about ready to go to lunch?"

"I'm starved," said Maggi. "I could go for a big greasy cheeseburger, rare."

Glen laughed, "Jennifer's not into your cuisine. We're going to Pizza Hut so she can order a salad."

At the restaurant, Maggi convinced Glen to share a Meat Lover's pizza with her while Jennifer savored her salad.

"What plans do you two have for the rest of the day?" asked Maggi.

Glen worried she might decide to join them.

"I need to stop by the nursing home to visit a friend."

"Gross. Count me out. You two can go play with the strange people; I'm not into that sort of thing. I think I'll pick up my dogs and head home."

Maggi had insisted on taking her own vehicle so she would have the freedom to return to her dogs.

"Tell me about your friend in the nursing home," said Jennifer after Maggi left.

"We really don't have to go by there right now. I can do it later or even tomorrow," said Glen. "My friend is a pistol of an old lady named Josie. She fancies herself an amateur detective. I had the pleasure of meeting her shortly after I moved here. You know the story. Remember when my neighbor was found dead?"

"The one with the white pickup?" asked Jennifer.

"Yeah. You told me it was no accident and you were right. Anyway, Josie and a couple of other women got a little too tangled up in that whole mess. Josie took a bad fall. She broke her hip and needs to stay in the manor until she's well enough to care for herself."

"You know, it's been years since I've been in a nursing home. I'm not sure what to expect. The last one I was in had some strange effect on me."

"I have to admit I was curious about that. I wondered if you'd be bombarded with dead people trying to talk to you."

"I am curious."

"Would you like to come along?"

"Actually, I believe I would."

"I don't want you to get creeped out. If something makes you feel uncomfortable just give me the high sign and I'll get you out of there."

"What sort of code word should we use?"

"Code word?" asked Glen.

"You know, something that wouldn't make your friend feel awkward if I needed to leave."

"I know. Why don't you ask directions to the bathroom and that'll get you out of the direct vicinity of whatever is bothering you. Then I'll quickly make an excuse about getting you back for a meeting or something. I'll meet you in the hall by the bathrooms. Will that work?"

"That'll be just fine, Glen," she smiled.

It had been several years since a man wanted to protect her and she found herself enjoying it.

On the way to Wallace Manor, Glen and Jennifer stopped by Winegard's Florist. Inside, a young woman offered her assistance.

"Where's Vanessa today?" asked Glen.

"She took the day off. She and her husband are going on a cruise. They leave tomorrow."

"Must be rough," said Glen.

"It's safe to assume you've never experienced the relaxation of a cruise," said Jennifer.

"Hell no. I take that back. My cruises are on a smaller scale. I have my own boat. Maybe I could take you out on it sometime," he suggested.

"I'm not sure, I'll give it some thought," replied Jennifer.

Glen felt badly, almost as soon as he extended the invitation, he remembered she lost her husband and son to a rafting accident.

"Did your employer and her husband plan to go alone or with a group?" asked Jennifer, making polite conversation.

"A whole group is going. There's them and Dr. Culbertson and his wife, and a couple lawyers and their wives and let's see, this time I think a couple of retired farmers and their wives are going."

"I didn't think you could make enough money farming to go on cruises," said Glen.

"Most don't, but when it's family land passed down from generations some can inherit a bundle and make that grow. What is it you said you needed today?" she asked.

"I'd like some red roses for a special lady," said Glen.

"My, aren't you the lucky one," she said to Jennifer. "Would you like to pick them out yourself?"

"Oh, they're not for me," she blushed.

"I'm sorry, I just assumed..."

"They're for an elderly friend in the nursing home," said Glen. "Can you give me about half a dozen?"

"Sure, I'll get right to those."

"I'm sorry, Jennifer. Seems everyone we come in contact with is causing you a little discomfort."

"Glen, don't be ridiculous. I find it all amusing. Your friend, Maggi, is well, a little over the top. But I already knew that when I met her in Omaha and she stayed with me for a short time. It's refreshing to see her spunk back. She had a long road to recovery and the way she suffered when she lost her dogs...I'm happy to see her this way. And this little incident could have happened to anyone. Actually, it is quite the compliment that she felt the flowers were from you to me."

Glen surprised, by her statement, welcomed the interruption when the clerk returned with the roses arranged in a vase.

When they arrived at the manor Glen extended his arm to Jennifer to walk her to the door. His protective side was showing again.

"Are you sure you're up to this?" he asked.

"Yes."

Just inside the door in the lobby, they stopped. Glen allowed Jennifer a moment to compose herself before moving deeper into the building.

"I need to use the bathroom," she said.

"Already? I thought maybe the ghosts wouldn't attack you the minute you walked in. Let's just leave. I can bring these back to Josie later."

He turned and opened the door for Jennifer.

"No, I really have to use the bathroom," she laughed.

Embarrassed, Glen showed her the way.

"Detective Karst, what a pleasant surprise."

Laura, looking as gorgeous as always, joined him in the hall.

"Are you here to see Josie?"

"Yes. I thought I'd bring her some flowers."

"I'm sure she'll be thrilled. She talks often about her handsome detective, as she puts it," she flirted ever so slightly.

Jennifer joined them.

Mind Your Manors!

"Jennifer, this is Laura. She's the Director of Nursing. Laura this is Jennifer, a friend of mine. I wanted her to meet Josie."

"It's nice to meet you," said Laura, anxious to leave knowing Glen had his girlfriend with him.

"Is everything okay? You still want to do this?" he asked.

"Glen, stop being a mother hen. I'm fine."

He led her down the hall to Josie's room.

"Knock, knock," he said as he gently rapped on her open door.

"Glen, what took you so long to visit? You said you'd be stopping by more often," she scolded him.

He and Jennifer entered the room.

"And who are you?" she asked.

"Josie, this is my friend, Jennifer."

"What kind of friend? Do you work together or are you one of his girlfriends?"

"Josie, you know you're my only girlfriend," he teased while he handed her the flowers.

"Oh, hogwash. With all these pretty women around here drooling all over you, don't you expect me to believe you don't take notice. You didn't answer me, dear."

"I do both. We are good friends and occasionally I work with him."

Josie squinted her eyes and cocked her head as she scrutinized Jennifer.

"She's the one, isn't she?" Josie asked.

"Which one would that be?" asked Glen.

"She's the psychic you work with, isn't she?"

"What'd I tell you, Jennifer. You can't pull the wool over her eyes, she's too keen when it comes to detective work."

Josie glowed.

As Glen and Josie talked about his work and her stay at the manor Jennifer withdrew from their conversation. She saw family members hovering over Josie. One by one, the room began to fill with the ghosts of residents from the manor, trying to reach out to her, trying to tell her something.

They were all attempting to communicate at once. Jennifer felt dizzy. She grew weak from the multitude of spirits clamoring for her attention.

Glen felt the urge to look at Jennifer. Her face had grown white. He recognized the feeling he experienced in the kitchen of the stabbing victim, Monica.

"Jennifer, are you alright?"

"I need to find a bathroom."

Chapter 10

Bill phoned Glen. "You're not gonna believe this," he said.

"Why? What do you have?" asked Glen while keeping one eye on Jennifer seated next to him in his pickup.

"Dr. Gruber's missing."

"What do you mean missing?"

"I stopped by the hospital today to have a chat with him and he was a no-show. I went to his home and talked to his wife and she said when she came home from a shopping trip, their bedroom was a wreck and his luggage and most of his clothes were missing."

"No shit. Did she offer any idea as to where he might have gone?"

"She's confused. She checked their in-home safe and all the cash was gone. So was his passport."

"He's on to us. We must've been too close for comfort when we were at the hospital asking questions about Carol. Have you checked the airlines to see if his name's on a boarding roster?"

"No need to. His wife says he only flies private."

"Does she have the name of the company he flies with?"

"Nope, he handles all that."

"Son of a bitch. We were so close and he slipped right through our fingers. Does she have any idea how much cash he left with? How long can he survive without more?"

"Negative."

"Don't tell me, I know," said Glen. "She leaves all of that up to him."

"Yep. She's got the look of a high maintenance babe who could care less where her husband is as long as the money comes in and now, if he's skipped the country, her lifestyle will change drastically. She's just as anxious as we are to find him."

"Good. Maybe the fear of poverty will jostle her memory or cause her to do a little digging through his files."

"You got that right. My guess is by now his home office is no longer recognizable."

"We've got nothing," said Glen. "It's no crime to walk away from your life and your job. No one can connect him to anything other than he had his phone number on Carol's cell. Old man Mertz may or may not be able to ID him from a driver's license photo in a mug shot line-up and still there's no law against knocking on someone's door. Did you happen to get some DNA from his house? Don't forget the cigarette butt I found."

"Not yet. His razor, hairbrush, toothbrush all the best sources were gone. All we have is a small bit of circumstantial evidence and a large chunk of instinct. I know this is our guy."

"Look, I've got to go. Keep me posted," said Glen.

Jennifer, with her head tipped back against the seat of the pickup, remained motionless with her eyes closed.

Glen reached over and took her hand.

"Hey, are you still with me? Is there something I can get for you?"

"No, I'm sure I'll be fine. I just feel as though all of my life energy has been drained from my body. I fear if you wouldn't have gotten me out of there when you did...well, I'm not quite sure what would have happened to me. It's difficult to explain."

"No need. I know exactly how you feel. Maybe not exactly, but I have a pretty good idea. It happened to me not too long ago during an investigation."

"Why, what happened?"

"I was at a crime scene. A woman had her throat slashed by an intruder. He left the knife at the scene. I stood over her body holding the knife. Jennifer, I swear I was her just before her death. I felt the fear; my heart pounded so loudly in my head I thought it would explode. I felt my pulse race like I'd been working out then I felt the touch of someone grabbing me from behind. I dropped the knife and turned to defend myself against my attacker, except there was no one there.

"I tell you it was so real. There were other cops there gathering evidence and I'm sure they thought I'd lost my mind. Even Bill thought I must have been having a damned heart attack by the look on my face. My color was completely drained. The same way you looked in the manor."

"I assure you, Glen, you are not losing your mind. Your gifts are growing. I believe in the correct setting under the right circumstances, you are going to actually go to the crime scene in your mind long enough to begin to see the face of the attacker. For the time being, the revelation is too much of a shock to your system and you quickly pull yourself back to reality. Give it more time. Congratulations."

"Congratulations is not the best word here. I felt sick as hell."

She smiled faintly, "I know."

"Would you like me to drive you home?"

"No, my car is at your house."

"Okay, I'm taking you home, but you're not driving yourself back to Denver until I say so. I don't want to be responsible for sending you on your way then find out you blacked out and had a car accident. I already feel bad enough for taking you there to begin with."

"I will agree to go to your house and believe me, I'm not up to driving anywhere at the moment. However, you are not to feel guilty about what happened to me today. I didn't prepare myself for the visit, I should have known better. Next time will be different."

"There ain't gonna be a next time, pretty lady, I can promise you that."

"No Glen, you're wrong. I must go back. There is an important message needing to be shared. I feel it's my duty to find out what it is. Those beings need my help."

"Holy shit. Don't tell me you plan to go ghost busting in Wallace Manor."

"I am telling you so."

"Then hell, at least promise me you'll only go there when I'm there to help you."

"That, my dear man, is a promise."

Inside his house, Glen convinced Jennifer to relax in his room with the shades drawn. Once again, he had to apologize for not having his guest room ready for, what now seems to be, a steady stream of women staying over. He made a mental note to move that chore to the top of his list.

Slipping into the kitchen to find something for her to drink, he opened the cabinets finding his bourbon, coffee and wine. At the refrigerator he checked the orange juice and, since he guzzles it out of the carton, he had no idea how low it had become. There was not enough for even half of a glass.

His bachelor pad was not conducive to the needs of someone like Jennifer. He filled a glass with water and returned to her side.

"Thank you," she said as she took a sip. "But you know what really sounds good..."

"A cup of tea?" he asked.

"Yes."

"I'm sorry, but..."

"I know. There's some in my handbag. If you bring it to me I'll find some for you."

"I feel really bad. I know how much you enjoy your tea. I should have a shitload of varieties in my kitchen just for you."

He took the tea packet from her then returned with a hot cup of tea. He sat on the edge of the bed while she sipped it.

"Is there anything else I can do for you?"

"Not at the moment. I would love to rest for a while in the darkness."

"I'm going to run back into town. I'll be back in a few minutes."

"That's fine, please take your time," she said as her eyes closed.

Mind Your Manors!

At the grocery store Glen ran into Cindy.

"What's up, Glen?"

"You wouldn't believe me if I told you."

"Oh, I don't know. Give it a shot. I think you're a pretty believable guy."

"I took my friend, Jennifer Parker, with me to visit Josie."

"Jennifer, your psychic friend?"

"Yeah, and she got bombarded by dead people. It wasn't a pretty sight."

"What do you mean bombarded by dead people? Do you mean ghosts?"

"Sort of…yeah, I guess that's what you'd call them. They came at her so fast wanting to talk to her because they knew she could see and understand them. There's probably never been a psychic in the nursing home before. Anyway, they all sort of ganged up on her and zapped her. I thought she was going to faint. She's at my place now trying to gain back her strength."

"That explains the tea," she said, taking inventory of his cart.

His basket contained every brand and flavor of tea available from the shelves of the small town grocery store. Fortunately, for his wallet, that collection was slim.

"What should I get for supper?" asked Glen. "She's not big into meat and potatoes type of food."

"And you're not much into vegetables," laughed Cindy. "You do have a dilemma."

"Can you help me?"

"Sure, let's get some salmon for her. You can grill it and then you can fix yourself a steak."

"I love salmon, great idea."

"Okay, then let's find some vegetables you can grill to go along with it."

"You lead the way," said Glen. "I'm not sure I know where the vegetable counter is."

He could always get Cindy to laugh. She knew he was teasing her but enjoyed his sense of humor.

As he checked out, he noticed a small cheesecake had been slipped into the basket. He glanced at Cindy in the next checkout. She smiled back. He winked.

***

Darrell made rounds during the evening meal at the manor. He introduced himself to the residents and their families.

At one table the daughter of one of the residents confronted him.

"What happened to Dr. Culbertson? I want him to take care of my mother. He's been her doctor for a long time. I'm sure she'd not be happy with a new doctor."

"I'm sorry, but not only is Dr. Culbertson away on a cruise, but he's also retired. I'll be taking care of your mother from now on."

Mind Your Manors!

News had spread fast throughout the community about the sudden change in the town doctor. The god-like praise that Darrell had hoped to taste was replaced with a bitter cup of negative gossip and lack of faith in his ability.

Not having come from a small town, he had no idea how non-trusting the citizens were of new folks moving in. Time, and a lot of it, is needed to gain that trust. Darrell, having a stern personality, was going to need more time than most.

Abby had tried to warn him, but he refused to listen. She suggested he work into the setting more slowly with Dr. Culbertson at his side until he gained the confidence of the people. Small towns don't welcome change, especially Wallace, where old time attitudes still prevailed.

Earlier in the day he had called a staff meeting at the manor. He expressed his interest in changing the evening medication regimen. No longer would he allow the administration of sedatives for the residents as a routine procedure. He wanted to be notified of every complaint each resident expressed, whether the nurse on duty thought it appropriate or not.

His experience during his internship at a nursing home in Denver taught him that many patients' problems are overlooked due to their mental state. He knew several residents could be hypochondriacs, but he wanted to be the one to make that ruling.

He asked to review all the files from deceased residents for the past three years. The manor had been recently purchased by Bangert Corporation. He planned to research their track record with other nursing homes. All complaints filed either to the state or to the Director of Nursing needed to be on his desk no later than Monday morning.

He implemented the one-two-three rule. Not showing up for work, consistently being late or being negligent of a resident on three separate occasions were grounds for dismissal. Wallace Manor was now to be run with a firm hand.

A group of staff members were talking in the dining area while Darrell schmoozed with the residents and families.

"I think he's a jerk," said Darcy.

"I agree," said Diane.

"Ladies, give him a chance," said Melody.

"Yeah, but I heard Laura say he's over-stepping his bounds. It's her job to run the nursing home according to the rules of Bangert. She said she's not going to ignore them and take a chance of losing her job. He has no authority to fire anyone," said Darcy.

Darcy stretched the rules to the limit more than any of the other staff members. She needed the money and planned to do the minimum necessary to keep her job. Now she felt like "big brother" would be watching.

Suddenly, one of the residents fell to the floor unconscious. The ladies hesitated, not knowing how to handle the emergency. One of them ran for the nurse on duty and alerted Laura on her way past her office.

Darrell rushed to the man, checking for vitals. With no pulse or respirations, he immediately started CPR. He looked around for assistance. He noticed the cluster of aides standing off to the side of the room.

“One of you get your ass over here, STAT!” he yelled.

Darcy took a step back and Diane rushed to his side. He counted, giving her instructions to breathe for the man while he administered chest compressions. The dining area went silent.

The nurse and Laura entered the room.

“He’s a DNR,” Laura called out.

Darrell continued his work. An expert in ER, he never gave any thought to a do-not-resuscitate patient. The man began to breathe on his own and Darrell found his pulse.

“Let’s get him over to the hospital,” he said.

The visitors to the manor stood speechless while a few of the residents applauded Darrell’s heroic measures, Josie included. The young doctor gained her trust in an atmosphere where she thought no one cared enough to save the life of an elderly person.

Darrell walked over to the group of employees, "When I yell for help I want to see each and every one of you jump to attention. Do you understand me?"

He turned and walked away, shaking his head. At the hospital, he checked out the man he saved. His heart rate was strong and his breathing returned to normal.

"Let's watch him overnight. If he's stable, return him to his room tomorrow."

He bought a Coke from the machine in the hall of the hospital. He rubbed the can over his forehead. Tonight he filled the shoes of the new town doctor with his first emergency. He stepped outside to get a breath of fresh air.

As he walked to his car across the parking lot he noticed how quiet the small town seemed at night. The full moon against the buildings and trees cast shadows upon the ground. He decided to take a drive in the country to re-evaluate his position. He had to wonder if he expected too much from the workers at the nursing home. They lacked the experience of his triage staff in ER. Everything in this town seemed to happen in slow motion. Maybe he was being too hard on them.

As he drove along the gravel road he made his way around a sharp curve.

"What the hell?" he said.

His eyes took a moment to focus. There in the ditch on the opposite side of the road he spotted a pickup turned upside down. He slammed on his brakes and pulled over to the side of the road so his car wouldn't cause another accident when an unsuspecting driver rounded the turn and came upon his parked car.

He rushed to the other side, pushing through the waist high weeds on the edge of the pasture. He heard moaning sounds of the passengers. The accident happened moments before he arrived on the scene. Two teenagers were thrown from the vehicle and one remained inside. No one responded to his voice. One appeared to be dead while the other two moaned in pain.

He used his cell phone to call for an ambulance not exactly sure where he was or how far out he had driven. The best he could tell them was to follow the highway east of town until they found him just past the curve in the road.

He ran back to his car for his bag. After examining the three boys his ER training told him one of the boys, the one who at first appeared dead, was bleeding out. He needed to open him up and repair the artery. There wasn't time to wait for the ambulance to get him to the hospital.

He rolled the boy over on the grass, ripped open his clothing and made his incision. He found the bleeder right away.

"Thank God," he said. Without the proper equipment, he had to guess where he thought it might be and his hunch proved correct. He stopped the bleeding.

The only two ambulances from town arrived with the volunteer fire department and the EMTs. They rushed to treat two other boys who now had regained consciousness and appeared to be suffering from broken bones and possible head trauma.

The crew marveled at the surgical procedure Darrell performed at the scene of the accident, saving the life of one of the boys.

Darrell accompanied the boy to the hospital to monitor his vitals. He'd lost a lot of blood but remained stable during the ride.

Once they arrived at the hospital, Darrell single-handedly treated each child. His presence at the accident site at that precise moment was the reason all three boys survived the crash.

News spread fast among the townspeople. Friends and families of the boys arrived at the hospital. Parents, sobbing at the near loss of their children, struggled to find the words to express their gratitude to Darrell.

He finally received the praise and recognition he longed for, but in the end, it meant much less to him than the elated feeling of saving lives. This was the reason he became an ER doctor in the first place. In a matter of a few hours he saved the lives of four people.

***

When Jennifer woke from her nap, she found Glen had prepared blackened salmon in white wine cream sauce, a salad and grilled zucchini, thanks to the advice and counsel of Cindy.

She joined him at the table.

"How about another cup of tea," he suggested.

"That sounds wonderful. I can't believe you went to all of this trouble."

"I like to cook for company, I just don't like to cook for myself. What flavor tea would you like?"

She looked across the room at the open kitchen cabinet and there, in the narrowest cabinet next to the sink, he had stacked the new boxes of tea.

She smiled, "Choose for me."

She helped him set the table, moving a small stack of books and magazines.

"You can put those in the living room out of the way," he said.

When Jennifer set them on the coffee table she noticed a note from Maggi under a horse sculpture.

"Did you read this note from Maggi?" she asked.

"No, I missed it. What's it say?"

"Thanks for lunch. Here's the lottery ticket. Don't spend it all in one place. Mags."

"Hell, I forgot about that. So she actually bought the ticket. We'll have to watch the news tonight for the drawing."

"Is that how you find out?" she asked. "I've never purchased a ticket."

"While you were asleep I cleared the bed in the guest room. Why don't you plan to spend the night and head home in the morning so you don't have to worry about hitting deer on the road in the dark."

"I suppose if we plan to watch the drawing for Maggi's ticket that makes the most sense."

After dinner they lingered in the kitchen to talk. Jennifer accompanied Glen when he fed the dogs and went for an evening walk. When they returned they continued talking. Jennifer and Glen seemed to not run out of topics to discuss, most of which, of course, had a spiritual nature to them.

He glanced at the clock.

"It's time," he said.

He and Jennifer made themselves comfortable in front of the television while the numbers were being drawn.

The announcer said, "Welcome to the Powerball drawing for September fifth and the numbers are: fourteen-four-seven-eighteen-one and the Powerball is twenty-three.

Chapter 11

The following morning at the café, the doughnut and coffee group of men were singing the praises of the new doctor when Tate entered.

"Hey, where the hell were you last night when all the excitement happened?" asked Kent, one of the farmers.

"I was off duty," explained Tate as he sat on a stool at the counter.

The waitress poured a cup of coffee for him and placed a cinnamon roll on a plate.

"How convenient," muttered Bob, another of the neighbors.

"What the hell do you mean by that?" asked Tate.

"Seems like since that detective moved in you've been letting your job slide a little," taunted Kent.

"That cocky bastard probably caused the accident, it was on his road after all," complained Tate.

"Nah, I'm sure if he would've been there he'd probably have taken care of those kids before the doc even got there. I think where he's from he's most likely had all kinds of emergency training. Being a cop in the city is a far cry from your cushy job here," Kent said.

"There ain't nothing he can do that I can't. We had the same damn training. I just don't go braggin' and showin' off like he does."

Tate sipped his coffee.

The door opened and in walked Darrell to grab one of the homemade cinnamon rolls the café was so famous for.

"Good job, Doc," said Bob as he tipped his hat.

"Yeah, good job," said Kent. "We were just telling the sheriff here that your buddy, Detective Karst, was most likely trained to handle stuff like you ran into last night."

Darrell counted out his change on the counter.

"You're right there. I've worked lots of ER cases when Glen's been first on the scene. He's got magic hands, no doubt about it. He's stopped more bleeding from accidents than I can count. He keeps his cool and knows his stuff when it comes to CPR and applying pressure to bad wounds."

"Yeah, the ladies like those magic hands," said Tate. "I saw he had another one spend the night last night. Damn Casanova, that's what he is."

"Look who's talking," said Bob. "Seems you do your fair share of visiting with the ladies and not all of them are the lookers that detective is seen around town with. Especially the one who spent the night last night."

"Yeah, or how about the black-haired one he had with them in Pizza Hut yesterday," added Tom, who had been quietly listening to the conversation. "She was pretty hot."

"Maybe you can ask him for his castoffs," said Kent, to Tate.

"I still think it's pretty damn strange death and accidents seem to follow him wherever he goes. I'm keepin' my eye on him. Don't be surprised if there's some kinda connection. When I find it, his ass is grass."

Tate grabbed the remainder of his cinnamon roll, wrapped it in the napkin then stormed out the door.

"He sure doesn't like your buddy, Doc," said Bob. "But Glen's a pretty good cop, isn't he?"

"The best," said Darrell.

"Can't blame a guy for having a way with pretty ladies. Hell, I'd like to be him just for one night with one of those lookers," said Tom.

The others laughed.

"What?" whined Tom.

"You'd like a night with anyone who'd take you," teased Kent.

"On that note, I'm out of here. Have a good day, gentlemen," said Darrell.

When he walked out to his car Sheriff Tate was leaning on it waiting for him.

"You know what I said in there goes for you, too. I'm not sure why you and Karst showed up in Wallace but you're not turning it into a two-man town. I haven't figured out how you forced Dr. Culbertson to quit but you can be damned sure I'll be watching you. I don't trust you any more than I trust Karst."

Darrell went by the hospital to check on his patients and release the elderly gentleman back into the care of the nursing home.

***

Glen called Maggi.

"Glen, what time is it?" she asked.

"I guess I woke you, huh?" he laughed. "Wake up and get your lazy ass out of bed. We're coming over to see you."

"Who's we?"

"Jennifer and me."

"Why are you and Jennifer out so early in the morning?" she said after she checked her alarm clock. "Did she spend the night?"

"Yes, but it's not what you're thinking."

"Yeah, right."

Mind Your Manors!

"Are you up or not? We're only a few blocks from your house."

"Yeah, yeah. I'll go unlock the door, let yourself in while I make myself presentable. I look like hell. I was up all night editing."

Glen drove up to Maggi's house along the tree-lined street. The broad expansive lawn appeared perfectly manicured and ready for a long winter's sleep. The last of her fall flowers were turning brown from the heavy frosts occurring during the nights.

"What a lovely home she has," said Jennifer.

"Maggi does all right for herself with her books. Have you read any?" asked Glen.

"I'm afraid not. I don't generally read fiction, especially crime fiction, given what I have to deal with in real life," she said.

"That's understandable. But not me. I work it, live it and still find time to read it," said Glen.

He opened the door and escorted Jennifer inside. He expected the dogs to greet them, but Maggi must have already put them in the back yard.

"Hey!" he yelled.

"Give me a minute!" she yelled back.

Glen winked at Jennifer. How he loved to tease Maggi. Jennifer quickly caught on to their love-hate relationship and knew that either one of them would risk life itself for the other. Glen had already proven that when he went beyond the call of duty and normal friendship to save Maggi's life, taking a bullet in the process.

"What's so damned important that it couldn't wait a couple of hours," she griped.

Jennifer looked up to watch the elegant Maggi Morgan glide down her large staircase dressed in a red silk robe, achieving the perfect foundation for her black flowing hair.

"She is quite beautiful," she whispered to Glen.

"Yeah, but don't tell her. She'll get a big head."

"Don't tell me what?" asked Maggi.

"Jennifer here, was just telling me she thought you had a big butt."

Maggi knew Jennifer was far too gracious to allow a catty comment like that to leave her lips. She scrunched up her face into a sneer in response to Glen's insult.

They followed her through the house to the kitchen where she poured herself a cup of coffee. Maggi enjoyed the luxury of a coffee pot on a timer, knowing full well she is not a morning person and does not want to hire a housekeeper to invade her privacy. After a long quiet sip she turned to the two of them.

"Okay, spill it."

Glen removed the lottery ticket from his jacket pocket.

"I believe this belongs to you and Jennifer," he said, waving it in the air.

She reached out to snatch it from him, but he was too fast for her sleepy movements.

"Why did you drive all the way here for this?" she asked. "I left it at your house as a joke for you two."

"No joke, Mags. You two are Colorado's newest Powerball winners."

Before Maggi hurled a new insult at Glen, she glanced at Jennifer. She read her face and it told her Glen was serious.

She set her coffee cup down and took the ticket from him.

"You did it?" she asked, looking at Jennifer. "You actually picked the numbers?"

"It appears so," responded Jennifer.

"How many did we get right?" she asked.

"All of them," said Glen.

"No shit? Don't play with me, Detective Karst."

"Go check the numbers on the Internet if you don't believe us," he said, faking a hurt tone to his voice.

"What do we do with it now?" asked Maggi.

"Hold onto it until Monday then go turn it in," he said.

She tossed it at Glen, acting like it was too hot to hold.

"I don't want it. You hold it. I'll lose it or something. Give it to Jennifer. I don't want the responsibility. How much did we win?"

"One-hundred and fifty," said Jennifer.

"Holy shit, we can buy a lot of dog food splitting one hundred and fifty thousand dollars," said Maggi.

"No, you numbskull, one hundred and fifty million," said Glen. "Didn't you check it out when you bought the ticket?"

"No, I bought it as a joke."

Monday morning Glen escorted both ladies as they turned in the ticket. They needed to wait two weeks to collect their winnings. Maggi began to call dog rescue groups while Jennifer made arrangements for scholarships to the psychic school in London.

The two weeks flew by and the ladies kept their promises and delivered the funds to the proper hands. They offered to give Glen a share to cover the balance on his mortgage or whatever other debt he might owe, but he refused.

Glen's puppies were becoming more labor intensive. The weaning process had begun and along with that, the mess made by a large litter of eight puppies was more than Mieke wanted to deal with. Glen found himself changing shredded paper twice a day. He paid Becky, a vet tech from the clinic, to come by on her lunch hour to handle the noon feeding. The puppies were up on their feet barking and playing.

The time had come to make plans to find them homes. He posted a notice on the bulletin board at work and before the week was out, he had all but one spoken for. The temptation to keep that one increased each day, especially with Cheyenne fading from old age. He told himself if that pup was not adopted by the time the others left, it was meant to be his.

He had developed a regular routine of stopping by the manor to visit Josie at least twice during the week. Today he planned to take a puppy along with him. After work he hurried home, did his chores and grabbed his favorite female puppy and drove into town with it sitting on his lap.

He carried the puppy into the manor. Nearly every resident he passed begged him to stop so they could pet the little dog. That cinched it for him. He considered the puppy his and she was destined to be a therapy dog for the manor. He'd bring her in as often as he could. Seeing the glowing faces of the otherwise lifeless residents warmed his heart.

He stopped by Laura's office to share the little puppy with her.

"Oh," she said. "Who's this?"

She stood from her desk to take the puppy from Glen's hands.

"I haven't named her yet. She's one from a litter of eight out of my German shepherd, Mieke. Is it okay if she visits here from time to time?"

"Yes, I'm sure the residents will love her."

The puppy pressed her nose against Laura's then gave her a big sloppy kiss.

"Puppy breath. I love puppy breath."

"Yeah, all women do. I don't get it. Maybe someone should make a men's cologne with the scent of puppy breath," he suggested.

"Meeting your girlfriend a few weeks ago tells me you don't need any help. She was very pretty."

"My girlfriend? Oh, you mean Jennifer. She's not my girlfriend. We're just friends. Sometimes we work together. She came out to see the puppies that day and I offered to take her to lunch. I wanted her to meet Josie."

Laura's eyes sparkled and a smile crept up on her face when she realized the handsome detective still remained single.

They chatted for a brief time then Laura walked with Glen to Josie's room. She carried the puppy the entire way then handed her off to Glen at Josie's door.

"Knock, knock," he said.

He extended his arm so the puppy would be all that Josie could see.

"What's that mongrel doing here?" she asked.

Glen stepped around to the doorway.

"What's the big idea calling my new dog a mongrel?"

"I don't like dogs. They belong outside. Now get in here and close the door."

Glen obeyed.

He could tell Josie was in a tizzy about something. He watched her wheel herself past him, nearly running over his foot. She opened the door again, looking both ways down the hall. He stepped further into her tiny room containing her bed, a dresser and a comfortable chair from her home. Cindy had wanted to bring in more personal belongings to help Josie feel more at home but she refused. She told Cindy someone would just steal them. Cindy thought it better to not push it.

"Josie, who are you looking for?" asked Glen.

"I don't want her to hear me."

"Who?"

"The sneaky one named Darcy."

Glen smiled. "And who is Darcy?"

"She's a thief. I caught her going through my purse the other day when she thought I was asleep. I pretended long enough to watch her take a five dollar bill."

"Did you report it?"

"Yes."

"And what happened?"

"Nothing. When I wheeled myself down to the office to complain she came back to my room and put it back in my purse. I couldn't prove a thing. You have to arrest her, Glen."

"Josie, I can't do that."

"Why not? Isn't that your job?"

In an attempt to calm the situation, he said, "Yes, it's my job, but Josie, this is out of my jurisdiction."

"Does that mean I'm gonna have to deal with that lame-brained sheriff?"

"Afraid so," responded Glen.

"I tried that already. He just patted me on the hand and told me I must've been dreaming. The stupid fool wouldn't notice if someone stole a shirt right off of his back," she said.

Glen chuckled at her dislike of Tate. She already knew he and Glen didn't get along.

"Here, look at this," she handed him her notebook. "I've been writing down all the items I hear the others talking about missing from their rooms. I know it's her."

Glen read through the list.

"I think I should take this to Laura," said Glen.

"It won't do you any good," she responded.

"I'm going to leave now to get this little gal home. I'll stop by the office to talk to Laura on my way out. We'll get to the bottom of this, I promise."

Glen kept his word. He stepped into Laura's office.

"Do you have a minute?" he asked.

"Sure, what's up?"

"Josie seems to think one of your aides might have taken money from her purse."

"Glen, we have that complaint all the time. When I took her back to her room the money was still in her purse. You have to understand it's difficult at their age to remember things correctly. Last week I had a gentleman come into my office at least a dozen times in one day to tell me someone had stolen his horse. He knew he had tied it outside the door and was only planning a short visit, but couldn't go home because his horse was missing. Or, the woman who came to me crying because someone stole her eyeglasses when she was wearing them at the time. When I tried to console her and pointed out the fact she was wearing her glasses, she told me those were not hers. The thief had traded glasses with her."

"Were they her glasses?"

"Well, actually, no. She had mixed them up with another resident's glasses, probably during dinner or one of the craft sessions. The point I'm trying to make is, things disappear and reappear for them all the time. The best we can do is weigh the situation and decide if they have a legitimate complaint or if their minds are playing tricks on them. It's all very real to them."

"Gotcha. I'll try to keep that in mind where Josie's concerned. Thank you for your time."

Glen wasn't sure which woman to believe. Josie might be old and might have had an accident but she appears to be in control of her faculties. He planned to keep alert while at the manor for Josie's sake.

***

Vanessa went over the books when she returned from her cruise. Sales had gone down drastically while they were away. Finding good help was the hardest part of running a business. She wondered what exactly had gone on in her absence.

She met her husband, Michael, for lunch at Fouraker's Steak House. She loved their Cobb salad and Michael thought they had the best steak sandwiches in the world. And he would know, since the two of them had traveled extensively with the high society crowd from Wallace.

Their clique of lawyers, Doc Culbertson and his wife, as well as a choice few farmers, got together nearly every week to play cards or attend a play or movie in Denver. They preferred the city for entertainment, avoiding rubbing elbows with the common folk in their small backward town.

All the members of their group made good money from the residents who refused to trust lawyers and doctors from the city. They might love to be entertained in the city, but they understood where their money came from and they had no competition. The situation worked well for all. Of course, they did give back to the town. It was that same group who sponsored the after prom party and made sure the school sports teams always competed in new uniforms. Community pride was important.

"It's hard to be home," she said as she ate her salad.

"I like to come home. It's relaxing," said Michael.

"A little too relaxing," she said. "Sales are down."

"Things were pretty quiet around here. Did you hear there were no deaths the entire time we were gone?" he asked. "I didn't have to pay Frank to handle one body for me while we were away."

Frank was a friend and mortician from Denver who filled in for Michael during his travels.

"Not one? Isn't that unusual?" she asked.

"Extremely so. It's good, I mean, for the community that no one died. But you know what that means?"

"What?"

"It means we're going to be swamped soon. There's going to be a cluster of deaths from the manor if no one expired while we were gone. Remember the last time that happened? It was hell trying to juggle all the services and then you had to hire more women at the shop to help with flowers. I like it slow and steady. I don't want that city pace out here."

"You're right. I suppose I need to plan for the inevitable rush. Besides, homecoming is nearly here. Gads, I hope the deaths don't start until we're past that."

That evening Dr. Culbertson paid a visit to the manor. He talked to the residents who were gathered around a table playing checkers.

Melody came up behind him and began rubbing his shoulders. He reached up and touched her hands.

"How was your cruise?" she asked.

"Wonderful. Relaxing, my dear. You would've enjoyed it."

"I'm sure I would have."

"How's everything here?" he asked.

"Okay."

"You don't sound like it's okay."

"It's different. Dr. Hooper stopped with the sleeping pills and now we have lots more to do at night. We've had to bring in extras. Bangert's not happy with the increase in payroll. They've been giving Laura a bad time. Everything's just more tense."

"Who did we lose while I was gone?" he asked.

Melody thought for a moment trying to remember when he had actually left.

"No one," she answered.

"No one?"

"We have a few that are hanging on by a thread. It's so sad. I can't stand to watch them suffer. It's so inhumane. When they are so close to death it's unfair to keep them around."

"I know, dear," he said as he patted her hand. "I know, but it's no longer my job to care for the sick and dying. I've retired."

"You are still planning to come by often, aren't you?"

"Yes, so many of the residents here were my friends or parents of my friends when I was growing up. I'll never desert them. I'll be around whenever you need me."

A buzzer sounded and Melody went off to assist a resident.

Dr. Culbertson continued to visit with his friends at the manor.

"Did you bring it?" asked one gentleman.

"I did," said Dr. Culbertson.

The two men went off into a corner of the room near a stand of magazines. The gentleman turned his wheelchair in such a way that he could see if anyone approached.

Dr. Culbertson reached into his pocket. He drew out his fisted hand and placed it over the open hand of his old patient who quickly raised his hand to his mouth.

At that moment, Dr. Hooper stepped in. He witnessed the transaction and rushed to the scene.

"May I have a word with you, Raymond?"

He didn't give him the courtesy of calling him doctor once he forced his retirement.

"What the hell do you think you're doing?"

"I beg your pardon?"

"I'll go to the medical board. I'll turn your ass in so quick it'll make your head spin. You have no right administering drugs to my patients."

"Your patients? You barely know any of them. They were my patients and I'll continue to come here as often as I want. You might have stopped me from practicing medicine in this town, but you can't stop me from giving them emotional support."

"Emotional support, huh? That's not what it looked like from where I stood. What did you give my patient?"

"You mean, Fred?"

"Yes, if that's his name. What did you give him?"

Dr. Culbertson laughed in the face of the angry young doctor. It was difficult to tell which of the two of them was angrier.

"Go ahead, turn me in," said Dr. Culbertson as he reached into his pocket and withdrew a bag of M&M's.

"Fred's a diabetic. He begs for candy and I supply a bit now and then, Doctor."

He slammed the bag down on the table spilling the M&M's across the floor and stormed off.

Chapter 12

Glen kept the promise he made to himself and routinely brought along his new little female puppy, Anka. Josie never did warm up to the idea of bringing the dog in for visits so Glen allowed the aides to take the puppy and show it to the other residents while he and Josie spent some time together.

"How's your hip doing?" he asked

"It pains me a little more than it should."

"Are they giving you anything for it?" he asked.

"They try but I'm not gonna let them drug me into a screamin' zombie like some of the others. I'm too smart for that. I'd rather deal with the pain."

"Josie, there's no sense in suffering if you don't have to. A little pain medication to take the edge off would make you feel so much better," he said.

"Dulls the senses. I'll bet when you were shot you didn't take anything for the pain."

Glen's thoughts returned to the bottle of pills he accidentally spilled on the floor of his bedroom. Those innocent looking yellow tablets could have finished him off if he was the type to take medication.

He looked at Josie. There had already been an attempt on her life. That's what caused her broken hip resulting in her confinement in the nursing home. How well she knew him, or at least how he would respond to a situation. Was he that transparent or does she have a touch of the same insight Jennifer is always talking about?

She feared someone would tamper with her drugs and push her over the edge. Glen refused to take drugs so he could remain sharp in the face of danger. The very action Josie feared most happened to him when his pills were switched by the killer. How could he justify telling her she was wrong...or was she?

He thought how badly he'd feel if something happened to her based on advice he had given her. She made it this long in life making her own decisions; he had no right to interfere.

"I guess you're right. The only thing I took for pain was bourbon. Would you like me to bring you some?"

"Heavens no. I'd hate to get tipsy and start dancing on the tables or some fool thing like that."

"Don't worry, with your bum leg, you couldn't get up there anyway," chuckled Glen.

The vision of Josie losing control and dancing on a tabletop caused him to smile.

"So how is your stay here? What do they have you doing?"

"Oh, we go out to the dining room for three meals a day. The food here is actually pretty good. I don't suppose it'll last. They'll probably fire the cook."

"What makes you say that?"

"There's lots of tension around here. The aides are getting upset about the increase in hours and some of them are quitting. Others are getting fired. That company that bought this place wants to cut corners more and save money. I expect we'll be on bread and water soon if they get their way."

"I'm sure things will work out for the best once they iron out all the problems," said Glen, trying to be more optimistic.

"Did you find out anything about our resident thief? Are they gonna fire her?"

"Nope, I haven't seen or heard anything to report back to you."

"I've been keeping my eyes peeled," said Josie. "She's been coming in on her days off, visiting with the residents."

"That's nice," said Glen.

"Nice hell, she's up to something. Mark my words. She don't give us the time a day when she's on duty. She can't wait to get out of here then she shows up all smiley-faced. She's up to no good."

Josie's comments ignited the flame of curiosity that flared up quite easily in the seasoned detective. He wondered what was going on with this Darcy person. The puppy would give him the perfect alibi to float around, visit with the aides and observe how they handle the residents.

"Well, sweet lady. I had better get myself and my little dog home. I'll stop back to see you again real soon," he squatted down and kissed her on the cheek.

"Can you come on Wednesday?" she asked.

"I work on Wednesdays, why?"

"There's someone I want you to meet."

"And who might that be?"

"His name is Josh, Josh Mackey. He works on the radio and he's such a nice young man. I think you'd really like him. He comes by here on Wednesdays to visit us and brings recordings of old radio shows. In the mornings he plays music for us old folks from when we were kids growing up. Not too many young men like him take time out of life to spend it with old people when he doesn't have to."

"I'll make a note of that. If I can get away some Wednesday, I'll stop by in the afternoon to meet him."

"Try to make it this next Wednesday, it's my birthday and he'll bring me a flower. He does that, you know, for everyone's birthday."

"I'll see what I can do."

Glen left Josie's room in search of Anka. He spotted an aide cleaning up the floor where the puppy had an accident. He rushed over.

"Here, let me do that," he said.

She handed him the paper towels, surprised by the handsome man who came to her assistance.

"You really don't have to do that," she said.

"Yes, I do. She's my dog."

"Oh, you must be Detective Karst."

"Glen, just call me Glen. And you are?"

"I'm Melody."

"It's nice to meet you, Melody." He extended his hand. "Have you worked here long?"

"Forever it seems."

"I have to commend you on that. It must be hard at times."

"It can be. The hardest part is when they're finished with life and it's time to move on but their bodies refuse to give up. If they have their minds about them they become so sad and humiliated to need the personal hygiene care. If their minds are gone it's so unfair that their bodies can't just go with them."

"I guess there's a place in this world for people like Dr. Kevorkian," said Glen.

"Exactly," said Melody. "If your little dog here was suffering and there was no way to help her, you'd do the humane thing. Wouldn't you?"

"Absolutely."

"That's my point. Why do we have to stand by and watch them suffer? It's just not right."

Melody suddenly appeared nervous as she looked past Glen. He noticed the expression on her face and turned to see what had caught her attention.

"I'd better get back to work," she said. She quickly disappeared down the hall and into a resident's room.

Glen watched her depart then walked over to Dr. Hooper, who had just entered.

"Darrell, it's about time I bumped into you. You'd think, as small as Wallace is, we'd be constantly stumbling over each other."

"You're right we need to spend more time together if we're gonna turn this burg into a two-man town."

"What the hell does that mean?" asked Glen.

Darrell's eyes scanned the room to see who was within earshot.

"I met up with your friend, Sheriff Tate, the other day. He says he has his eye on you. He thinks you're somehow involved with every death that takes place here, in Wallace. He plans to catch you in the act. So watch your back, old buddy."

"Yeah, I've heard the rumors. He thinks I'm some damn serial killer. He swears there's been no crime here until I moved to town. The truth is, he's turned a blind eye to everything going on."

"I gathered that. But now I'm your accomplice. He says he's going to watch my every move just because you and I are friends. He thinks we're up to something and that's why we both left Denver to move into his private domain."

"Asshole. I hope he doesn't cause you any grief getting your practice started."

"You and me both."

"How is the practice going? I was surprised when Culbertson just up and quit the way he did. I thought those old docs kept at it until they ended up in a place like this."

"Let's just say he was Tate's counterpart when it comes to competency. I merely pointed out his unorthodox way of practicing medicine and he agreed to step down and let me take over."

Glen thought there must be more to the story than Darrell was willing to share at the moment. He filed it away in his mind to bring up at a later date in a more private setting.

Darrell reached across and petted the puppy in Glen's arms.

"What brings you on my turf anyway?" he asked.

"One of your residents, Josie. I come by on a regular basis to visit her. She fancies herself an amateur detective, so watch your step. She's got an eye on everything that goes on here," chuckled Glen.

"Oh, she does, does she? That could prove interesting. Has she shared anything important with you?"

Glen thought Darrell's question to be a little odd.

"No, not really. There's one aide that she doesn't have much use for. But then you can't judge her based on the opinion of an old lady. Hell, she's always on my case about something. She's full of piss and vinegar, that gal is," said Glen.

"What's the aide's name?"

"I'm not saying. Like I said, there's probably nothing to it. Josie has a criminal mind and a great imagination. Let's just leave it at that. I'd better go. I've got to get this pup back to her mother."

"See ya around then," said Darrell.

He watched Glen walk across the room and out of the door before taking his eyes off of him. Then he went to the nurse's station to find out which room Josie occupied.

He walked past a group of residents with their walkers making their way to the dining room for supper.

He politely greeted each of them. When he went to Josie's room it was empty. He stepped back out into the hall, realizing that one of the residents he passed could have been her.

He headed back to the dining room, stopping along the way to assist a resident who had her wheelchair parked in front of the doorway to another resident's room.

"Can I help you?" he asked.

"No, I'm fine."

"Don't you want to get a bite to eat?" he asked.

"Yes, but I want to see what's going on in there first," she said.

"Why? Is there a problem?"

She finally took her eyes off of the aide caring for the resident to look up into the face of the man with whom she'd been carrying on the conversation.

"You're the new doctor."

"Yes, ma'am. I'm Dr. Hooper. It's nice to meet you and you're...?

"My name is Josie."

"Josie. It is so nice to meet you."

His eyes turned to the view ahead of them in the resident's room. Now that he knew there was a spy among them he wanted to see what had her attention.

"Stop, don't touch me. I don't like you," said the resident.

"Come on. Let me get you cleaned up so you can join the others for dinner," said the aide.

"No, I don't like you. Go away."

Dr. Hooper stepped in to help.

"Is there a problem?"

"I don't like her. Can you help me?"

"I'll take care of her," said Darrell. He checked the nametag worn by the aide. "Darcy, go ahead and help Josie to the dining room, I'll finish with..."

"Her name is Helen," said Darcy. "She's a tough one."

When Darcy stepped out into the hall to help Josie she noticed her heading for the dining room as fast as she could manage in her wheelchair. She continued past Josie, allowing her to take care of herself. She knew that Josie had turned her in for stealing. She wasn't very fond of her. Actually, she wasn't very fond of any of the residents. Josie had that part right.

Darcy stepped outside to smoke a cigarette while she knew Dr. Hooper was occupied.

"How's your wing tonight?" Diane asked Darcy, noticing her agitated state.

Diane had come a long way since her first day when she helped Melody with the death of her dear friend, Kate. She became one of the better aides at the manor. Melody had taken her under her care and taught her compassion and concern for the well-being of the residents. She taught her to learn about them and their previous lives to help understand why they sometimes behaved the way they did.

Diane came to feel the same as Melody about the extended pain and suffering being so unnecessary.

“Shitty as always. Literally,” said Darcy in response to Diane’s question. “That Helen can really be a witch sometimes. I suppose I got my ass in trouble because of her. Dr. Hooper was standing outside of her room and I didn’t know he was there. She started screaming at me. She told him she didn’t like me. That’s probably strike one.”

She dropped her cigarette to the ground and stomped it out.

“Don’t worry about it,” said Diane. “I’m sure he realizes Helen can be pretty moody at times.”

The two aides returned inside as Dr. Hooper finished pushing Helen’s wheelchair up to her table.

He walked past the two aides and into Laura’s office.

“What’d I tell you?” said Darcy. “He’s going in to complain. I guess I’d better go stuff some food down that bitch’s throat before she starts wailing again.”

***

Glen’s cell phone rang on his way to work.

“You have to get me out of here.”

“Josie?”

"Yes, get me out of here. She's on to me."

"Who's on to you?"

"Darcy. I saw her in Helen's room being mean to her and she knows I saw her."

"Josie, darlin'. Calm down. We'll talk about it tonight. I'll stop in to see you on my way home from work."

"I've gotta go, here they come. I'm not supposed to use the phone. I have to tell you, she killed Helen."

The phone went dead.

"Shit, Josie," said Glen as he pulled over to the side of the road.

He called Bill.

"Hey, I'm gonna be a little late. I have to check something out before I get to the office."

"Anything I can help with?"

"No, I'll tell you about it later."

Glen turned his pickup around and headed back to Wallace.

When he entered the manor something was different. He noticed there were no residents roaming the halls. The doors to the rooms were closed and the aides were watching the small group in the commons area.

He sped his pace as he headed to Josie's room. One of the aides stood to stop him.

"Can I help you?" she asked.

"I'm just here to visit someone."

"Could you wait here for a few minutes? We have an incident to take care of."

"No, I'm in a bit of a hurry."

"Well, then can you make sure whoever you're here to visit remains in their room until further notice?"

"Yeah, sure," he said wondering if the 'incident' was Helen's death as Josie said before she disconnected.

Then, before he got to Josie's room, he witnessed a body being wheeled out on a gurney.

He slipped into Josie's room closing the door quickly behind him.

"I knew you'd come. Let's get me out of here."

"Whoa, hold on there. I can't take you out of here; you have nowhere to go. Tell me what happened."

"It's that Darcy. I was going to dinner last night and I heard Helen yelling. I parked outside her room and watched. She was trying to get her ready for dinner and she was being mean to her. I think she slapped her, but I'm not sure."

"Who slapped who?"

"That's what I'm not sure of. I suppose Helen could've slapped Darcy. All I heard was the slap. I stayed outside the door to watch so I could tell someone if Darcy was hurting Helen."

"Then what happened?"

"Dr. Hooper came along and took over. Darcy stormed past me and went outside to cool off and smoke a cigarette. Then this morning Helen turns up dead."

"Are you sure?"

"Yes, I'm sure. I was up early and went out in the hall. I watched an aide come out of the room quickly, then the nurse went in. Then they started to close all the doors. They do that when someone's dead, like we're not supposed to know what's going on.

"I hurried back to my room before Darcy knew I was wise to her. I think she already knows I'm watching her. I think I'm next. You have to get me out of here."

A tear rolled down her cheek.

Glen felt sorry for her. What a difficult situation developed for her. Josie, a tough cookie, had been self-sufficient her entire life. Then because of a fall, a fall he felt partly responsible for, she found herself among the old and dying when she still had so much spunk left in her. He knew he couldn't cope as well as she has thus far.

"I'm going out in the hall to learn more," he said. "I'll be back."

He watched as Michael Winegard, the mortician, loaded the body into his vehicle. He went down the hall to the nurses' station in search of Laura when he ran into Darrell.

"Hey, what happened?" asked Glen.

"We lost one."

"Why?"

"Well, I guess it was her time."

"Had she been ill?"

"I'm just going through her chart. Helen's been here for about three years. She came in with congestive heart failure. She also had diabetes. There's been some problem for the last six months keeping her sugar level under control. Diabetes is a nasty disease. It attacks internal organs as well as eyesight. According to her chart, she has been in and out of the hospital for the past few months trying to regulate her blood sugar and remove fluid from her lungs. It was a toss up which would get her first, her diabetes or her heart condition. The heart took her."

"Will there be a post-mortem?" asked Glen.

"Not unless the family orders one. I can suggest strongly, but I can't force them. I hope they agree to it. I like to put complete closure to my cases leaving, no stone unturned. I want answers, but out here the community has a different opinion about autopsies, especially on their family."

"So this didn't come as a surprise to you, then?" asked Glen.

"A little. I was with her yesterday afternoon. She had herself worked up over an aide. I suppose she could've stressed her heart. But after reading her chart a sudden death could be expected in her condition. Why all the questions?" asked Darrell.

"She was a friend of Josie's. She's a little concerned about the details. How much do you want me to tell her?"

"Tell her the truth. Her heart stopped."

Josie wasn't happy with Glen's evaluation of Helen's death, but after she calmed down she realized there was not much he could do to change her situation. She tried to focus on the upcoming Wednesday and her birthday.

Wednesday finally arrived. During Josh's show he bid a happy birthday to Josie. Then after the show he went by Winegard's Florist to pick up a red carnation for her.

The shop was busy when he arrived, he didn't mind waiting. He spent so much time at work he rarely had the opportunity to browse the wares of the local merchants.

He picked up the stuffed teddy bears wishing his budget would allow him to purchase those for birthday gifts. Vanessa already gave him a discount for his flower gifts knowing they went to a good cause.

He sampled a slice of chocolate from the serving tray on the display case. As he savored the rich taste of the dark chocolate with coconut filling he read the labels on the chocolates behind the glass.

His eyes caught the sugar free section.

"Hi, Josh, are you here for your flowers of the week?" asked Vanessa.

"Yeah, just one this week. When did you get the sugar free chocolates in?"

"Today. We thought we'd see how they go over. Did you try one?"

"I did. Was that one sugar free?"

"Yes."

"Wow, I couldn't tell. I don't suppose I can talk you into extending your discount to those as well?"

"Are you wanting to take them to the manor?"

"Yeah. I take sugar free treats to pass out on Wednesdays, but they don't compare to the taste of these."

"I think we can work something out. Let me talk to Michael about it. I'll let you know. Who gets your flower?"

"Make the card out to Josie."

He looked around the store while she filled out the card.

"Sure is busy today."

"It's been pretty quiet until today. There was a death at the manor last night and the orders for flowers have been pouring in. You knew Helen, didn't you?"

"Sure, of course. Is she the one?"

"Yes, and she has a huge family. She had twelve kids of her own and then there's the grandkids and great grandkids. They all want flowers. This is probably going to be one of the largest funerals Wallace has seen in quite a while."

"Maybe I should take some of these chocolates with me today. On the days someone dies, I've noticed the others are more somber."

Josh arrived at the manor bearing chocolates and a flower for Josie. The residents were already seated in a circle waiting for Josh and his entertainment for the day. He worked later that day at the radio station so he didn't have time to put on a costume. He hated that, but he knew his audience would understand.

He passed out the candy then they all sang happy birthday to Josie. He knelt by her side and said, "A pretty flower for a pretty lady," then kissed her on the cheek.

"Thank you, sweetie. A kiss from you is always welcome. Can I ask you to take my flower to my room for me? I don't want to spill the water on my lap during your show."

"How about I set it on the table here, right next to you?"

She motioned for him to come closer.

"I think someone will steal it if you leave it there. My room is 128."

"I'll be right back, ladies and gentlemen."

He jogged down the hall to Josie's room. Her door was closed. He opened it and, as he stepped inside, he startled Darcy and she dropped Josie's handbag, spilling the contents onto the floor while she gripped cash in her hand.

Chapter 13

Bill dropped a folder off on Glen's desk.

"What's this?" asked Glen.

"Looks like this guy made a clean getaway," said Bill.

While Glen thumbed through the case involving Dr. Gruber and the arson, Bill noticed a box of donuts being added to the coffee counter.

"My gut tells me he's our guy. Do we have anything to connect him to the slashing?" asked Glen.

"Uh, just a minute. I'll be right back."

Glen watched Bill make his way through the maze of desks and people walking around to be one of the first to the donut trough.

"It's easy to understand where some cops got the name pig," Glen mumbled under his breath.

He quickly cleared the important paperwork from his desk knowing full well that somehow, some way, Bill would manage to spill jelly or coffee all over it. He opened his drawer and took out napkins. Then he shoved his chair away from the desk to give Bill a wide berth for his food and coffee.

Bill returned with a cup of coffee so full Glen wondered how he carried it across the room without spilling the hot liquid on his hand. Especially while biting into the powdered jelly donut, not able to wait until he was seated.

Another officer nearly stepped in the jelly that plopped onto the floor with the first bite. Bill, both hands full, had no way to clean up his mess.

"Hey, can you wipe that up, buddy?" he said to a rookie detective passing by him.

Reluctantly, the new guy plucked a couple of tissues from a nearby desk, squatted to the floor and started to clean up the jelly before another unsuspecting cop stepped in it.

Glen stopped him and said, "Tell him to do it himself."

The young detective finished anyway and hurried off.

"Thanks," said Bill with his mouth full.

"You're such a slob," said Glen.

"I know, but a loveable slob."

"That line's getting old. I don't think you're so damn loveable. I think you're damned disgusting, to be brutally honest with you."

"Now, where were we?" asked Bill. He placed his jelly donut on the desk.

Glen picked it up and threw it in the trashcan, enough was enough. Bill started to protest angrily, but the look Glen gave him told him to hold his tongue. Bill knew all too well when not to push.

"Oops, sorry," said Bill. "Oh yeah, I was telling you this is going to be an unsolved case, cold case or whatever the hell you want to call it. Until this doctor returns to the States our hands are tied. He's a free son of a bitch living the high life in Brazil."

"Brazil, huh? How'd you find that out?"

"His old lady did some checking and found out he had a friend with a private jet take him there. The guy had no idea he was a fugitive. He thought he was going on vacation."

"Without his wife?"

"Yeah, they always took separate vacations, according to her. She's anxious for him to come back so she can help throw his ass in jail."

"Why?" asked Glen.

"He left her without much money. She's gonna have to sell that big fancy home they've got. Seems he's spent the last couple of weeks transferring money to his bank down there. She had no idea. I believe her when she says the minute she gets wind of him returning to the States we'll be the first to know. Without a divorce she'll have access to his funds and she plans to exercise that right."

"Can't say that I blame her," said Glen. "I just wish he wouldn't have slipped away so easily."

"Money makes things happen," said Bill.

""You've got that right," said Glen.

His mind wandered to how his life might be different if he had taken the offer made to him by Jennifer and Maggi to share the lottery winnings and pay off his debts. His strong sense of pride to make his own way may have interfered with a little financial gain.

"Oh shit," said Glen noticing the time. "I've gotta go."

He grabbed his jacket from the back of the chair.

"Hot date?" Bill called out as Glen darted across the room.

"You could say that."

Josie peered across the room to the entrance, hoping Glen would arrive to join in her birthday celebration and meet Josh. The show was nearly finished and she knew Josh made a quick exit to return to work. Disappointment clouded her cheery mood.

She turned her focus back to the show, not wanting to miss any comments Josh made as it ended. Convinced Glen was probably on a case, she decided to forgive him.

Not having enough time to stop by Winegard's for a flower, Glen called and asked them to send a couple roses to the manor for Josie.

"Hello, pretty lady," came a familiar voice from behind her wheelchair.

He squatted down and kissed her cheek.

"Glen, you made it."

"Of course, I wouldn't miss spending time with the birthday girl."

"I want you to meet Josh before he leaves. Don't let him get away without talking to you."

"I promise. I'll tackle him if I have to."

Josh spared himself the assault by Glen when he stopped at Josie's wheelchair to wish her a happy birthday one last time.

Glen stood to meet him.

"Josh Mackey, I'd like you to meet Detective Glen Karst."

"Detective Karst. Are you here to arrest this nice lady? Whatever did she do wrong?"

"You'd be surprised the trouble this lady gets involved with," teased Glen.

"Oh, now, stop it before someone hears you," said Josie as she slapped Glen on the leg.

"Josie, you didn't tell me I had competition for your affections," said Josh.

"Now just listen to the both of you. I'll swear. Behave yourselves," she pretended to be embarrassed, but loved every minute of the attention from the two younger men.

Josh noticed Glen's gun when he stood to straighten his jacket.

"I see you have your gun, but I didn't bring mine so the duel for the hand of this fair lady will have to be postponed."

Josie cackled at the thought.

Glen noticed Vanessa walk in carrying Josie's roses.

"Excuse me a moment," he walked to the door to meet her.

"I really must go," said Josh. "I'll see you next week."

"I sure hope so. One never knows if next week will come in a place like this. You heard about Helen, didn't you?"

Josh looked across the room at Glen.

"I really do need to go."

He left Josie's side.

Josh joined Glen and Vanessa at the door.

"Josh, how'd the show go?" she asked.

"Great as always. My fans love me, what can I say?"

"I can speak for Josie and I know she certainly is fascinated with you," said Glen.

"Do you two know each other?" asked Vanessa.

"We just met," said Josh.

"I'd better get back to work," she said. She turned and quickly left the building.

"I'd better get these roses to my girl before some other guy steps in on both of us," said Glen.

"Wait, can I talk to you a minute?" asked Josh.

"Absolutely. Is there something wrong?"

"Can you walk with me to my car. I don't want to talk here."

Glen followed Josh to the parking lot.

"What's up?"

"Actually, I'm feeling a little foolish now. With you being a detective and all. I don't want you to think I'm trying to play crime fighter with you."

"Let me be the judge of that," said Glen.

"Earlier this afternoon, before I started my program for the residents, Josie insisted I go immediately to take the flower I gave her and put it in her room. She said she worried someone would steal it. I thought that was a pretty odd thing to say, especially when we were all sitting right there.

"I learned a long time ago when I started coming here it's best to not argue with them, but give in whenever possible. It seems to give them a sense of control. Heaven knows that's something most of them have been forced to give up."

"What happened next?" asked Glen, aware Josh was having difficulty getting to the point.

"When I went into her room, I startled an aide, causing her to drop Josie's handbag spilling everything all over the floor."

"Why did she have Josie's purse?"

"I'm not sure. Maybe she was just tidying up the room and I scared the crap out of her when I came barging in. I was in a big hurry to get back to my program."

"There has to be something else that has you concerned enough to speak to me about it. Just spill it."

"She had cash clutched in her hand before she dropped the bag."

"Did you catch her name?"

"I did. I checked her nametag. Her name is Darcy. I didn't want to go to the office and report her just yet. I thought since you're a friend of Josie's and a cop and this isn't your territory...well, I thought maybe you could tell me what to do."

Glen thought about Josie and her fear of Darcy. His concern for her safety forced his decision.

"Why don't you sit on the information for a little while. Let me nose around a bit. I'm glad you came to me with it. I'll get to the bottom of it."

"Thanks, I feel better. I didn't want to get someone in trouble if I misjudged the situation. Small town stuff, ya know."

"I absolutely know. Let's keep this between us for now."

Glen, armed with his roses, went inside to find Josie.

She had positioned herself near a window where she could observe Josh and Glen during their discussion.

"There you are," said Glen when he stepped inside and saw her at the window.

"Did Josh tell you?" she asked.

"Tell me what?"

She looked around then motioned for Glen to come closer.

"Did he tell you anything about Darcy?"

"What about her?"

"Before I left my room I set my purse on my bed table. I saw her go into my room when Josh arrived. I sent him there with my flower knowing she was in there. Josh came back with a strange look on his face and I saw her rush out of my room."

"And what do you think happened?" asked Glen.

"I think he caught her red-handed. Let's go back to my room to check."

Glen handed her the flowers, which, at this moment, seemed of no interest to her. He wheeled her down the hall to her room. Inside he pushed her next to her bed table.

She reached for her purse.

"See, she did it," said Josie.

"Did what?" asked Glen. "Are you missing money?"

"No," she said as she counted it. "But I put each bill in a special order. One right side up, then the next upside down and continued that way with the ones and the fives and the tens. Look here, they're all still in the same pattern except the tens. Someone moved them then put them back. Ha! I foiled her a second time."

"Josie, I understand your desire to catch her by setting her up, but I really think you should focus more on getting better so we can get you out of here safely. Don't rock the boat. You said yourself she comes in here after hours to visit with the residents. No one would think twice if she got fired and still came for visits. Something is not setting right with all of this.

"You be careful," he scolded. "Let's work this case together. You be my eyes and ears here. I couldn't live with myself if something happened to you."

"You mean like Helen?" she asked.

Glen hated to believe Darcy may have had something to do with Helen's death, but in his line of work he knew better than to trust anyone completely. Often the most seemingly innocent can be the most deadly. If Josie happened to be right then her life could be in danger once again.

***

When Abby brought in the mail for the day she noticed a large orange envelope the size a greeting card might fit into. Once she noticed it was a local return address she became excited. After their move to Wallace she felt out of place. Many of her friends from school had gone on to have families and were busily taking care of them or working during the week. She found herself becoming more and more lonely as time went on. Darrell spent more hours in the clinic, the hospital and the manor than he did when he worked ER in Denver.

Slowly he gained favor with the residents. He enjoyed his new life. Now, if only Abby could become pregnant she, too, would have her days filled doing what she so longed to do, care for a child.

Inside the envelope she found an invitation to a masquerade party from Vanessa and Michael Winegard. They were hosting it at their mortuary and the theme was "Death". She thought it a little strange, but then she often found the people of Wallace to be quite different from their friends in Denver.

The invitation stated the date and time. It also reminded the guests about the tradition set long ago to dress as couples having something to do with the theme.

Too anxious to wait for Darrell to arrive home she phoned his office.

"Hi Honey, what's up?"

"Well, Dr. Hooper, you and your beautiful wife have been cordially invited to attend a masquerade party as guests of the Winegards."

"You've got to be kidding. I don't want to go to some stupid masquerade party," he said. He was working hard on his image and felt dressing up in a costume would be a foolish thing to do in his attempt to gain respect.

"Oh, please, Darrell. It sounds like fun," she begged.

"Who are the other guests?" he asked.

"I have no idea."

"Let me think about it," he said. "I need to get back to work. I have a patient."

When he finished with his patient he called his receptionist, Betty, to his office.

"Hey, what do you know about the masquerade party at Winegard's? Is this an annual thing?"

"I don't know a lot about it. We little people aren't invited."

"So this is an annual event?"

"Yes, sir. It switches homes every year from one big fish to the next. I heard they're always trying to outdo the other."

"Any idea who might be on that guest list?"

"Pretty much the same group every year. Dr. Culbertson and his wife, the Winegards, a couple of rich old farmers and, of course, there's the lawyers...oh, you know, the upper class of Wallace."

"What about Sheriff Tate?"

"Now that you mention it, he does attend and last year they invited Josh Mackey from the radio station."

"Why do you suppose they invite him and Tate?"

"Josh is a local celebrity and, if they invite him, he can talk about it on the radio the next morning and Tate...well, who knows why they invite him. Did you get an invitation?"

"Yes, I did, but I'm not sure I'm going."

"If you want to be one of the big shots around here you should. The town doctor is expected to attend the big social happenings."

"I'll give it some thought."

Darrell gave Glen a call.

"What's up, Doc?"

Glen smiled at the Bugs Bunny reference every time he was able to say that to Darrell.

"Abby and I just received an invitation to the big gala masquerade party sponsored by the Winegard's. Did you get one?"

"Hell, no. I'm not a social butterfly around here like you. They wouldn't want me. What's the problem?"

"The problem is Abby really wants to go."

"Then take her."

"I'm not sure I approve of the guest list."

"Why?"

"Dr. Culbertson will be there and so will Tate."

"No shit, they invited that slimebag? What's the matter with those people?" said Glen, wondering what the real motive was. Cops were often viewed as merely useful to the wealthy. "What are you gonna do?"

"I don't know. My receptionist thinks it'll be good for business if I go, but can you imagine trying to be sociable with Tate?"

"Hell, you might like him after a few drinks."

"I've seen him after he's had a few, no thanks," said Darrell.

"No, I mean after *you've* tossed some back," laughed Glen.

"Want to go with Abby and me?"

"Me, in a damn costume? Ain't happenin'," said Glen. "If you don't want to go then don't."

"I'll talk to Abby about it and decide later."

The night of the party arrived and Darrell had buckled under pressure. He and Abby arrived as Dracula and his beautiful lady victim. They already owned costumes from a party they attended at the hospital last Halloween in Denver.

Dr. Culbertson and his wife were dressed as angels. Raymond wore a black tuxedo with white angel wings and his wife dressed in a white robe with matching wings. Abby introduced herself to Mrs. Culbertson.

"I've been wanting to welcome you to the community," she told Abby. "Seems time got away from us with our cruise and other busy projects now that Raymond has finally retired. I'm so grateful your husband convinced him. I've been trying for years."

"I love your costume," said Abby.

"Thank you. I'm a guardian angel and Raymond is the angel of death. With the blood running down your neck I'm guessing you are Dracula's victim."

"You're right," said Abby wishing her costume covered a little more flesh for this conservative community. She felt better when she saw more couples arriving and noticed some of the younger women were also dressed more provocatively.

Josh Mackey arrived without a date. Dressed as the Lone Ranger he always preferred to stand out by not being part of the theme. The costume came from his Wednesday afternoon at the manor collection. He wore this particular costume often when the radio show was the Lone Ranger.

The host and hostess came by to greet the new doctor and his lovely wife.

Michael dressed as the Egyptian god, Anubis, with the body of a man and the head of a dog. His job was to weigh the souls of men as they pass through to the afterlife. At his side, Vanessa dressed as the Egyptian queen, Cleopatra.

Another guest, Gary Powers, an attorney, wore the Grim Reaper costume and his wife came dressed as an old lady. Finally, in walked Tate dressed as an old west undertaker with a saloon girl on his arm.

Darrell watched his wife mingle through the group of people. She seemed happier than she'd been in a long time. He felt glad he gave in to her pleading.

Actually, he found himself enjoying the evening as well. He'd not had much of a chance to visit with many of the aristocrats of Wallace. He assumed most of them went to Denver for their medical care.

"I guess your detective buddy didn't get an invite," said Tate.

Not wanting to give Tate the satisfaction of knowing he was right, Darrell responded, "Glen's not much into costumes. It's just not his style."

"He's probably got himself some lady friend to spend the night with," said Tate.

"You know, I'm not quite sure what Glen has planned for the night. I don't think it's any of my business."

"You can bet I'm keeping my nose in Karst's business, every chance I get," said Tate, as he puffed up his chest and walked away, hoping he impressed his date for the evening.

"You'll regret that," Darrell mumbled under his breath.

Glen did have a date. He planned to spend a little time with Josie.

He brought Anka with him so as not to draw attention to him singling out Josie. He wanted everyone to think his visits were to share the pup with the residents. He walked through the commons area, letting residents he met stroke the squirming young dog. The rest of the litter had gone on to their new homes.

Glen introduced himself to the aides. He left off the title of detective; he didn't like to use it. One by one, he worked his way through the residents and aides. Finally, he saw a young woman sitting with an elderly gentleman. He watched as she wheeled him down the hall to his room. Soon she stepped back out into the hall with him and returned him to the group then left.

He didn't think too much of it until he caught Josie's face. She made eye gestures to Glen pointing out the young woman. He went to Josie and she actually placed her hand on Anka's head while she spoke with Glen.

"The only reason I'm touching this cur is to not look suspicious. Did you see her?"

"Who?"

"Darcy."

"Where?" he asked.

"That was her with Rex over there. She's gone now."

"I did see her," said Glen.

***

As the party at the mortuary continued Darrell received a call from the manor.

"I've got to go," he told Abby.

"Why?"

"We lost another resident at the manor tonight. Do you want to stay or come with me?"

"I want to stay."

"Okay, I'll come back by to pick you up."

Darrell hurried to the manor. He saw Glen in the hall with Josie as he darted into the room where Delbert had just died.

Glen excused himself from Josie to follow Darrell.

"What the hell are you doing here dressed like a vampire?" asked Glen. "Aren't you afraid you're gonna scare one of these old folks to death?"

"That's why I'm here."

Glen looked over at the face of the dead man lying on the bed.

Melody stood next to Darrell.

"What happened?" he asked.

She responded, "I'm not sure. He seemed fine earlier this evening. He was a little more anxious about his Alzheimer's than usual, but after he spoke with Dr. Culbertson, he calmed right down."

Chapter 14

Back at the party, Abby approached a group of women.

"Let me introduce Abby Cooper to you," said Vanessa.

The other ladies extended their hands as Vanessa announced their names individually.

Abby quickly noticed along with each name came the title of their husbands. She was positive these women would not have wanted to associate with her had she not been married to a doctor.

Karen Powers, wife of attorney Gary Powers, asked, "Where will the two of you be vacationing for the holidays?"

"I'm sure we'll be right here," said Abby. "Darrell would have a difficult time pulling himself away from his patients."

"You'll just have to see to it that he does," said Alice Culbertson, wife of Dr. Raymond Culbertson.

"Heaven knows if I didn't put my foot down with Raymond, we would never have left Wallace."

"Michael says we might not be going to the Bahamas with all of you this year," complained Vanessa.

"Why on earth not?" asked Alice.

"Business has been a little slow for the past few months," she explained.

"Slow? How can things be slow at the mortuary?"

"Things have been the same for us," said Karen. "I didn't want to mention it here at the party, but Gary said we might skip taking a whole month off for the holidays and cut it back to a week or two."

"What's this I hear about you all not going to the Bahamas with us?" asked Julie, wife to William Benge, a local well-to-do farmer.

Alice responded, "Can you believe it? Raymond finally retires and now some of our favorite people can't make it for our Christmas get-away. Vanessa says it's slow at the mortuary."

"I guess your husband is to blame for that," said Julie to Abby.

Her comment took Abby completely off guard. She couldn't tell by the tone of her voice if she was making the comment in jest or if she meant it. How she wished now that she would've left with Darrell.

"I'm not sure I understand," said Abby.

"Why dear, it's simple," said Julie. "These people make a living from the dead and your husband has dropped the mortality rate in Wallace."

"I beg your pardon?" said Abby.

"She's just playing with you," said Alice. "Just ignore her. When Raymond was still doctor they used to accuse him of killing people to keep them in business so they could all party together."

Everyone laughed. Abby forced a chuckle then excused herself to the powder room.

On her way she met Tate.

"Where's your hubby? Off chasing some nurse?"

"No, he received an emergency call from the manor."

"What kind of an emergency?"

"I'm not sure. He didn't tell me."

"Something's up at the manor?" asked Dr. Culbertson who overheard their conversation.

"Yeah, the new doc is over there. Shall we take a drive over and see if there's anything we need to help with?" asked Tate.

"I don't know if that's such a good idea," said Dr. Culbertson.

"Why the hell not? We've got every right to be there. Just because Dr. Hooper stepped in and shoved you out of your practice doesn't mean he can control where you go and who you see. You need to stand up to the cocky bastard."

Abby gasped then turned and walked away.

Tate, who enjoyed baiting Darrell, drove Dr. Culbertson to the manor.

When they went inside, Culbertson knew instantly by the lockdown procedure there had been a death.

"Someone died," he whispered to Tate.

"Well, then, let's find out who."

Tate marched up to the nurses' station.

"What's all the commotion? Who died?"

"Delbert," she responded.

Tate returned to Culbertson.

"She said Delbert passed away." Tate's voice softened in a way totally out of character for him. He knew how fond Culbertson was of his cousin Delbert and how it pained him to see the man linger so unhappily.

Culbertson headed down the hall to Delbert's room with Tate on his heels.

Along the way he met Darrell and Glen.

"What'd you give my patient?" accused Darrell.

"Hey, buddy, watch what you're saying," Tate piped in.

"You keep out of this. The conversation is between the two doctors," said Glen.

"I should've known you were here," said Tate, glaring at Glen.

"I'm everywhere," said Glen.

"What are you talking about?" asked Culbertson in response to Tate's comment.

"Just look for death anywhere in this county and you can bet Karst will have something to do with it," said Tate.

Glen simply smiled, staring at Tate until he looked away.

Culbertson turned to Darrell, "What happened to Delbert?"

"Suppose you tell me," he replied.

"I don't know what you're getting at," said Culbertson, shaken by the entire episode.

"When I left here this afternoon Delbert was fine. Then I found out you were here to see him and now he's dead. By the way, your angel of death costume is so appropriate. You put him out of his misery, didn't you?"

Melody stepped into the hall when she heard the arguing.

Her eyes caught Dr. Culbertson's. She quickly returned to Delbert's room.

"I did no such thing," said Culbertson.

"We'll see about that," said Darrell. "I'm going to order an autopsy as soon as I find the next of kin."

"Ha!" said Tate. "You're lookin' at him. Doc's Delbert's cousin and last remaining relative."

"I'm not going to let you butcher Delbert to appease your own sick whims," said Culbertson as he shoved past Darrell to Delbert's room.

Tate followed, intentionally bumping his shoulder into Glen as he passed by.

Glen's desire to tear Tate into tiny pieces and flush him down the toilet surged, but his powerful self-control stopped him from following through. The day will come, he thought.

Darrell's cell phone rang.

"Abby, what do you need?" he said in an angry voice, not having had enough time to cool down properly from his encounter with Culbertson and Tate.

"How much longer will you be?" she asked.

"A while. Why?"

"I want to go home. I'm not feeling well."

"Honey, I've lost a resident tonight. I have paperwork and procedures to follow. I wish I could pick you up..."

Glen cut in, "Does she need a ride? I can pick her up from wherever she is."

"Honey, Glen says he'll pick you up. While I have you on the phone, can you find Michael and tell him to send someone over?"

"Sure. I'll do that."

"Okay, Glen will be there in a few minutes. How sick are you? Do you need me to send something with him?"

"No, I'll be okay once I get home and into a hot bath."

The following day Glen stopped by the manor again. Josie had physical therapy that day and her discomfort showed on her face.

"Can't I get you something for that pain?" he asked.

"No, I've told you before. I need to stay alert. I won't even take a damned aspirin. I'll manage."

He understood the pain made her more cranky than usual.

"Would you mind if I brought Jennifer back to see you? She's really great at getting pain to ease up."

"And how does she do that?"

"I'd rather not explain it. She calls it Reiki. It's pretty damn amazing. She's used it on me to get rid of migraines. No drugs involved."

"At this point, I'll try anything that you think might help, as long as you promise me it won't dull the senses."

"I promise."

He sat in the commons area with her trying to keep a conversation going to take her mind off of the pain.

They both stopped talking when Darcy walked in armed with packages. She met up with Rex again and the two of them headed back to his room.

"Let's go find out what that's all about," said Josie.

"I don't think you're in any shape to be playing Dick Tracy tonight," said Glen.

"Don't give me any crap. Are you going to wheel me down the hall or not?"

"Okay, but you let me do all the talking."

"Fine."

When they reached Rex's room, Glen parked Josie outside the door and went in.

"Excuse me, I was wondering if you could get a blanket for Josie's legs. She's having some discomfort from her therapy today and I think maybe her circulation might be a little slow tonight."

"I'm not on duty tonight," said Darcy.

"Can you tell us where to get one or who to talk to?" he persisted, purposely being annoying.

"Wait here, I'll get one."

She stormed off to Josie's room and grabbed the folded blanket from her bed. When she returned, Rex was busy showing Glen and Josie the Christmas gifts Darcy had selected for his kids and grandkids.

"You must be quite the Wal-Mart shopper," said Glen in a complimentary tone.

Not wanting to continue the conversation, she attempted a polite response, "Yes, I love to shop. Now if you'll excuse me, I need to finish here so I can get home to my kids."

Glen wheeled Josie back to the commons area. They moved to an empty corner of the room.

"I don't get it," said Josie. "What's she up to?"

"I'm not sure," said Glen. "If she's as cold and nasty as you say then what's in it for her helping these residents out with their Christmas shopping?"

"I'll visit with Rex tomorrow when she goes out for a smoke. I'll find out what's happening," said Josie. "Then I'll report back to you."

"I'll stop by tomorrow," said Glen. "Maybe if Jennifer is free she'll come with me and we can see about easing your pain."

Glen phoned Jennifer.

"Hello, Detective Karst," she said. "What can I do for you?"

"I have a big favor to ask, but please tell me if you don't want to do it, okay?"

"That sounds very mysterious," she laughed.

"My friend, Josie, is in a lot of pain and won't take any drugs. She's afraid someone at the manor will try to kill her or something if she loses her edge."

"And you would like me to try Reiki on her?"

"Yes. Do you think you can? I know you can, I mean, do you think you'll be able to visit the manor again after what happened to you last time?"

"Yes, I believe I can. I will need to prepare myself by imagining a gold ring around my body or bathe myself in white light before entering."

"I don't know what the hell that means, but if you think you can help her, I'd sure like you to try."

The following day Glen made arrangements to pick up Jennifer when he got off of work. He had no intentions of letting her drive herself home in case there was a reoccurrence of dead people attacking her, desperate to be heard, draining her of all of her strength.

They found Josie reading a book in the library when they arrived.

"Hello, Jennifer," said Josie. "Glen, can I talk to you alone a minute please?"

Jennifer busied herself studying the selection of books on the shelves. She smiled at the thought of donating some of her books and wondering how well they would be received.

"Can she read our minds?" asked Josie, concerned that Jennifer would learn of their investigation.

"No. But even if she could, she can be trusted," said Glen. "What'd you find out?"

"Darcy went Christmas shopping for Rex and he paid her twenty dollars to do it. She's been doing the same for other residents. Then if they want to pay her more she'll also wrap the gifts. She has quite the racket going."

"I really don't see anything wrong with it," said Glen. "She's not breaking any laws and if she can earn a little extra Christmas money helping them out, I'm all for it. Could it be possible she's not as bad as you think?"

"I know I'm right about her," pouted Josie. "I think she's extorting money from them and, if they don't work with her, she's killing them like she did Helen."

"Don't you think that's a risky motive?" asked Glen. "You, of all people, should know if she's going to commit homicide there has to be a better reason than that. Let's dig deeper."

He wheeled Josie closer to Jennifer. How different today's experience appeared to be for Jennifer. She remained in total control.

Glen asked, "Any problems?"

"No, none," she replied. "Shall we begin?"

"Josie," said Jennifer as she knelt in front of her wheelchair. "If you would like me to ease your pain with the energy of Reiki I'd be willing to give it a try. You might find my hands getting a little warm. If they get too hot and you'd like me to stop, please just say so."

"How long will this take?" asked Josie.

"It's different for everyone. Maybe twenty minutes."

"Okay, let's give it a try," said Josie.

Glen wandered off leaving the two women alone. Jennifer pulled a chair up close to Josie and held the knee of Josie's painful leg between her own knees, then reached up to her thigh and cupped one hand on either side of her thigh with her thumbs touching. She closed her eyes and focused on bringing in healing energy. Soon her hands began to tingle, Josie felt it through her slacks.

"What's that?" she asked.

"It's just the flow of energy. Sit back and enjoy it."

Josie also closed her eyes, as she did her body began to relax. The tension from the therapy sessions released from her sore and aching muscles. The women sat in silence for twenty-three minutes. Glen looked in on them from time to time, but didn't interrupt.

He bumped into Rex watching television.

"How's the Christmas shopping going?" he asked.

"Fine. That Darcy sure is a big help. I liked everything she bought."

Jennifer wheeled Josie in to meet Glen.

"Well?" he asked.

"I don't know what she did, but I sure feel better. I did peek a couple of times though, because I was sure she slipped a heating pad onto my leg, but it was only her hands. Any time you want to bring her along I'd be happy to have her try it again."

Jennifer smiled, "I'll stop back with Glen on occasion, but I can do it from a distance also."

"You can what?" asked Josie.

"With your permission, I can focus on sending healing energy to you from my home. It's sort of like a prayer connection only more directed."

"I ain't much for prayers, but if they work this good, maybe I should reconsider."

Glen smiled at Jennifer. He felt a warm glow knowing she helped Josie and he felt honored to be such good friends with her. If he would not have been so open-minded, he would've missed out on learning how much she has to offer as a person, a healer and a psychic. Too bad the rest of the world remains so close-minded to the gifts some people have bestowed upon them. In time, he thought, it will become more mainstream. He believed the younger generation to be more open-minded and ready for change.

Josh stopped by Winegard's to pick up flowers for his Wednesday program.

"Have you had a chance to speak to Michael about the chocolate discount?" he asked when Vanessa appeared at his side.

"I did. This is not a good time for us. We're experiencing a little drop in income. We're going to have to let our delivery person go. I hate to do it before the holidays like this, but you have to do what you have to do."

"I'm sorry to hear that," said Josh.

"I'm also sad to have to tell you we can't give you such a big break on the flowers until things pick up."

"Isn't there something we can work out?" he asked. "I don't want to go to the manor empty handed on birthdays. They've come to expect it and my budget can't keep all the residents in flowers and candy."

"Wait a minute, let me call Michael," she said as she went into the back room.

She returned with a smile on her face.

"We have a proposition for you. If you could find a few hours every day between your shows to deliver flowers around town for us, we might be able to keep that discount up and that would include the candy."

"How many hours are we talking about?" he asked, knowing his schedule was already tighter than he'd like it to be.

"How about two hours a day and you pick the hours?"

He bit his lip in thought.

"Okay, it's a deal. Let's give it a try for a couple of weeks. If it doesn't work out then I'll just have to come up with a different way to please the residents."

"I'm sure you just being there is pleasure enough for them. Now how many flowers this week?"

"Two and enough chocolates so that they can each have two pieces, make sure it's sugar-free."

That evening Vanessa and Michael were to have dinner with their clique at the home of attorney Gary Powers. When they arrived, they were surprised to see that not everyone had been invited.

"Where's Alice and Bill?" asked Michael.

"We wanted to discuss financial problems and they certainly made enough farming that they don't have to rely on the local community for support like we do," said Gary. "I thought if we could put our heads together we could find a way to boost the economy here in Wallace without having to expand into Denver, or worse, move there."

"What kind of ideas have you got brewing?" asked Michael.

The wives sat back to listen.

"Some of the guys at our firm have noticed the cut in monthly income putting a pinch on their budgets as well," Gary explained. "We had a meeting to discuss the problem. Turns out a great deal of our revenue comes from handling estates. With the advance of medicine we can see our seniors living longer. We thought, at our firm, it might be a good idea to approach them while they're younger to encourage them to do more estate planning while they're still mentally alert and have more control over their money. We're going to offer to handle their finances for them for a set fee until they pass away, then finalize the details we outlined with them earlier."

"That sounds like a good idea," said Dr. Culbertson. "A package deal might be the ticket. While I still practiced I had a couple of discussions with Laura at the manor. She said the Bangert Company, who took over Wallace Manor, has set up a package of their own. They give discounts to families who pay six months in advance for care. The discount is considerable. It works great for both parties because the families shell out less money and Bangert can count on the resident not being moved to another facility in another town."

"What happens if they die before the six months is up?" asked Vanessa.

"That is the only downside for the family. They don't get a refund. But for every six months they remain alive, it's well worth it."

"Are there many families going for it?" asked Michael.

"Yes, there seems to be," said Culbertson.

"I wonder what kind of package we can offer?" asked Vanessa.

"We'll have to talk about it when we get home," said Michael. "We really appreciate you guys sharing your plans with us. Sounds like it's a win-win for everyone."

"We asked you to dinner to discuss it and were wondering if you'd like to put something together within the next few weeks. We'd like to begin setting up meetings with potential clients and make them an offer from the business men...and women," he nodded to Vanessa. "Sort of make it one-stop shopping. They could get their finances taken care of, their trust funds, wills, funeral expenses and if we can talk to Dr. Hooper, maybe he can throw in some long-term health care package. Why, if we play our cards right, Wallace can become a model for other small towns when it comes to taking care of their elderly residents."

"I say let's do it," said Michael. "I can talk to Darrell tomorrow if you'd like me to."

"Okay, then it's settled. Let's eat," said Gary.

That same evening after Glen took Jennifer home, he received a call from Darrell.

"Glen, do you have time to go out for a drink?"

"Always."

"Unless you're busy. I need someone to talk to."

"Sure, not a problem. I'm on my way home from Littleton right now. I can meet you in the bar in twenty minutes."

Darrell arrived first. He sat at the bar and ordered a beer while he waited for Glen.

He barely had time to take his first swallow when he saw Glen walk in. The women in the bar couldn't help but look up when he entered wearing his black cowboy hat and long black duster. His strong body and clean-shaven face looked like he stepped off the set of a photo shoot for Stetson cologne.

Darrell smiled as he watched the women checking out Glen. That is, until he noticed a table toward the back of the bar where Tate sat with his lady for the night, who also had her eyes upon Glen.

Glen ordered a double bourbon, neat.

“Don’t look now, but Tate’s date checked you out big time when you walked in and he didn’t look too happy about it.”

“I can guarantee he’s not going to let us sit here without hurling an insult or two,” said Glen. “Man, you don’t know how bad I want to wipe up the floor with that bastard. He and I will have some fun, one day.”

“Don’t let him get to you,” said Darrell. He knew full well Tate would be no match for Glen if he pushed him too far. He’d heard stories from the other cops around the ER about Glen’s abilities with Russian martial arts keeping a steady flow of bad guys coming in to be checked out. Miraculously, the excruciating pain came from minimal damage...most of the time.

“Don’t worry, a bottom feeder like him can’t get to me. I can outlast his insults. What’d you want to talk about?”

“Dr. Culbertson. I’m not positive, but I think he’s been giving drugs to some of my patients at the manor. I don’t want to point the finger until I have more proof, but I think he might be putting the ones who are past the point of wanting to live out of their misery."

"No shit?"

"I have nothing to base it on. I could be way off and this damn town has such a backward attitude toward autopsies. I might..."

"Well, if it isn't the deadly duo," said Tate as he stood behind Glen and Darrell.

Glen sipped his bourbon, ignoring him.

"What's that smell?" asked Glen.

"What?" asked Darrell.

Glen turned around, "Oh, it's just Tate. I thought someone shit his pants."

"Watch it, Karst, I'd hate to beat your ass here in front of the whole town."

Glen settled his hat and continued to sip his bourbon. Darrell, on the other hand, felt uneasy not knowing what to expect from either of them.

"I'm talking to you, Karst."

Glen continued to drink his bourbon, laughing a little, knowing full well that laughing at a bad guy is fuel for the fire.

Being ignored infuriated Tate. He stormed across the room shoving men out of his way. Unfortunately, for him, he shoved the wrong group of guys. It was corn harvest time in Wallace and some of the men on the custom harvest crews were exceedingly rough around the edges, big, burly men who hadn't shaved in days. They'd started drinking hours ago and they had no idea Tate was the town sheriff. All they knew was some puny excuse for a man irritated them.

One shoved Tate backwards into another. They began the game of shove the weenie. Tate was out of uniform and had left his gun in his jacket pocket on the back of his chair. He swung at one of the men, hitting him squarely on the jaw. Then, before Tate could defend himself further, four men were at him.

Glen watched the entire event from his spot at the bar. He took a long sip of his bourbon then removed his cowboy hat. He walked over to the fight and grabbed one man by the shoulder, turning him around. When he raised his arm to hit Glen, in one swift move his arm was wrapped around his back as he dropped to his knees. Glen spun in a fast half circle catching the man under the chin with his free arm, knocking him across the room.

One by one, he worked over the four men who soon lay broken and unconscious on the floor. Then he walked over to Tate and extended his hand to help him up. Tate, blood pouring from a gaping wound on his face, turned away from Glen.

Glen returned to the bar, put his hat back on and finished his bourbon.

"Look's like you're gonna be busy with a few patients, Doc. We can continue this conversation later."

Mind Your Manors!

The bar was silent. Glen straightened his duster and walked out tipping his hat to the other patrons.

Chapter 15

With Christmas approaching, Glen decided to do a little shopping. He stopped by PetsMart to pick up new toys and treats for his dogs. He planned to purchase chocolates and flowers for Cindy and Josie. A nice wreath and a pot of his beef short ribs and cornmeal dumplings would be good for Darrell and Abby. He kept his Christmas shopping list short. He didn't need a holiday season to give him reason to remember his friends. He did so throughout the year.

The grocery store in Wallace would be closed when he drove through town so he stopped by Wal-Mart to stock his kitchen. A turkey to smoke, deli meat, bread, chips, milk and cookies would keep him a while. He grabbed a bag of potatoes and a couple cartons of juice then headed for the checkout counter.

The lines were longer than usual and he gave his decision a second thought. There were no lines to contend with in Wallace. He thumbed through a magazine from the rack while the line crept forward so very slowly. As he waited, he noticed a familiar face arrive with lots of packages to return. His keen memory immediately recognized the person as Darcy.

He knew she did the shopping for the residents. She must've bought things one of them didn't like and had to return them. He thought it would be a good idea to watch her and when he finished checking out, he'd walk over to her for a chat. He always likes to throw the person he's observing off guard when the opportunity presents itself.

By the time he worked his way through the long line, Darcy had already made it to the return counter. He watched as she unloaded the bags: an electric mixer, a couple of digital cameras, three DVD players, an electric drill and other various electronic items.

Odd, he thought, those are the same items she purchased for Rex.

"Darcy, back at it, huh?"

His voice startled her.

"What? Oh yeah, shop, shop, shop," she said, trying to be upbeat.

Glen immediately picked up on her nervous movements.

"Those look like the things you bought for Rex the other night."

"Yeah, he decided he didn't like them. So here I am, standing in line to return them. You know, those old goats can be a real pain in the ass sometimes."

"I suppose they can," said Glen. "Have a Merry Christmas if I don't see you at the manor between now and then."

"Sure, the same to you."

As Glen loaded his packages into the car his thoughts turned to Josie's words about Darcy being up to something.

On his way home he stopped in at the manor for a quick look around. Something didn't sit well with him.

He didn't notice Josie in the commons area. Rex was nowhere to be seen either. Josie found Glen as he walked down the hall toward Rex's room.

"Hey, I'm back here," she called out.

"Shhh," he said as he continued forward to Rex's room.

Poor Josie wished she could move more quickly, but she had recently graduated from her wheelchair to a walker and her movements were extremely slow.

Glen rapped on the door to Rex's room.

"Come in, young fella, come in. What can I do for you?"

"I was out Christmas shopping and remembered you had a couple of nice digital cameras in your shopping collection. I thought I might take a look at them. I have a nephew who might want one."

"Oh darn. I had them wrapped already."

Now Glen's instincts were on high alert. Were those wrapped packages that were stacked in the corner of his room empty? Was that Darcy's scam?

"That's too bad, I really wanted to look at them," pushed Glen.

"Well, if you think you can fix the wrapping paper, you're sure welcome to open one and check it out."

"Thanks, Rex. I'll make sure I wrap it back up good as new."

Glen gently removed the paper and the box inside was for a digital camera. He opened the box and the contents were intact. He fixed the wrapping paper just as he promised then made it a point to restack the entire collection of gifts. Each box appeared to be full.

"Did Darcy get everything you wanted?"

"Yes, and more. Why, I don't know what half of this stuff is, but she assured me my kids and grandkids would love them. I planned to give them cash like always, but she convinced me a personal gift would mean so much more."

Glen patted him on the back, "I think you made a wise decision. Have a good night."

He met Josie in the hall.

"What's this?" asked Glen, referring to her walker.

"They told me in physical therapy the sooner I can get around with this thing the sooner I can go home. What'd you want with Rex?"

"You look tired and it's a long way to your room. Do you want me to carry you back?"

"Don't be silly. Just get a wheelchair from the front and I'll meet you there."

Glen found a spare wheelchair and met Josie on her way to the front hall. He helped her place her frail body gently on the seat. He folded her walker and tucked it under one arm and used his free hand to push her back to her room.

"Okay, now spill it," she said.

"I was out doing a little shopping and I ran into Darcy. She was returning the gifts she bought for Rex. I thought it was a little odd so I wanted to check it out. He still has all of his packages, but now they're wrapped. My mind has a tendency to remember everything I see and I recognized the returns in her basket immediately. When I asked her about them she said Rex didn't want them any more."

"I don't get it," said Josie.

"Me either, but I think you're right when you said she's up to something. Now I need to find out what."

"What're you going to do?"

"I think I might tail that girl a little while," replied Glen. "I want you to find out when she works and see if you can watch to see when she brings gifts in. I need to know if all the bags are from Wal-Mart."

***

Michael kept his promise to the other businessmen and took Darrell to lunch.

After the two men ordered, Michael said, "Dr. Hooper..."

"Just call me Darrell," he said.

"Okay, Darrell, some of the other merchants and I were talking at dinner and came up with a plan to improve the commerce in Wallace. We wondered if you might like to get involved."

"That depends," said Darrell. "Tell me more."

"Several of the attorneys around town would like to put together a one-stop-shopping package for the elderly. It would help them with their estate planning when they're younger, while helping their families at a time of stress."

"What would be in it for the attorneys?"

"Well, they could keep the estate planning here in Wallace instead of some other area where the families of the old folks might live. Vanessa and I came up with a plan that includes the complete funeral package, together with flowers, if paid in advance."

"There's nothing unusual about that," Darrell pointed out.

"I know, but we also planned to add remembrances while they're still alive. We want to be known as the mortuary with a heart. Vanessa will have flowers delivered once a week to the elderly who are signed up for the package, as well as some other goodie or treat. She'll sign a different family member's name to the card each time they're delivered so the recipient will feel they're being remembered by someone who can't personally come to see them."

"That's a kind gesture," said Darrell. He thought the plan would help relieve some of the depression he had to deal with among the residents.

"Many of the older folks in the community have saved their entire lives and can afford to send themselves flowers even if the family members can't. We both know they don't always live long after they're left all alone."

"You don't have to sell me on the idea, I like it," said Darrell. "Where do I fit into this project?"

"We were wondering if you would like to add a medical care package to the bundle. You could charge a fee and guarantee to stop in more often or give more physicals or whatever you feel is right to make the families of the manor residents feel confident that their loved ones can receive better one-on-one care in Wallace than they could in the city."

"I don't think you left anyone out except the pharmacy," said Darrell.

"We're already planning to approach them as well."

"What gave you the idea for the elderly package in the first place?"

"We were tossing the idea around, but when Dr. Culbertson said that Bangert already had a package in place and it appeared to be successful, we felt we should give it a try."

Darrell's curiosity piqued.

"What package does Bangert offer?"

"They let the family or resident pay six months in advance and then give a huge discount. Lots of them are already signed up for it."

"What happens if the resident doesn't live six months?"

"That's what I asked. Bangert keeps the money."

"So it's in Bangert's best interest if they die early?"

"I suppose you could say that," replied Michael. "Why?"

"Oh, nothing, I'm just thinking out loud. I'm sure I can come up with a package that would fit right in with your plan. How soon do you need me to put something together?"

"Would next week work?"

"Sure. That should be fine."

After lunch, Darrell stopped by the office at the manor. Before he knocked he drew in a deep breath. He still had no idea why Laura made him drool like a schoolboy and lose his train of thought, but she did.

He tapped on the doorframe.

Laura looked up. "Dr. Hooper, please come in. How can I help you?"

Laura was totally unaware of the spell she cast on the young doctor. She, on the other hand, feared his professional attitude and each time he came to the office she felt her job could be questioned. Today was no exception.

"I would like to see the records of the residents since the manor was taken over by Bangert, both living and dead," he said.

"Is there a problem, Doctor?"

"No, I just want to familiarize myself with how a large company handles every aspect of running a manor and I wanted to start with patients' charts and payment records."

"I'm afraid I don't quite understand what you're getting at," she said.

The request made no sense to her and Darrell didn't want to include her in his concerns. He wondered if somehow Culbertson was tied in with Bangert.

That night at home he learned more about Bangert. He had originally thought they were a large corporation who took over nursing homes across the country. Instead, he discovered they were a small company just beginning with only a handful of nursing homes. Now he needed to find some connection between Culbertson and Bangert to confirm his theory.

***

Laura stopped Darcy in the hall.

"How's your shopping for the residents going?"

"Fine."

Darcy knew she was not well liked among the residents or staff. She really didn't care. She also didn't like Laura's pretence of being friendly whenever she saw her.

"Josie was asking about you. Maybe you should stop in and visit with her before you leave tonight. She may have some shopping for you to do."

"Josie?"

"Yes, she was asking about your work schedule and when you did your shopping for the others."

"I'll talk to her," said Darcy.

She didn't trust Josie any more than Josie trusted her. After Josh walked in on her attempting to steal money from Josie's purse she kept waiting for that bomb to drop at the office. Josie had already turned her in once. There were several times she felt Josie watching her.

Before she checked out for the evening, she stopped by Josie's room.

"Laura said you were asking about me," said Darcy.

Josie's eyes scanned the doorway behind Darcy as she planned her escape. She feared Darcy meant to harm her.

"I don't remember," lied Josie.

"She thought you might want me to do a little Christmas shopping for you."

Josie quickly went along with that opening.

"Oh, yes. I would like to purchase a few gifts. Let's see, there's my neighbor lady Cindy and Detec...er...Glen, and my nieces and nephews and their kids."

"Do you have a list?"

"No, I was hoping you'd know what to buy them. I thought maybe a nice fruit basket or flowers and candy. Maybe gift certificates for the younger ones."

"You know, Josie, like I told the other residents. Gift certificates are so cold and impersonal. What people want today are gifts of electronics or for the men, tools."

"Do you really think so?"

"Yes, I do."

"Okay, if you say so. I can write down the list of names and ages and give you my credit card."

She knew Glen would be upset with her for getting involved too deeply, but she felt she had to go with it when the opportunity presented itself.

"I think it's better if you give me cash."

"Cash?"

"Yes, with security as tight as it is, I can't use your credit card."

"Oh, I see. How much cash?"

"That depends upon how many people."

Josie handed her the list she had jotted down.

Darcy was quick to notice how Josie differed from the other residents. She had her mind about her and her dexterity. She wrote the list as quickly as a younger person and her memory did not seem to falter as she had implied when Darcy first questioned her about her conversation with Laura.

"I would say five hundred dollars should cover most of your list. Unless you wanted to spend more?"

"What's your fee?"

"Twenty dollars for one trip."

"That's fair enough. Here's my bank card so you can get cash."

"Do you have more than one?"

"Why would I have more than one?"

"I can't get more than three hundred dollars out at a time unless you call the bank."

"When will you be doing my shopping?"

"How about tomorrow evening? I have to go to a school program for my kids tonight."

"Can't you take three hundred out on your way home today and get the rest tomorrow night before you shop?"

"That'll work," said Darcy.

She eyed Josie with increased suspicion, aware of how quickly her mind works.

"Can you bring my packages in tomorrow night?"

"It could be late," said Darcy.

"That's okay. What time do you think you'll be shopping?"

Annoyed with all the time-related questions, she thought the sooner she finished with Josie's purchases the better.

"I'll leave here at five tomorrow and be in Denver by six. I'll shop for an hour and be back here by eight. Will that work for you?"

"Yes, ma'am, that'll be just fine."

Josie's heart raced inside the chest of her frail frame. Every cell in her body told her she just had a conversation with an evil woman and she wasn't sure Darcy trusted her.

She needed to speak with Glen. Not having a cell phone or a phone in her room made that difficult. She walked herself to the nurses' station.

"Can I use the phone?" she asked.

"No, Josie dear, it's time to eat supper. Why don't I help you find a seat," said Diane.

"I really need to use the phone," she insisted.

"Not now, doll. Let's go."

"I'm not going anywhere until you let me use the telephone!" she yelled.

"What seems to be the problem here?" asked Laura when she heard the commotion.

Diane walked over to Laura.

"Josie's a bit agitated tonight. I think it might be Sundowner's. How do you want me to handle it?"

"Try to get her to calm down or take her back to her room so she doesn't disrupt the others," said Laura. I'll call Dr. Hooper and see if he'd like her to have a tranquilizer."

Josie had already wandered off, asking all the visitors if they had a cell phone. Of course, they responded the way they would to any resident who appeared to be irrational. No one wanted to help.

Diane found her and when Josie refused to go to the dining area, she placed her in a wheelchair and returned her to her room. Melody watched from across the room. After Diane left Josie alone, Melody slipped in. She liked Josie and feared the others would soon label her a troublemaker. That reputation made it difficult to be heard in nursing homes.

"Josie, what seems to be the trouble?"

"I need to use a phone and no one will let me."

"I'll tell you what. Why don't you relax in here and let me bring you a tray. Then after you finish eating, if you still want to use the phone I'll take you there myself."

Melody went to the kitchen to get a tray for Josie. Just outside Josie's door she stopped and stirred a sedative into her mashed potatoes. It worked. After her supper was finished, Josie could barely hold her head up. Melody helped her into her night clothes and tucked her in for a good night's sleep, just the way Dr. Culbertson had taught her many years ago when she started at the manor.

After supper, Glen stopped by to check on Josie. He didn't find her at her usual table visiting with her friends.

"Where's Josie?" he asked.

Margaret said, "She had a bit of bad episode. She lost her temper. Something about wanting to use the phone. They couldn't calm her down so she ate in her room tonight. Poor thing."

Glen rushed down the hall to Josie's room. When he opened the door he found her in a deep sleep. He touched her shoulder; there was no response.

"Josie, it's me, Glen."

Still no response. He knew immediately she'd been drugged. He called Darrell.

"Glen, thanks buddy, for leaving me with that mess at the bar. I did enjoy the show though."

"Darrell can you come over to the manor right away?"

"Sure, what's wrong?"

"It's Josie."

Glen sat next to her bed hoping whatever had been given to her was not fatal.

About twenty minutes later Darrell arrived.

"What happened?" he asked.

"I can't get her to wake up."

"Did you call the nurse?"

"No, I called you."

Darrell took her vitals.

"Everything seems to be okay. I'm not sure why she's in so deep of a sleep."

"I think someone drugged her," said Glen.

"Why would anyone want to drug her?" asked Darrell.

"I'm not sure. Can we get her out of here?"

"I can take her over to the hospital and draw blood if you want me to. We can keep her there overnight."

Darrell called over to the hospital to make arrangements. He went to the office to speak to the nurse on duty. On his way back to Josie's room, he saw Dr. Culbertson talking to Melody in the library.

When he returned to Glen and Josie, he said, "If she's been drugged, I know who's responsible. Culbertson just happens to be in the building."

"Why would he want to drug her?"

Darrell shook his head. "I wish I knew."

Chapter 16

Early the next morning, Glen went to the hospital to check on Josie. When he stepped into her room a nurse had just finished helping her sit up in bed to prepare for her breakfast tray.

"Glen, do you have any idea what happened?" she asked as he approached her bed.

"I was hoping you'd tell me."

"All I can remember was asking to use the phone to call you and no one would let me. I did get a little testy and the next thing I knew I was sent of to my room like a spoiled kid. Melody brought supper to me and by the time I finished my meal, I couldn't stay awake. I woke up here."

"How do you feel?" he asked.

"Fine. Do you know what happened?"

He looked over his shoulder to be sure they were alone.

"Someone drugged you."

"Are you sure?"

"Yes, I had Dr. Hooper draw blood last night and check."

"Why did someone drug me?"

"Just how cantankerous were you last night?"

"Oh, not bad. Well, maybe a little. Okay, I got real mad. No one would listen to me."

"Why were you wanting to reach me?" he asked.

"I have Darcy's schedule for you and I know when she'll be shopping at Wal-Mart."

"How'd you find that out without asking her?"

"I did ask her."

"You what?"

"She showed up in my room because Laura told her I was asking about her schedule. I convinced her I wanted her to do some shopping for me like she does for the others. I know she bought it. I gave her my bank card."

"You did what?"

"I gave her my bank card so she could get cash. She's going to be shopping tonight between six thirty and seven thirty. Then she's going to bring my packages back. I insisted she bring them tonight so I would know her whereabouts."

"Josie, that was one hell of a dangerous move on your part. Now we have to figure out why someone drugged you."

"I don't think Darcy did it. I didn't eat or drink anything other than what Melody brought to me. And she's such a sweet thing. I'm sure she didn't do it."

"The fact of the matter is you were drugged, but the reason is what escapes me. I'm not comfortable with you going back to the manor."

"That's fine with me. Are you taking me home with you?"

Glen, chuckled, "Why, Miss Josie, I never dreamed you'd ask me to take you home."

She swatted his arm. "Don't you be getting fresh, young man. You'd better mind your manners!"

"Yes, ma'am."

He stepped aside when her tray was brought in.

"I'm a little afraid to eat this," she said.

"I'll stay with you until you're finished to see how you feel. I really do think you're safe in here. I'll give Cindy a call and see if she can spend more time with you at the manor for the next few days. Maybe Becky will agree to being a watchdog as well. I can't always be with you. I'm not sure who on the inside can be trusted."

"Thanks, Glen. That'll make me feel better."

That night Glen stayed in Denver to wait for Darcy to do her shopping. He positioned himself in clear view of one of the entrances. As the time ticked away, he realized she probably entered through the other set of doors. He wandered the aisles of the store looking for her. He remembered the purchases she had made for Rex came mostly from the electronics department.

As he rounded the corner toward the camera counter, he spotted her. He turned quickly and walked in the opposite direction. He placed himself at a safe distance to watch her. After many years of surveillance on drug busts, he knew exactly how to melt into the scenery and not be noticed by the subject.

He had left his cowboy hat and duster in the truck. He grabbed his jean jacket that he kept behind the seat for dirty work like changing tires. Inside his pocket he found a stocking hat that he slipped on to change his appearance to one Darcy would not recognize.

As she made her way through the store he kept his distance, taking note of the items she placed in the basket. He noticed she placed two of every item in the cart. For a woman, she shopped at a very deliberate, precise pace. She appeared to know exactly what she was after.

He shopped the aisle behind her as she stood in line to check out.

Odd, he thought. I wonder why she's staying in the longest line?

Finally, she made her way through the checkout, not speaking or making eye contact with the girl who ran the cash register, then wheeled her purchases out the door. He waited a few moments then followed.

She loaded the packages into her car and drove off.

He ran through the parking lot to his pickup. He raced out into the street and headed toward Wallace. With his driving skills he could arrive before her. He knew Josie returned to the manor earlier that day.

When Darcy stepped into Josie's room she found her having a cup of tea with Glen.

"Look, Glen. She has my packages. Now, don't you peek. There should be something in there for you," warned Josie.

Glen stood to step out of the way.

"Just put them in my closet, please," instructed Josie.

"Here's your change," said Darcy.

Josie took the remaining money. She picked out a ten-dollar bill and handed it to Darcy.

"I've already taken my share out," she said.

"I know," said Josie. "I wanted to give you a little bonus for bringing them in tonight."

The kind gesture from Josie surprised Darcy. Glen watched the expression of confusion on her face. But that's all it seemed to be. Her face did not register guilt.

Darcy turned to leave the room. Glen stepped out into the hall to watch her departure. Then he went down the hall to be sure she left the building and finally he watched her drive her car out of the parking lot. He hurried back to Josie's room where the two of them searched through the packages.

To Glen's surprise, he found one of every item in the bags, not two. He searched for a receipt, but found none. He made a quick inventory of what he thought the cost of the items might be. Then he checked Josie's cash.

"How much did she take from you?" he asked.

"She took my card, remember?"

"Can you call the bank in the morning and ask how much has been withdrawn from your account, then call me?"

"How can I call you or the bank? No one wants to let me use the phone. I'm just a crazy old lady with no one to call who loses her temper."

"I thought of that earlier today. I stopped by the cell phone store and picked this up for you. It's a second line on my account. Let me teach you how to use it."

"Glen, you didn't have to buy me a phone. Let me pay you for it."

"No, that's okay. We'll work something out later when you're out of here, if you decide to keep it."

He sat on the edge of her bed to show her how to call him.

"I programmed my number in so you just have to open the phone like this, and press the number two. Then press this green button and listen for my voice."

Josie took the phone from Glen. He closed it as he handed it to her. She opened it, pressed two and the green button and the phone in his pocket began to ring.

"Perfect," he said. "I put your phone on vibrate, so no one will hear it ring, but you'll be able to feel it."

"On what?"

"Your phone will vibrate instead of ring."

Glen called her so that Josie could understand.

Her phone vibrated repeatedly. She looked at the phone in her hand.

"Just open it up and start to talk," he said.

She followed his orders. He stepped out into the hall so she could get a feel for the sound of his voice to be sure she could hear it or if he needed to adjust the volume.

"Now remember, you call the bank in the morning. Do you know the number?"

"Yes."

"Just dial it in like you would any other phone and press the green button. You should be set. Remember, call me after you talk to the bank and don't let anyone know you have this phone."

Josie turned the phone over in her hand to admire it.

"This is almost as good as the Dick Tracy wrist watch," she smiled.

"Now, can you tell me Darcy's schedule?" he asked.

"I found out she works days this month. She gets off at five."

"I'll be here at five to watch her leave the building. I'll follow her home or wherever else she goes. I need to know what she's up to."

Glen followed Darcy home for the next three days. On the fourth day she drove to Denver, back to Wal-Mart. He watched her carry packages inside. He observed her returning the duplicates of the items she purchased for Josie. She collected the cash then went shopping again.

She filled the cart with duplicate electronic items and power tools. Again he watched as she went to the same clerk to be checked out. He was on to her and her accomplice now.

When she left the store he went to the store security office.

He knocked at the door then stepped inside.

"Hello, my name is Glen. I'm a detective for the Denver PD and I think you may have a shoplifting team in your store."

***

On Wednesday, Josh appeared dressed as one of Santa's elves. He passed out chocolates and flowers for the birthday people. He played lots of sing-a-long Christmas songs, encouraging the residents to join in. He couldn't help but notice many of the residents had invited their family members to come to visit during his performance. His celebrity status increased as the months progressed. Breaking into a new community is a difficult task. Josh, with his winning personality and oddball antics, paved the way for his early acceptance into the social circle and now, among the general population of Wallace.

Glen mistakenly called Josie during the show. She quickly answered the phone putting him in his place, "Not now, Josh is here."

"I'll call you later."

Cindy and Becky had agreed to make more frequent visits to check on Josie's well being, improving her sense of security. Josie worked hard each day taking many walks up and down the halls to strengthen her legs, hoping to return home as soon as possible.

The plan set in place by the businessmen of the community was well accepted. During the Christmas season, while more family members returned to Wallace signing up their elderly relatives for long term health and financial care, Wallace began to flourish once again.

Glen and Josie touched base that evening before she went to sleep. She felt safer having the phone tucked under her pillow and he felt more assured to know she could reach him at any time.

The next morning when she went to meet her friends for breakfast, she noticed Rex had not joined the men at the next table. She glanced back down the hall in time to watch the familiar shutdown procedure.

She turned to Margaret and whispered, "Where's Rex?"

"He might be the one," she responded. The men and women who had their wits about them knew exactly what it meant during the lockdown, as they called it.

"I didn't know he had any problems other than not being able to walk well," said Josie.

"I didn't think he did," said Margaret. "But he must've had something go wrong."

"Maybe it's not him," said Josie hopefully.

After breakfast she headed directly to his room. She found his family removing the Christmas gifts. They cried knowing before he left he made sure they each had a gift.

"It's almost as if he knew," said his daughter.

Josie left the scene and went to her room to call Glen.

"Morning, Josie. How's my favorite lady this morning?"

"Rex is dead."

"What?"

"You heard me. She got the money she needed out of him and now he's dead. I'm probably next."

"Calm down. Nothing's gonna happen to you. I'm on to her. I found out her scheme. I'm ready to catch her in the act. Let me call Dr. Hooper and get back to you."

He dialed the phone.

"Darrell, what happened to Rex?"

"Hell if I know. He appeared fine. Then he complained last night about severe stomach pains. He had all the symptoms of food poisoning according to the nurse on duty. She tended to his needs planning to wait until morning to call me in. Then he died before she called."

"You're gonna run a post, aren't you?"

"I'm going to try my hardest to convince the family to agree to one. Can you do anything, you know, since you're a cop and all?"

"Not my jurisdiction. You need Tate."

"I was afraid you were gonna say that."

Glen didn't know if he should inform Darrell of Josie's suspicions. He knew Darcy was involved in a shoplifting scheme, but he had nothing to make him think she was capable of murder, nothing more than Josie's fears. Old people die at nursing homes all the time. He knew better than to start something he had no evidence to back up.

Darrell asked around the manor to find out whether or not Dr. Culbertson had been in. Laura informed him that Dr. Culbertson made it a point to come in every day for a visit.

Darrell knew he could put Dr. Culbertson at the scene for nearly every death, but without autopsies he had no proof. Determined to get a family to comply with his suggestion for an autopsy, he went to visit them at Rex's home where they stayed during the holidays.

He knocked on the door.

Alice, Rex's daughter, answered the door.

"Yes? Can I help you?"

"I'm Dr. Hooper. I'd like to talk with Rex's family. Are you his daughter?"

"Yes, I am. Come in."

She quickly introduced him around the room to the rest of the family including her three children and her two siblings.

"First of all, I'd like to express my sympathy for your loss," he began.

"Before you give us your sympathy," said Rosemary, Alice's sister. "Maybe you can explain why Daddy died so suddenly. We thought he was getting wonderful care here. Then we found out Dr. Culbertson no longer practiced and you moved in and now he's dead."

"That's the reason I'm here. I'd like to ask you to allow us to do an autopsy to find the cause of death."

"Lack of proper medical care is most likely the cause of death," said the grief stricken Rosemary. "I just saw him yesterday and he seemed fine. He was all excited for me to come to watch that Josh Mackey guy from the radio station give them a little program and then this morning he's dead. What did you miss?"

"I don't feel I missed anything. I have to agree this came as a complete surprise to me as well. Won't you please consider the autopsy?"

"I'm not too sure about that," said Alice. "Daddy's been through enough already."

"I agree," said Rosemary. "Maybe you should just leave. I don't believe you're welcome here."

Shocked, Darrell let himself out.

He sat in his car wondering how to deal with this dilemma.

After months of lowering the death rate, residents were beginning to die once again. The following week he lost another with many of the same symptoms. The DNR papers made it impossible for him to get them to hold on so he could run tests.

Glen continued to keep Darcy under surveillance, wondering when she would return the items she purchased to the store. Finally, after the holidays and her kids were back in school she made a trip to Wal-Mart.

Glen went directly to the security office.

"Okay, the scheme's in motion. The person in question is at the customer service counter returning the merchandise. If my instincts are correct, she'll take the cash then go shopping with it. Keep an eye on register fourteen. You have a young woman there with red hair and black roots. I believe she's involved."

They monitored the security cameras and stationed one plain-clothes security guard at the exit nearest register fourteen. Just as Glen predicted, Darcy shopped, gathering two or three of each item. Then she stood in line for register fourteen. They watched the clerk scan the merchandise.

"I don't see anything wrong," said the head of security.

Glen watched the camera more closely.

"Look. Check out where the barcode is on the item, then when she scans the same item the second time she's turning it to avoid the bar code. She's faking it."

"Son of a bitch. I think you're right."

They watched the entire process. No conversation or eye contact occurred between the two women. Darcy had her back to the customers behind her while she skimmed through a magazine, blocking their view of the transaction. After paying, she proceeded to the door with her basket full of bagged merchandise.

The security guard at the door snatched her as soon as she left the building. A second guard made his way through the store to the red haired checker at register fourteen.

"Come with me," he said. "They want to speak to you in the office."

"I can't just close my register. I have customers."

"Finish with the one you're with."

He turned to the line of customers, "Ladies, and gentlemen this register is closed. I'm sorry. Can you please move to another register? Thank you."

As Darcy was escorted to the security office she noticed Glen leaving by the back stairs.

One quick check of the cash register receipt revealed there were more items in the bag than were purchased. Both ladies were taken into custody.

The next day was Saturday. Glen stopped by Winegard's to buy something for Josie as a reward for her detective skills.

Vanessa stepped out from the back room to assist him.

"What brings you here?" she asked.

"I need some candy for my lady friend."

"Anyone I know?"

"You might."

"You're not going to tell me are you?"

Glen smiled. "They're for Josie over at the manor."

"So you two are quite the item I hear."

"What do you mean?"

"There's talk that you're always hanging out with her at the manor. What gives? You're not family, are you?"

"No. Just good friends."

"Sort of an odd friendship, wouldn't you say? With the age difference and all."

Glen didn't appreciate the interrogation. "So how about those chocolates?"

Vanessa opened the glass case containing the chocolates.

"What kind does she like?"

"I don't have a clue. Just give me a nice assortment."

"In that case, let me grab a box from the back that's already packaged. I like to give soft centers to the residents at the manor. No toffee or nuts for them."

"That's a great idea."

She returned with a bright gold foil box.

"Will there be anything else?"

"No, that should do it," he responded while he took cash from his pocket. "How's business these days?"

He couldn't help but notice the two women helping in the back with flower arrangements.

"Good. Business is good. Things are picking back up."

Glen took the chocolates and the Dick Tracy book he'd purchased earlier in the week to Josie.

"Where have you been, stranger?" she complained when she saw him approaching.

"I've been on a stakeout, thanks to you, and we got our man. Well, in this case we got our woman."

"You nailed her?"

Glen smiled at the vocabulary used by the frail little lady.

"Yes, ma'am, we nailed her. Thanks to you. I brought you some chocolates and a book as a reward for a job well done."

"Chocolates, huh?" she said as she opened the golden gift box. "I don't eat the stuff, but thanks anyway. Let me see the book."

"I had no idea. I thought all women ate chocolate."

"Most do, just not this one. Can I see my book or not?"

Glen handed the other package to her. He watched her face light up as she gently stroked the cover of the book, remembering the old series from her youth.

"Let's go to my room where we can talk in private."

He followed her down the hall. Her ability with the walker improved daily. He felt sure Darrell would allow her to go home soon.

Once inside her room she turned anxiously to Glen. "Well, what happened?"

He explained about the initial purchase made with cash. He told her how Darcy would buy multiples of the same item and have a friend at the checkout only ring up one of each, passing the others through without charging for them. Then Darcy would keep the items she wanted for herself, take the paid items to the residents like Josie then return the rest for a cash refund that she undoubtedly shared with her accomplice.

"I knew, it. I knew she was a bad seed," said Josie. "What happens next?"

"She and her buddy spent the night in jail. They'll have to go before the judge and then a court date will be set. I imagine they'll both do a little time. The security department is going to have to go back and review the tapes and returns to find out how much they stole. Based on that, they'll know if the total is high enough to make felony charges stick."

"I know my stuff, don't I?" she boasted.

"Yes, Josie. You know your stuff."

The two of them had a nice visit then Glen returned home to spend time with his dogs. He felt he'd been neglecting them lately by following Darcy around. He knew he couldn't have gone to Tate with his suspicions.

***

Tuesday morning when Josie stepped out of her bathroom she found Darcy standing in her room.

"What're you doing here? I thought you were in jail?"

"I'm out on bond waiting to go to court to see how much time I have to serve. Now I know it was you and your detective friend who ruined my life and had my kids taken away. You can tell him for me that I always return favors. And I know where both of you live."

Chapter 17

Darrell, frustrated by the families not working with him to prove his theory, turned his attention to Josie who remained alive after her unauthorized drugging.

He went to her room and found Darcy with Josie.

"Good morning, Dr. Hooper," said Darcy as she slipped past him into the hall.

"She just threatened me!" said Josie. "Call Glen."

"Now, Ms. Josie. I'm sure you just misunderstood. Why don't I help you back into bed and we'll talk about it."

"I don't need your help and I'm not getting back in that bed. I need to get out of here. She threatened me, I tell you. She's an evil one. Just ask Glen about her. He had her arrested. What's she still doing here?"

"What do you mean he had her arrested?"

"Just ask him. Here, talk to him."

She pressed two on the phone and handed it to Darrell.

"Hi, Josie," said Glen.

"Glen, it's me, Darrell."

"Darrell, what the hell? Did something happen to Josie?"

"No, she's fine, but she told me you had Darcy arrested?"

"Yeah, sort of. She was involved in a shoplifting scheme. She got picked up on Friday night. As far as I know she's still in jail. Why?"

"I just bumped into her in Josie's room and she told me Darcy threatened her."

"No shit. That bitch. I wonder how she connected Josie to her arrest? We've got to get her out of there. How much longer does she have to stay?"

"Does she have someone to watch her twenty-four seven?"

"No."

"I'm sorry, Glen. She needs to be a little more mobile. Maybe another couple of weeks. I can see to it that Darcy's not allowed in the building any longer. Can I get a protection order?"

"I suppose, but that's only a piece of paper you know."

"I'm going to talk to Tate," said Darrell.

"Why?"

"I want him on my side. I need him to help me with the families around town. I know something's not right."

"Go ahead, but the asshole's not gonna listen and remember, he parties with the people who make their living from death."

"Good point, but I want to try. Maybe it will flush something out."

"Tell Josie I'm coming over when I get off duty."

Darrell went to Laura to explain the circumstances surrounding Darcy. He encouraged her to inform the remaining staff and to be sure she wouldn't be allowed inside the building again. Then he went to the sheriff's office to confront Tate.

Tate watched Darrell from his office window as he approached the building. When the dispatcher told Tate he had a visitor, he told her to make him wait.

He had the upper hand. Darrell was on his turf and he wanted to be in control. After thirty minutes he stepped out of his office.

"Dr. Hooper, what brings you here?"

He remembered the scene at the bar and how Glen humiliated him in front of Darrell and the other patrons.

"Can I speak to you in private?"

"Of course, come into my office."

Darrell closed the door behind him. He knew if Tate chose to, he could destroy his career in Wallace by spreading his theory around town.

"So, tell me what you and your buddy are up to now? Some new killer running around Wallace that you need to tell me about?"

Darrell considered getting up to leave, knowing this conversation would go nowhere, but if he was right, he wanted a record of having gone through the proper channels.

"I'm wondering. I think you should know one of the residents of the manor was threatened today by an ex-employee."

"And who might that be?"

"The resident or the employee?"

"Both."

"The resident is Josie..."

Before Darrell could give her last name Tate cut him off, "Isn't that old broad a close friend of your detective?"

"Yes, I suppose so."

"So, you're all in on this then?"

"Look, are you going to listen or not?"

"Okay, okay, cool your jets. Give me the facts."

Tate leaned toward his desk and took out a pad and pencil.

"Darcy, one of the aides, was arrested on Friday for shoplifting. She's out on bond and came by the manor to accuse Josie of being involved."

"Was she?"

"What do you mean?"

"Was Josie somehow involved in her arrest?"

"She and Glen figured out her..."

"Aha, Glen's involved too. I knew it. Let there be a crime in Wallace and he's somehow connected. Where was this supposed shoplifting and why didn't I hear about it?"

"Look, you can discuss that with Detective Karst. I'm here to inform you that Darcy threatened Josie. Are you going to make note of it? She's not to be seen in the manor any more. If she shows up there I've instructed the staff to call you. I wanted to inform you of the situation so you could send a car over. It's called trespassing."

"I know what it's called," sneered Tate. "Is there anything else?"

"Possibly."

"What does that mean?"

"I've had some unexplained deaths at the manor recently and I'm suspecting foul play."

"I knew it. You and Karst are turning natural cause deaths into homicides. Aren't there enough in Denver to keep him busy? Why does he have to invent more here? He wants to prove he's some damn hero, doesn't he?"

"Glen's not involved with this. I am. I want an investigation into some of the deaths."

"What do you want from me? What kind of proof do you have?"

"None, without an autopsy or two."

"So, you have no proof. Old folks are dying and you want me to shake up the town and force grieving families to have autopsies performed to appease your curiosity. And suppose you're wrong. I'd look like a jackass for going along with your crazy game."

"You are a jackass!" said Darrell as he walked out the door, slamming it behind him.

At the end of the day, Darrell returned to the manor to make his rounds, a new routine to keep a closer watch on his patients. He went to Josie's room last.

"Josie, how're you doing? I made sure Darcy's not allowed in the building in the future. I hope that makes you feel a little safer."

"I'll never feel safe here. I don't think it was Darcy who drugged me; she wasn't even here. She was off at some school thing for her kids."

"You know, that's been on my mind a lot lately," said Darrell. "Any chance you took something on your own, thinking you were taking an aspirin or something for pain?"

"No. I won't take anything. I need my wits about me to live in a place like this."

"Can you give me all the details of that night, please?"

"Sure, I already told Glen. I needed to call him and no one took me seriously. It was dinnertime and they told me to eat dinner and make my call later. It was important I reach him right away. I got a little cranky and boom, the next thing I know one of them drugged me."

"One of who?"

"I don't know. Somebody."

"Who did you see?"

"Diane took me to my room and made me stay there. Melody brought me a tray and then I remember waking up in the hospital."

"Did you see Dr. Culbertson that night?"

"Raymond? No. Well, he was talking to some of the residents, but he didn't talk to me or come by my room, if that's what you mean."

"You saw no one other than Diane and Melody? And it was Melody who brought your tray?"

"That's right."

"Okay, sweetie. You've been a big help."

"Have you seen Glen? He said he was coming tonight, right?"

"Yes, I'm sure he'll be along shortly."

Darrell got up to leave when Josie stopped him.

"Say, does your wife like chocolates?"

"Yes, she does."

"Glen bought this for me and I don't eat them. There's not enough to pass out to all of my friends and I don't want to be accused of playing favorites. So could you take these home with you?"

"Why, thank you. I'm sure she'll appreciate them. She's been a little under the weather lately. I think she's coming down with a bug, so these might cheer her up."

Darrell set off to find Melody. At the end of the hall, he found Glen talking to Josh Mackey.

"Good evening, gentlemen. What are you two up to?"

"Josh was just telling me he's the new delivery man for Winegard's."

"Is that a fact?" said Darrell.

"Yeah, Vanessa said business was a little slow and they let their regular delivery girl go. So long story short, I'm here every day dropping off flowers and candy to the residents who signed up for their 'Mortuary with a Heart' program."

"I know all about that program. I'm all for it. Well, don't let us stop you from making your deliveries. I guess we'll be seeing you around here quite a bit."

"Guess so."

"Nice kid," said Glen, as Josh walked away.

"A little nutty, but the residents really like him. I'm all for him spreading a little sunshine around here," said Darrell.

"How'd your visit with Tate go?"

"How do you think?"

"I tried to warn you."

"I know, but I thought he might have a fragment of a brain in that empty skull. I don't know how in the hell he gets re-elected all the time."

"No one else wants to run against him. Once again, remember who he rubs elbows with."

"Why don't you?"

Glen laughed one of his big hearty laughs.

"Now, that would be funny. I should, just to shake him up then drop out of the election at the last minute. I'll have to give that some thought. Sweet!"

"Can we talk?"

"Sure, let's sit in the library. I guess we never did finish our discussion, did we?"

The two men made their way through the residents with walkers and wheelchairs swarming around the commons area. The library frequently remained empty. Most of the residents with dementia and vision problems were incapable of reading books, while others like Josie, Margaret and her other friends, chose to take them either back to their rooms or into the sun room.

"You look troubled," said Glen.

"I am. I know some of these deaths here are to be expected, but damn it, Glen, I can't be missing everything. I swear some of these people are in good health except for lack of mobility, like Josie. Her heart is strong and so is her mind. She's not had a sick day since she got here, she just can't walk very well and even that's getting better. If she showed up dead tomorrow I would have the right to wonder why."

"Still no takers for autopsies?"

"Nope."

"Can you run any tests while they're still alive?

"I could, but on who, and why? There are new residents coming in to fill every opening the same day we lose one. How could I predict who I need to run tests on? Besides, if I tried to do it to all of them I'd be accused of padding my pockets."

"You really do think someone is killing these people?"

"Yes, I do."

"What would they have to gain by it?"

"I think it could be mercy killings."

"But who?"

"I still think it's Culbertson."

"Can you prove it?"

"Not without tests."

"Has he been here for all the deaths?"

"Yes."

"Shit," said Glen. "Your hands are tied."

"I know. Josie is adamant about Darcy being so evil. Do you think she's involved?"

"In a mercy killing?" said Glen. "She's not the type. She'd be more apt to kill for money and, even at that, it's a long stretch from stealing to killing, even for someone like Darcy."

"I need to get home to Abby. She's been complaining she's not seeing enough of me lately. And I know Josie's waiting for you. Let me know if you come up with any ideas to help me out."

"Sure thing, Doc."

Melody walked past the entrance to the library.

Darrell called out, "Melody."

She popped her head in the doorway as Glen got up to leave.

"You wanted to speak to me?" she asked.

Laura had noticed Melody in the hall and started toward her when Melody stepped inside the library with Darrell. She waited in the hall.

"Can you tell me about the other night with Josie?"

"What night?"

"The night you took her a tray in her room."

"Oh, she was just a little agitated. She ate her dinner then fell asleep."

"Don't fool around with me," he said. "I know that you and the entire staff talk. I had her taken over to the hospital for observation when we couldn't wake her. She had a sedative in her system. What you know about that?"

"I don't know anything."

"I think you're lying. You were the one who took her the tray; you were the last person with her before she fell into a deep sedated sleep. Who else could've slipped her a drug?"

"Are you accusing me of drugging Josie?"

"Yes, I am."

"Well, you're wrong," she said, as she stormed out of the library.

Laura followed her down the hall to the bathroom. She heard Melody crying in one of the stalls.

"Melody, it's Laura."

"What?"

"I heard your conversation with Dr. Hooper. Can we talk?"

Melody stepped out.

"I wanted to talk to you about a missing bottle of sleeping pills from inventory. Do you know anything about them?"

"Oh, now you're accusing me, too."

"Look, I'm just asking," said Laura. "Even if you did help Josie sleep that night when she was irrational, I'm okay with it. Sometimes we know more than the doctors about what the residents need. We're the ones who have to deal with them all day and all night while the docs just pop in and make rounds, not really knowing what's going on."

"I wish Dr. Culbertson still worked here. He knew what was best," said Melody. "Why make them suffer even one minute if we can take that stress or pain away from them?"

"I agree," said Laura as she hugged Melody. "Let's drop this discussion about the bottle. No harm's been done. Josie had a good night's sleep, that's all. Don't let Dr. Hooper get to you."

***

The next afternoon Vanessa and her ladies group had lunch at Fouraker's Steakhouse. The other ladies had already ordered when Vanessa arrived.

"We'd almost given up on you," said Karen Powers.

"I thought we'd never get caught up," she responded. She grabbed her menu and gave her order quickly to the waitress who patiently stood by.

"Is business picking back up?" asked Karen.

"Yes it is, thank you."

"Ours too. Gary says the new program for estate planning is working really well. The best idea he's had in a long time."

"Michael's not selling lots of funeral packages yet, but he expects that to pick up. I've been busier with flowers and the idea to deliver them weekly to the residents will be better when we get a smoother system down and can delegate the work more efficiently," said Vanessa.

Mrs. Culbertson chimed in, "Raymond says we can leave for a two month vacation starting in March."

"Two months," said Karen. "Where in the world are you going?"

"He wants to start in Hawaii, then off to Europe. He's always wanted to go Germany and you know how badly I've wanted to go to Italy."

"I don't get it," said Vanessa. "I thought he hated to travel."

"He doesn't hate to travel, he's just content to stay home. I'm not sure what's gotten into him, but I'm not going to question it."

"I thought with him retiring, you'd be watching your finances more closely," said Vanessa.

"Nessie, that's none of your business. I'm sure they have a tidy nest egg set aside. Why shouldn't they travel as much as they want?"

"When can we count on all of you joining us?" asked Mrs. Culbertson.

"I'll talk to Gary. I'd love to go to Hawaii in March. What about you, Vanessa?"

"Italy sounds good. I'll talk to Michael and see if we can do both Italy and Hawaii."

"Can you afford to be away from the shop for so long? I don't mean money, but who can you trust to run it?"

"I'm sure we can make it work. We really do need a break."

After lunch Vanessa drove to the mortuary to talk to Michael. She couldn't wait until he came home that night.

"Hi, honey," she said when she walked into his office. "Are you busy?"

"Not at the moment." He slipped his arms around her waist giving her a long passionate kiss. "We're here all alone and I don't have any appointments for the rest of the day."

"Oh no, Romeo. The last time we tried to have sex here the Arnold's showed up with all of their kids to give them a tour of the mortuary. I learned my lesson."

She pushed him away.

"If you didn't come here for my body then why are you here?"

"I wanted to talk to you about going on vacation."

"Where to?"

"The Culbertson's are going to Hawaii and then to Europe. I told her we might join them for Hawaii and Italy, but then we'd have to get back to work. They plan to be gone two months. I figured we could only be gone three weeks."

"When?"

"They're leaving in March."

"Vanessa, sweetie, I'd love to, but we're not out of the woods yet. We had a pretty long dry spell. I think we need to build up reserves again before we blow all we've got left in savings on a vacation. Then there's payroll while we're gone."

"Can we give it six months and see where we're at?"

She gave him her famous pouty face.

"Don't start that. I'm serious."

She dropped the pout and slipped her arms around his neck. "Okay, you're the financial genius in the family. But six months is it. Then you'd better take me someplace special."

"I promise. Now get back to work. You've been whining about how busy you are, so go make us some money."

***

That afternoon, Josh came by for his Wednesday radio program. Glen had asked him if he could find an old detective show to present to the group. He told him how much Josie would enjoy it.

"Today, ladies and gentlemen, I have a special treat for you. I've gotten my hands on Dick Tracy for your listening enjoyment. I'd like to dedicate this series to our own local detective, Josie. I've heard from Detective Karst that you are one clever gumshoe."

"And don't you forget it," said Josie.

Glen slipped in quietly to watch. He had taken a few hours off for the day to see the expression on Josie's face. She was in her glory. Josh caught sight of Glen and smiled. Glen gave him a thumbs-up.

A hand rested on Glen's shoulder. He instinctively turned in one quick move, ready to defend himself.

"Geez, Glen, you're a bit jumpy."

"I'm always prepared, so watch it," he said when he realized it was only Darrell. "How's it going?"

"No change."

"Any more deaths?"

"No, but there's a nasty bug going around here, so don't breathe too deeply."

"What kind of bug?"

"Must be some intestinal thing. Lots of vomiting, diarrhea and stomach cramps."

"Do you treat them here or take them to the hospital?"

"I think it's best to keep it contained, so we're treating the symptoms here, unless they really need to be hospitalized."

"Thanks for the heads up. How's Josie dealing with it?"

"Not bothering her in the least. None of the staff either. Strange, it'll probably hit them all at once and then we'll have a big mess to deal with."

Glen kept his visit with Josie short after the program. He wanted to get out of the building as quickly as possible. He might have spent many days in his youth puking his guts out from drinking, but now he'll go out of his way to avoid it.

Darrell was right about the epidemic spreading through the facility. The residents were getting sicker each day. Determined not to lose any additional patients he spent the next few days putting in extra hours at the manor.

He fell asleep on the sofa in the library from sheer exhaustion. The night nurse touched him on the shoulder.

"Dr. Hooper, you're needed at the hospital."

Darrell shook his head to wake himself.

"What? Huh?"

"I said, you're needed at the hospital. Your wife's there."

"My wife? What's Abby doing there this time of night?"

"She called an ambulance."

"For who? Why didn't she call me?"

He checked his phone and it was dead, the battery had lost its charge.

He raced to the hospital to check on Abby.

As he rushed into the emergency room, he bumped into Dr. Culbertson leaving.

"Come with me, Darrell," he said, putting his hand on his shoulder.

Darrell jerked away. "What're you doing here?"

"One of the nurses called me. No one knew where you were and you didn't answer your phone."

"I was at the manor, I fell asleep. My phone was dead. Where's Abby?"

Dr. Culbertson took a deep breath.

"I'm sorry, son. She didn't make it."

Chapter 18

Darrell finally had a body on which to perform the much-needed autopsy. However, the high price he had to pay for it was not worth it. He lost his desire to fight for what he believed in at the manor. He made up his mind that as soon as he laid his wife's body to rest in her family plot he'd pack up and return to Denver.

He regretted the long hours he took away from their time together. He cursed himself for not paying closer attention to her when she complained of feeling ill. Perhaps he was wrong about the manor, maybe he had no business being a doctor and maybe he should quit practicing altogether. After all, it was obvious he couldn't recognize a life-threatening illness or the other symptoms his dying patients exhibited.

When Glen knocked at his door there was no answer. He let himself in. He found Darrell sitting on the floor in the living room looking through photo albums of the short life he and Abby shared. He hadn't shaved since the day Abby died and by the number of empty bottles on the floor, Glen surmised he also hadn't stopped drinking.

"What do you want?" he asked.

Glen responded, "Hey, man, you've got to pull yourself together. I came by to see if I could help you in any way. I'm so sorry."

"No, I'm the one who's sorry. A sorry excuse for a husband, a sorry excuse for doctor and a sorry excuse for a friend. I want you to leave. I want to be alone."

"I'm sure you do, but we need to talk about this."

Glen took the glass from his hand and helped Darrell to the sofa then went into the kitchen to make coffee.

He handed a cup to Darrell, who spilled the hot liquid on the floor as his hands trembled when he raised it to his lips. Glen assumed he hadn't been eating. Who could at a time like this? Glen stopped for sandwiches on his way.

"Here, eat this," he said.

"No, I don't want it."

"I know, but eat it anyway. You owe it to Abby to pull yourself together. Winegard's called to ask me to speak to you about Abby's final arrangements. Michael said you're not answering your phone or the door."

"I let her down, Glen. I let her down when she needed me the most."

"You were only doing your job. Hell, I'd probably still be married if I hadn't put so much of myself into my job. That's just part of who we are."

"I can't handle the details. I'm not up to it."

"Okay, then. Let me do it. I'll make all the arrangements. You will be attending, won't you?"

"I don't want a public service. I can't face anyone. I want to be alone."

"I'll see to it, if that's the way you want to handle it. I have to ask, do you want a casket, or did she prefer cremation?"

"A casket. A pretty one, Glen, make sure there's lots of pink. Oh, and lots of pink flowers."

"Did you get the results of her autopsy?"

"No. I haven't checked."

"Did you send her to Denver?"

"Yeah."

"Let me call."

Glen had carried the mail in with him. Darrell got up to pace while Glen made his call. He thumbed through the stack on the desk. He found the newspaper and opened it to the obituary section to read about Abby. To his surprise, he noticed since her death, Wallace had lost five other residents.

"See what I mean?" said Darrell, handing the paper to Glen.

"I killed them all."

Glen read the names.

"Do you know all of these people?"

"Yeah, they're from the manor."

"Darrell, I think something's terribly wrong here."

"That's what I've been saying. I'm a terrible doctor."

Glen's cell phone rang. The pathologist returned his call.

"Detective Karst, I have the results on Abby Hooper for you. It appears she's been given a lethal dose of arsenic."

"What? Are you absolutely sure?"

"I ran the test myself. It's conclusive."

"Thanks."

Now Glen paced the room. He looked at his friend, an empty shell of the man he once knew and respected. Setting aside the friendship, his instincts as a cop allowed him to scrutinize Darrell's body language. He knew from deep within Darrell had no idea of the cause of his wife's death. In a case such as this, when a spouse is poisoned, the remaining spouse is the first suspect. How would he break this news to his suffering friend?

Glen walked over to him.

"Darrell, let's go back to the sofa to sit down. We need to talk."

Obediently, Darrell allowed Glen to guide him across the room to be seated. His head sank deeply into his hands as he sobbed over the loss of his wife.

Glen rubbed his shoulders.

"Darrell, I hate to be the one to tell you this, but Abby's pathology report found arsenic poisoning to be her cause of death."

Quickly, his head lifted and turned toward Glen.

"What did you say?"

"She's was poisoned, Darrell. Could she have been working in the garden shed, or cleaning something out, accidentally exposing herself to arsenic? You know how it is around these old farms. Hell, it could've been in some container that wasn't labeled properly."

"That would explain her symptoms," said Darrell.

"Let's have a look around. Are you up to it?" asked Glen.

With a sudden flood of strength Darrell rose to his feet. He wiped his eyes and led Glen to the garden shed out back. They tore the shed apart searching. Abby's grandmother kept it meticulous. In just moments, they had looked in every container on the shelves. Out in the yard, Glen's eyes scanned the garden and the empty trash area. Nothing. They walked to the garage. It was more empty than the garden shed.

"Was it this way when you moved in?" asked Glen.

"Yeah, her grandmother was a clean freak like you," said Darrell.

"How about the basement?"

"We can check, but it's going to be more of the same."

They searched there anyway, coming up empty-handed. The only place left would be where Abby kept her cleaning products and they found the same dead end.

"Has anyone been here to see Abby that you know of?" asked Glen.

"No, she kept to herself. I think that added to her depression."

"She was depressed?"

"It's not what you're thinking. She wouldn't have done this to herself. She wanted a baby and we were having difficulty conceiving. I spent so much time away lately that she felt lonely."

He burst into tears again.

Glen helped him back to the sofa.

"The pathologist is going to have to turn this in. Tate will be first man on the case. You need to prepare yourself for his interrogation, and I strongly suggest you lawyer up and say absolutely nothing. In fact, I insist."

"Damn, I don't need Tate in my face at a time like this. I'm going to be suspected of killing my wife, aren't I?"

"I'm afraid so. At least, that's the approach Tate will take. We have to find out who did this. Have you upset anyone lately?"

"Of course, there's Tate and Culbertson and lots of the staff at the manor aren't too pleased with me breathing down their necks all the time. But no one there should want to take it out on Abby. I'm the one they'd want to poison. You know, Culbertson was with Abby when she died."

"I guess we can start there," said Glen.

Soon after Darrell buried his wife, Tate showed up at his door.

"Dr. Hooper, we need to talk. I understand your wife died of arsenic poisoning. Can you shed any light on that?"

"I won't speak to you without an attorney present."

"I see. May I ask who gave you that advice?"

"That's none of your business."

"Okay, then bring your attorney downtown this afternoon. We'll talk then."

Tate started to leave then turned back to Darrell, "Leave your detective buddy out of this. You're in my jurisdiction."

Darrell called Glen to ask him to recommend a good attorney.

That afternoon Darrell and his attorney, Gene Winchester, reported to Tate for routine questioning.

Winchester did a great job handling Tate. Darrell thought it almost comical how easily he intimidated Tate. Glen waited outside.

"How'd it go?"

"This guy's a blooming idiot," said Darrell's attorney. "I don't think he'll give us much trouble. Now we'll have to wait and see if anyone comes up with any damning evidence to frame Dr. Hooper."

Glen enlisted the help of his buddy, Martin, at CBI to investigate the questions Darrell had about the deaths at the manor. He knew that Tate had neither the skills nor the desire to conduct a proper investigation and CBI sent Martin on a fact-finding mission, under the guise of assistance to the local agency. They started with Dr. Culbertson.

Martin went with Glen to visit Dr. Culbertson.

Raymond answered the door, "Good afternoon, gentlemen. How may I help you?"

"Dr. Culbertson, this is Martin Harmon, from the Colorado Bureau of Investigation. He'd like to ask you a few questions."

Culbertson answered questions about the night he treated Abby. He was annoyed when the line of questioning turned to the hours he spent at the manor. He was smart enough to realize where they were heading. After they left, he called Tate.

"What's going on?"

"What do you mean?"

"Why was CBI here asking me questions?"

"Karst has his nose out of joint because his friend killed his wife with arsenic and he's trying to blame someone else. I'm going to turn over every rock and plant on his property until I can prove he killed her."

"I've had it with all the accusations. I could tell they think I'm some mercy killer. I can't let this get around town. What do I have to do to get Delbert's body exhumed?"

"Why would you do that?"

"Hooper wanted an autopsy and I refused, so let's get one done now. If they think I've been killing people with arsenic it'll still be in his body."

Tate contacted CBI with Dr. Culbertson's request.

Meanwhile, Josie called Glen.

"Josie, I'm sorry I haven't been by to see you, but I've been spending time with Dr. Hooper since his wife died."

"Glen, get me out of here. They're dropping like flies."

"What do you mean?"

"Three more just last night."

"What?"

"Yes, three more died last night and lots of the others are near death."

Mind Your Manors!

Glen and Darrell spent so much time on Abby's case they were unaware of the happenings around town.

"Josie, are you absolutely sure?"

"Yes, damn it, Glen. You have to believe me. It's not safe here."

"Let me make a few calls and get back to you."

Glen called Winegard's Mortuary.

"Michael, Glen Karst. I heard through the grapevine there've been more deaths at the manor. Can you expand on that for me?"

"It's been hell, Glen. I can't believe it. I'm here day and night and I can't keep up. Whatever this bug is has spread through the manor like a wildfire. I'm having to recruit some help from my colleagues in Denver."

"Has anyone turned it in to the CDC?"

"I don't know, should I?"

"Hell, yes."

"Okay, I'll make that call right now."

Glen called Martin next.

"There's been an unusually high incidence of deaths at the manor that are worth looking into," said Glen.

"We're already on it. Some woman called it in."

"Who?"

Glen heard the rustle of papers. "An ex-employee, named Darcy Clark."

"No shit?" said Glen.

"You know her?"

"Yeah, she's out on bond waiting to get her court date. I'm responsible for getting her fired and picked up for shoplifting."

"Could she be involved?"

"Anything's possible. She's been banned from the manor, but maybe she has someone on the inside. Hell, I don't know."

"It's not just the manor any longer."

"What do you mean?" asked Glen.

"We've got a recent head count and three other people from Wallace, in no way connected to the manor, have died of the same mysterious symptoms. Our lab shows arsenic's the cause in all the cases."

"What the hell? No way."

"We're sending an entire crew over. We've got to close that town down and find the killer."

"Let me take some personal days and I'll be there to help. God knows Tate will be worthless."

"Thanks, Glen we could use another good man. Besides, you live there and know your way around. You can go places and talk to people easier than we can."

Glen made arrangements for the CBI crew and Darrell to meet at his house for a brainstorming session. An investigator with the Colorado State Department of Health was present as well.

"Gentlemen, I'd like to introduce you to Dr. Hooper. He lost his wife to this arsenic epidemic. He's the one you should speak to regarding this investigation. He's felt for some time there were too many unexplained deaths at the nursing home."

"Dr. Hooper," said Martin. "What have the lab reports told you about the previous deaths?"

"Nothing, I can't get the folks around here to authorize autopsies."

"Why the hell not?" asked one of the other CBI men.

"It's just the local mindset, especially where the elderly are concerned."

"That makes them the perfect target," said Martin.

"Exactly," said Darrell. "That's what I thought."

"Do you have any suspects?" asked Martin.

"I've wondered about Bangert."

"Who's Bangert?" asked Martin.

"Bangert is the name of the company who recently purchased Wallace Manor. When I first moved here I noticed there was a high incidence of deaths. I blamed Dr. Culbertson, the doctor who practiced here before me."

Martin asked, "What would they have to gain? Do you think they were working together somehow?"

"I do," said Darrell. "I think he's been performing mercy killings. Bangert stands to make a lot of money with a fast turnover of residents."

Darrell then went into the lengthy explanation of the price reduction package Bangert offered.

"So, you think they were offering Dr. Culbertson a kickback and he got to choose the residents to die, based on his desire to stop suffering?" questioned Martin.

"That's my theory," said Darrell.

"Then why your wife?" asked the other CBI agent.

"Maybe to get back at me because I've been asking too many questions or pushing so hard for autopsies. Maybe they thought I'd leave."

"I need a list of all the suspicious deaths at the manor for the past three months. We'll start there," said Martin.

"I'll get that for you," said Glen.

"What's your plan?" asked Darrell.

"We're going to exhume the bodies and test them for arsenic. We need to know how long this has been going on," said Martin.

Glen spoke up, "What can we do to protect the remaining residents?"

"First, we determine if the sick ones are suffering from arsenic poisoning," said Martin. "I think we should make arrangements to move them out of Wallace Manor and into other nursing homes throughout Denver. Doc, are you ready to go back to work?"

"I'll do anything I can to help."

"Okay, get blood tests ordered for the remaining residents. Then lets get them out of there. The samples will be sealed, initialed and go straight to our lab. Glen will show you the procedure."

"Let's start with Josie," said Glen. "I want to go get her right now."

Glen convinced Cindy to take a few days off of work and stay at his house with Josie.

Not to cause panic in the town, CBI worked through Darrell. When the tests came back most, but not all, of the residents had varying levels of arsenic in their bodies. Josie, along with a few other residents, had none.

The food supply in the kitchen at the manor was checked thoroughly. No arsenic was found. Colorado Department of Health officials were all over the town, finding nothing. It appeared more and more to be intentional poisonings.

Another group meeting at Glen's brought up more questions.

"Someone on the inside has got to be our killer," said Martin. "We've had someone posted in the parking lot watching who goes in and out of the building. Very few family members have been visiting over the past few days, probably because of the illness inside."

Josie stepped out to join them.

Glen introduced her. "Men, this is my good friend, Josie. She might be able to offer some assistance. She's got an eye for details where crime is concerned."

The others looked disbelievingly at him.

"What can I help with?" asked Josie.

"First of all, you were right. Someone is killing the people at the manor," said Glen.

"I told you," said Josie.

"Now we need your help to discover who," he said.

"I thought it was Darcy, but she's not been there since the day she threatened me."

"Is that the same woman who filed a complaint with us about the manor?" asked Martin.

Glen answered, "Yes, that's her."

"She threatened you?" asked Martin.

"She did. But then she never came back."

"Can you tell us of any other regular visitors?" asked Glen.

"You mean other than the aides and Dr. Hooper?"

"Yes."

"Well, Dr. Culbertson's there a lot. There's a number of preachers, and sometimes teachers bring kids in to sing songs."

"Preachers?" asked Martin.

"They comes in a couple of times a week," said Josie.

"Does anyone bring in food?" asked Glen.

"No. Well, maybe a family member brings in something once in a while."

"Do they bring in enough to share with others?"

"Not usually," said Josie. "I'm not being much help, am I?"

"You're doing just fine," said Glen. "Let's keep going. Think about the food, Josie. Why is it that you and some of the others have not gotten any of the arsenic? Does the same person take the trays to the tables?"

"No, they're different all the time."

"What about the cooks in the kitchen?"

"They're the same two ladies all the time."

Glen bit his lip. There had to be something they were missing.

"Wait, don't forget there's been a few others who are not connected to the manor. Whoever our killer is must be getting braver. He's obviously gotten by with it so far. But what the hell's the motive?"

"Do all serial killers need motives?" asked Josie.

The other men looked at her in surprise.

"No, Josie. You're right. Could be our perp is escalating for the thrill of the kill," said Glen.

Just then Martin's cell phone rang.

"Hey, there's a delivery guy who just went inside. Do you want us to grab him?" asked the agent stationed in the parking lot.

"What's he delivering?"

"Flowers and small boxes."

"What kind of small boxes?"

Josie turned to Glen. "They must be talking about Josh. He wouldn't hurt anyone."

"Hold on a second," said Martin. "Josie, do you know this guy?"

"Sure, he's Josh Mackey, from the radio station."

"What's in the boxes?" asked Glen.

"Chocolates."

"Grab him," said Martin.

Josh barely made his way past the front desk when two plain- clothes agents stopped him. One stood in front of him and the other behind. A badge was flashed quickly then put away.

"Please come with us, sir."

"Why? What'd I do?"

"Just come with us. We need to go have a little talk."

Once they had Josh securely in the backseat of the car with one of the agents they called it in to Martin.

"Okay, we've got him. Where do you want us to take him?"

"Take him to the sheriff's office. We'll be right there.

The agents walked Josh into Tate's office.

"What's going on?" asked Tate.

"We need to hold this man for questioning," said one of the men.

"Why? What'd he do?"

"We'll discuss that when the agent in charge gets here."

In the meantime, Martin instructed them to confiscate the chocolates and get them to the lab in Denver for testing.

Cindy stayed behind with Josie who protested loudly about being left. She wanted to be there to defend Josh.

Josh refused to answer questions. He knew his rights and asked for an attorney.

Two hours later while Josh and his attorney, Gary Powers, chatted privately, Martin received a call from the lab. The chocolates tested positive for arsenic.

Martin said to the others. "The chocolates are loaded."

Glen said, "That'll get us a search warrant. I'll get it started."

Martin will review and sign the search warrant as he has statewide jurisdiction.

Glen looked to Tate and said, "Would you be so kind as to notify your judge that we'll have a search warrant for his signature in forty-five minutes. Surely he's seen so many from your office that this one will be a breeze."

Martin turned away to hide the smile on his face flashing Glen a look that said what he was thinking. You just can't help yourself can you?

Tate sneered and barked out the order to his assistant, who incidentally, also hid her smile.

The Miranda rights were read to Josh and he was escorted to a cell.

"Will someone tell me what the hell's going on?" complained Tate.

Martin took him aside to fill him in on the details while the search warrants were being applied for.

With the completion of the search warrants Josh's house, car and the radio station were checked out and cleared. Josh was released.

As the days passed, the deaths at the manor continued. Darrell explained the deaths were a result of the high concentration of arsenic in the frail bodies of the elderly, who were not strong enough to fight off the effects.

Finally, the results from the exhumed bodies were in. Much to the surprise of the investigation crew and Darrell, the arsenic poisoning appeared to be a very recent occurrence. No evidence could be found in the bodies of the residents that Darrell had previously suspected were victims of foul play. His accusations of Dr. Culbertson were unfounded. The cause of those deaths would remain unanswered.

Josh continued to deny tampering with the chocolates. The remaining chocolates from Winegard's Florist were confiscated from the glass display case and tested. With no trace of arsenic present Josh's guilt seemed apparent, but there was not enough to arrest him.

With the crisis slowing down but still unresolved, Darrell decided to go forward with his plan to leave Wallace. Glen stopped by with Cindy and Josie to help him remove Abby's belongings. He'd not slept in their room since she died. He took his clothes into the guest room. He couldn't bear to look at her dresses hanging in the closet.

Cindy carefully took them down and placed them in boxes for charity. Josie moved around the room slowly with her cane picking up small items, placing them in a box. When she tired she sat on the bed for a break.

Glen walked in to offer his assistance, allowing Darrell time to be alone. He opened the drawer of the nightstand, finding items that belonged to Darrell. He closed the drawer and went to the other side of the bed, near Josie.

"What's wrong?" he asked.

"It's so sad. She was so young and beautiful. She had her whole life ahead of her."

"I know," sympathized Glen.

"I still can't believe Josh did it," said Josie.

Glen stood next to the bed looking at Josie. His mind raced. All of his instincts agreed with Josie. Why was he paying more attention to the evidence than his inner self? He paced around the room then stared out the window.

He turned around quickly, scanning the room.

"What?" asked Cindy, noticing his agitated state.

"Josh didn't do it and the answer is in this room," said Glen.

"Why do you say that?" asked Cindy.

"It's my gut," said Glen.

Josie perked up, excited to watch him work.

He opened the closet and checked boxes and bags. He stepped back and almost as if he heard a voice, his head spun around to the spot where he stood talking to Josie. He went to the bed table and opened the drawer.

There it was, the evidence to clear Josh. He reached down, lifting a gold foil chocolate box to the top of the table. He opened the lid. All but one piece had been eaten.

"Oh my," said Josie. "I gave that box to Dr. Hooper for his wife."

"Yes, but I gave the box to you. And I know Josh didn't have a chance to tamper with it. Did he?"

"No, I don't believe so," said Josie "I'm sure of it. I had it tucked away in a drawer until I gave it to Dr. Hooper. He wouldn't have known it was there."

Glen called Martin.

"Meet me at Winegard's Florist Shop. I have some new evidence on the case."

"I'll be right there."

The two men met at Winegard's.

"What do you have for me?" asked Martin.

"I bought this box of chocolates myself. I gave them to Josie and she doesn't eat chocolates. That's probably what saved her life. Anyway, she gave them to Dr. Hooper for his wife, who ate them and died. Don't you see? Josh was not connected to this box."

"You think they were tampered with before they left the store then?"

"Exactly," said Glen.

They tried the door, but the store was locked before closing time.

"That's odd," said Glen. "Let's go next door to the mortuary and see if they're in."

The lights in the front of the mortuary were off, but a glow came from the backroom where Michael worked on the bodies. The door was open; the men walked in.

They stopped suddenly when they heard a woman crying. Both men drew their guns and moved through the shadows to the backroom. While standing off to the side, they observed the figure of a woman sitting on the floor cradling the head of a man.

Waiting before entering the room, they heard Vanessa say, “I’m so sorry. I didn’t mean for you to die. All I wanted was more money. Why did you have to eat the chocolate? Why Michael? I’m so sorry, I’m so sorry.”

Now it's time to test "*your*" ability as a detective. Can you find the "Elusive Clue"?

It's a word puzzle hidden within the story.

The answer to the puzzle will spell out the name of the killer.

To Solve the puzzle:

A. You must locate the page or pages containing the puzzle.

B. Locate the letters you will need to unscramble the name of the killer.

I hope you enjoyed the book. For more exciting mysteries and once again the challenge of finding that "elusive clue" try my other books in the "Elusive Clue Series". (see next page for details.)

Patricia A. Bremmer

See ya on my website!

www.patriciabremmer.com

Additional Books
by
Patricia A. Bremmer

Tryst With Dolphins

Dolphins' Echo

Death Foreshadowed

Victim Wanted: Must Have References

Crystal Widow

Clinical Death

Mind Your Manors!

The Christmas Westie

(a children's picture book)